THE HAUNTED HEART

What Reviewers Say About Jane Kolven's Work

The Queen Has a Cold

"In Jane Kolven's romantic comedy *The Queen Has a Cold*, true love blossoms in a tiny European country. ...The fate of Montamant seems tied up with Remy's relationship in the cathartic conclusion, which brims with warmth, tenderness, and comedic wit. *The Queen Has a Cold* is a nonconforming romance that's fun and lighthearted."
—*Foreword Reviews*

"*The Queen Has a Cold* is everything that you could want in a book of this sort, and Kolven manages to thread the needle between social commentary and light-hearted romance."—*Queens of the Bs*

The Holiday Detour

"Kolven is a talented writer, no doubt; *The Holiday Detour* is a compelling and entertaining romance, for sure. This book showcases her ability to use dialog effectively and masterfully. She can create tension and drive the plot forward in the most amusing and engrossing ways. I would encourage anyone who loves fun, quirky romances to read *The Holiday Detour*. It's a highly entertaining and completely satisfying read."—*Lesbian Book Blog*

"Kolven has a keen eye for what makes a narrative work and, just as importantly, she handles everything with a light touch. There were several points while reading this book that I actually smiled or laughed out loud."—*Medium.com*

"It's a wonderful read about respect and genderqueer representation. ...The story leaves you with a message about making mistakes when knowledge or sensitizing lacks. This book shows the importance of a learning process, a lesson about respect, and a call on how much we need more education not only outside but within the LGBTAQ+ community."—*Rainbow Literary Society*

"Kolven has a keen eye for what makes a narrative work and, just as importantly, she handles everything with a light touch. There were several points while reading this book that I actually smiled or laughed out loud."—*Books Are Our Superpower*

Visit us at www.boldstrokesbooks.com

By the Author

The Holiday Detour

The Queen Has a Cold

The Haunted Heart

THE HAUNTED HEART

by

Jane Kolven

2022

THE HAUNTED HEART

ISBN 13: 978-1-63679-245-3

This Trade Paperback Original Is Published By
Bold Strokes Books, Inc.
P.O. Box 249
Valley Falls, NY 12185

First Edition: September 2022

CREDITS
EDITOR: CINDY CRESAP
PRODUCTION DESIGN: SUSAN RAMUNDO
COVER DESIGN BY INK SPIRAL DESIGN

Dedication

In loving memory of Aaron Brady

CHAPTER ONE

It took three attempts at buzzing the building manager before anyone answered, and then it was a voice too gruff and full of static for Kara to understand. She looked around the 1970s-styled lobby of her new building. Surely, the manager was going to come down and let her in? Or at least buzz her through the interior lobby door? If another tenant came out, maybe she could slip in after them.

She pulled out her phone. It was nearly six thirty, almost two hours after she'd expected to arrive and half an hour after she'd promised to text her mom that she'd made it safely. Stupid Chicago traffic. Mom would be worried, especially since Kara had rejected her offer to take the day off work and drive with her. But Kara had imagined hours of Mom poking into her life and no, thank you.

Made it to the new place. Talk after I get settled.

She put her phone back in her coat pocket.

This was ridiculous. She had already paid her first month's rent and signed the lease. She had a legal right to enter her new apartment. She put her finger on the buzzer again and left it there.

A moment later, a man of about fifty or sixty with silver hair combed sideways over a bald spot burst through the locked interior door. He glared at her, and Kara yanked her finger off the buzzer.

"You are Kara?"

Who else did he think she might be?

"You come." He barely waited for her before letting go of the door and turning away. "The apartment is this way, top floor. Is very nice."

"It looked nice in the pictures."

The manager, who hadn't bothered introducing himself, led her to the stairs and bounded up them two at a time. Kara was fit enough to keep up, but it had been a long day, and she was feeling grouchy by the time they reached the fifth floor.

The apartment was smaller than it had appeared in the pictures on the website. Online it had seemed charming, but in person it was old and funny-smelling. The wooden floors looked sticky with too many years of wax, grit lined the edges of the molded baseboards, and a cold draft made Kara shiver as she stepped inside.

The manager smiled and nodded. "Is nice, yes?"

"Uh...."

"You need to sign the papers." He unfolded a bundle and set it on the laminate kitchen counter. Then he took a pen from his shirt pocket and uncapped it.

Kara had asked the management company multiple times to email the lease for her to review, so she could sign it electronically in advance of arriving. They had eventually done that, but the day before someone from the office had phoned to say that she needed to sign the papers in person. She had politely explained that people signed documents electronically all the time, and they were still legally binding. It hadn't mattered.

Her concern was that they were trying to pull a fast one, to change the terms of the lease she'd already agreed to. But a thorough look showed her the paper lease seemed fairly standard, nothing different. She signed and slid the papers back to the manager. He folded them in thirds and tucked them into his pants pocket. She was going to have to call the office tomorrow morning to get an executed copy for her own records. She wondered with frustration if all leasing companies in Chicago sucked or if she'd just had the misfortune of working with the worst one.

From a different pocket, the custodian produced two silver keys on a simple metal loop. He gave her a wordless nod and let himself out.

The first thing Kara did was open all the windows. The radiators hissed in protest, but the air inside the apartment felt stale and... weirdly still. Fresh air was definitely needed, cold weather or not.

After that, it was time to start moving in. She'd had to park the moving truck two blocks away. She carried box after box from it to the lobby, where she dumped everything in a heap. Once she was ready to take a load up, she realized the building manager hadn't said anything about the freight elevator, and, sure enough, it was inoperable. She had to use a box to jimmy open the door of the tiny two-person passenger elevator while she crammed as many other boxes inside as she could. Once full, she rode it up to the fifth floor, pushed everything out in the hall, and went back to the lobby to repeat the process a hundred more times. If she took too long before letting the elevator door shut, an alarm went off. Once, she let the door shut to quell the alarm, and her boxes made their ascent alone. They came back, right about the time the stairwell door burst open, and two people who had probably hoped to ride the elevator glared at her before heading out into the night.

So far, her big Chicago adventure was awful.

She managed to haul in everything but the one piece of furniture she still owned, a couch, which would have to stay in the truck until she could get help.

Moving was always awful, but she'd been dumb not to pay for professionals or at least accept her brother-in-law's offer to come with her. Independence had its drawbacks, but it would be worth it once she was settled and ready to start this new life.

After looking up the nearest pizza place and ordering delivery, she sent her mother another text: *Moved in. Unpacking. Very tired.* Mom texted back a heart and a good night message instead of calling. She must have sensed that Kara wanted to be left alone.

And she did. She threw herself into cleaning and unpacking, and by the time the pizza arrived, she felt she'd earned her rest.

But by midnight, she lay wide awake on the air mattress that would serve as her bed until she could buy furniture. Every creak and noise in the apartment seemed to echo off the bare walls. In Eau Claire, the most common noise she'd heard at night was the sound of drunk college students on the weekends. Here she could hear the squeal of tires and the honking of car horns. Every few minutes an automated voice kindly announced to passengers they were on the Route 50 bus. In Eau Claire, she and Hilary had lived on a tree-lined street. At night their room was dark. Now the room was bathed in the glow of the streetlamps. She vaguely remembered having to adjust during her time in Madison for law school, but she and Hilary had moved away from the city center after her first year and spent the rest of the time in a darker, quieter residential area.

Kara took a few deep breaths. She tried to imagine Mom saying, *Just close your eyes, even if you don't feel tired*, the way she had when Kara was little and had a nightmare. Sure enough, after a few minutes, her muscles started to relax. She started to enter the delicious state of floating weightless, all cares and concerns muted into dream phenomena that could no longer hurt or worry her. She imagined Hilary sitting in the eating nook of this new apartment, calling out bus stops. Dream Hilary looked at Kara and asked if she wanted something to drink, but before Kara could answer, a clanging—a different one from the radiators—jolted her awake.

She opened her eyes and strained to listen while trying to keep her breath quiet. She went through her situation: she'd locked the front door, and she'd closed and locked the windows before going to bed. She was on the top floor. If someone managed to get past the locked lobby, it was unlikely they'd decide to take the elevator up five floors. If she'd forgotten to close a window, it would be difficult for someone to climb up that high. She was just hearing apartment noises she wasn't used to yet.

Swoosh. This time it sounded exactly like the refrigerator door being shut.

Kara sat up.

She looked around the bedroom for something to use in self-defense. Her cell phone was resting on the nightstand. She could call the police. But what if it was just a rat? Wasn't Chicago supposed to have a lot of rats? She didn't want to seem like an overanxious country bumpkin when the cops showed up.

She held her breath as the floorboards outside the bedroom door creaked. Her heart began pounding in her ears, and she was sure the intruder could hear it, just as surely as she could hear the slow *eek-eek-eek* of their footsteps.

The doorknob squeaked as it began to turn. Kara covered her mouth with her hands to prevent herself from screaming out loud.

The door opened halfway.

She froze in terror. This was it. Whoever it was, whatever they wanted, she was trapped now. Here they came.

But nothing happened.

She waited a long minute, but the apartment was quiet again, with only the noises of the city coming from outside. Her breathing started to even out, but her hands were shaking.

"Hello?"

She felt lightheaded. She knew she'd heard someone approaching. Maybe they were in the hallway. Maybe they were waiting to lure Kara out of the bedroom.

"Who's there? I have a gun!"

Nothing.

After what felt like an eternity, she rolled off the air mattress and got to her feet. She took a timid step to the doorway. The floor creaked. Her bare feet stuck to the ages-old wax as she took another step. She reached carefully for the doorknob because despite her threat, she didn't have a gun.

She hoped like hell no one was there.

The hall was empty. There was no one in the bathroom, which didn't yet have a shower curtain to hide behind. No one in the living room either.

She made her way to the kitchen and turned on the light.

The refrigerator door was closed, but a carton of orange juice sat on the counter. Kara looked at it with curiosity. Her mother had sent her with a cooler of a few fresh food items, but had there been any orange juice? And had she drunk some of it before going to bed? She didn't usually drink orange juice, except occasionally at brunch with champagne in it. She returned the carton to the fridge.

She looked around the living room again. The front door was still bolted. The windows were all still closed. If someone had broken in, how had they done it?

She returned to the kitchen. Why would someone break into her apartment to steal orange juice in the middle of the night? There were no dirty glasses. She hadn't even unpacked the dishes yet. She'd eaten the pizza straight from the delivery box, which was still on the counter. She opened it and peeked inside. The remaining slices were still there. If someone had come in, why would they bother opening the refrigerator when there was food sitting out in the open? If they opened the refrigerator, why would they drink orange juice? Had they drunk directly out of the carton?

Kara opened the refrigerator again and took the orange juice out. She stopped short of tossing the carton into the garbage. A peeping tom with a craving for vitamin C? That didn't make a lot of sense. Usually the most logical explanation to a problem was the simplest.

I probably just don't like being alone in a strange apartment in a new city. I probably forgot the orange juice when I put the other food away earlier.

She must have taken the carton out of the cooler and gotten distracted from putting it in the fridge. It had probably been sitting on the counter all night. That was the simplest explanation.

Gently, she set the carton back on the shelf in the nearly empty refrigerator.

It's an old building, she reminded herself. Their house in Eau Claire, which had originally been constructed in the 1960s, had been renovated only a few months before she and Hilary had moved in. This building hadn't been renovated since the mid-1970s, if the lobby decor was anything to go by, but it had been built decades before that. Kara probably wasn't accustomed to the quirks of old architecture. She tested the bedroom doorknob, and, sure enough, it didn't latch properly against the strike plate.

See? Just your imagination and an old door. Nothing to worry about.

She rooted around for something to use as a weapon to make her feel safer, but all she could find was a butterknife.

Great, I'll just spread someone to death.

Back in the bedroom, she found her phone and contemplated calling Mom or her sister Becca, but that would only create more problems. If she woke them up in the middle of the night, they'd panic, too. And when she told them she didn't actually find an intruder, they'd say she was paranoid and this was why she shouldn't have tried to strike out on her own, far from them and the comforts of the place where she grew up. They'd tell her to come home.

Instead, she opened a streaming app and pulled up an old episode of the British baking show. Somewhere between bread week and pastry week, she finally fell asleep.

By the next morning, cold logic prevailed. There were three possible scenarios to explain what had happened. Scenario one: a draft in the building caused doors and windows to creak. As for the orange juice, she'd either forgotten to put it away when she'd unpacked the cooler, or she really had imagined it. After all, she'd been dreaming about Hilary being in the kitchen. Maybe her mind wanted to see evidence of that.

The second and third possible explanations were that someone had actually come in. Scenario two: the locks in the building were so old that the keys worked universally. Someone who lived in the building had come home, probably drunk, and accidentally let themselves into the wrong apartment. They'd helped themselves to something to drink before they realized their mistake and fled, embarrassed and worried about getting caught. Scenario three: someone had a key to Kara's apartment specifically. Maybe someone who had never lived in the building, a friend the previous tenant had given an emergency key. They might not have known their friend—brother—whoever— had moved out a few days earlier. They'd come over, had some orange juice, and been ready to crash in the bedroom where Kara was sleeping when they realized their mistake. That seemed like a reasonable enough explanation, something innocuous but nonetheless a violation of Kara's privacy that would need to be curbed.

After a quick shower, she set out to find the building manager to ask if he would help move the couch and to get a read on the likelihood of the three scenarios. The man, whom Kara found tinkering with one of the washing machines in the basement laundry room, agreed to help her, but as they carried the couch from the moving truck to the lobby, he didn't seem all that concerned about the possible break-in.

"You want I change lock?"

"No, the lock's not broken. I just want to know if there's ever a problem with drafts making doors open and close. Or maybe the key to another apartment works in my lock, and someone stumbled home drunk or something? I was wondering if maybe someone else has a key to my place, like you, or—"

"Yuk-use? Yuk-use?"

It took Kara a moment to figure out what he was saying. "No, I'm not accusing you."

"I live ten years in America! I never have problem. I work hard. I do job. Everybody think, okay, is immigrant, is liar. Is thief. No have papers."

The elevator dinged open on the fifth floor, and they wrestled the sofa into the hall through a feat of geometry. At least the guy wasn't yelling anymore. Kara considered it real progress in their relationship.

"So are you from Poland then?"

"Poland? Poland! I am from *Ukraine*!"

"Sorry, I just thought—"

"I have work to do." He stabbed the elevator button, and the door jerked open. He stepped inside and pointed a finger at Kara. "Yuk-use, you go to Eric, say him Oleg is thief. He say no way, is honest. You see."

"I'm not really interested in going to Eric." Whoever Eric was. "Never mind."

"Never mind," he repeated, his voice tinged with sarcasm. He pushed a button on the panel inside the elevator.

The doors closed as Kara shouted, "Thank you for your help, sir!"

The couch was still yards away from her apartment and the next geometry puzzle of getting it inside the door. She sighed and began to push it inch by inch down the hall.

CHAPTER TWO

The sun that morning warmed Nisha's soul. She could tell it was going to be a good day, full of hope and happiness, and she welcomed the change of pace after such a dreary week. Although the temperature outside was only in the fifties, she decided to go for a run. She resisted the urge to put on a scarf and hat, knowing that once she started moving, her body would warm up plenty. She didn't need extra clothes. She would run to wake her body and her mind and to greet the morning, and that would set her up for a successful day.

"Setting yourself up for success" was one of the pearls of wisdom Carter, her new yoga teacher, often shared. The irony of an Indian woman having a white yoga teacher wasn't lost on her, but she'd never studied before and Carter had a calming presence she responded to. They always said things like, "Let go of whatever is going to leave anyway, and focus on what remains," and "Set yourself up for success and peace today." Nisha hadn't realized how often she used to set herself up for failure, how her choices had subconsciously been made to self-sabotage. So much of the heartache she'd caused to others and endured herself had been because she hadn't thought about how to set herself up for success. But this was a new era. A new Nisha.

"Setting yourself up for success" meant anticipating any problems that might arise from a choice and adjusting your actions as needed to ensure those problems didn't happen. It also meant expecting good things to happen, not bad, and welcoming them when they came along—and these days, that wasn't often.

That wasn't true. Good things were coming more often now than they had in the past year.

No, that wasn't right either. Good things happened all the time. Positivity was a state of mind. She had to acknowledge the good instead of focusing on the bad, and it would change her mindset. The more she welcomed positivity into her life, the more its effects would grow.

She ran the short distance to Foster Beach, where she took a few minutes to catch her breath in the cold air and watch the waves of Lake Michigan lapping at the shore. Nisha had lived in Chicago her entire life, and although she'd spent time at the lake in the summer, this experience of staring at the open water and connecting with its rhythms was a relatively new thing for her. It was funny to think how much she'd taken the lake for granted in the past. Now, looking at where the waves met the sky made her feel rooted to the earth under her feet. Small and insignificant compared to the vastness of the water, and lucky to be alive on such a beautiful planet. Being at the lakefront was spiritual. It was the temple of nature.

A seagull glided overhead and squawked, as excited for today as she was.

Nisha smiled at it before closing her eyes and turning her face to the sun. She stood with her arms out, palms upward. Behind her eyelids glowed a wall of red, and it heated her to the core.

Today is going to be a good day.

She repeated the mantra to herself three times, and then, after one more big breath in and out, she turned and ran the distance home.

After showering and dressing, she picked up her phone to check the time and saw a text from Oleg.

New tenant in your old apartment.

Nisha's heart gave a flutter of excitement. The last time someone had moved into her old apartment in Wicker Park, she had dreaded it. It had still felt like home, and a new tenant had been an unwelcome invader. But now a new tenant meant an opportunity, and she understood what the sun and the seagull had been trying to tell her.

This time, she was going to find her missing ring.

What are they like?

Very rude, he texted back. *You want me to ask about ring?*

Nisha hesitated. If the new tenant wasn't nice, they might not be receptive to a bunch of questions about their new space. Maybe an old-fashioned letter would work better. That way, then they wouldn't be blindsided, and they could take their time looking and responding.

Of course, it would take a few days for a letter to reach them, and Nisha wasn't sure waiting that long was a good idea. People usually took some time to fully unpack and get organized in a new space, but once they had, it was unlikely they'd be able to find anything that had been left before their move-in, especially something so small as a ring.

No, the best thing to do would be to leave a note directly on the door, or maybe Oleg could give it to the tenant when they got home from work. That way, Nisha could be assured her note arrived, and she might even get a faster response than if she had to wait for the mail.

And it would give her a chance to visit the old building.

Can I leave a note for you to give them? she texted Oleg. *I can come over this afternoon.*

Oleg agreed easily. He was required to be in the building all day anyway, and he probably welcomed the chance to socialize a bit during what was otherwise a very isolating job. Most people in the building treated him as if he were invisible. They'd only talk to him when they needed something fixed, and, from what Nisha had witnessed when she'd lived there, they rarely thanked him afterward.

On her way to the old building, she would stop at the Eastern European bakery on Division and get him a treat in appreciation.

❖

She puttered around the condo all morning, cleaning and tidying up. Although Suni and Maddie had told her many times that taking care of their messes wasn't her responsibility, Nisha couldn't help feeling it was the least she could do. Her schedule at the theater was lighter now that the latest show was up, and she had her days free while Suni and Maddie were chained to their desks at work from nine to five. The rent she paid for their spare bedroom wasn't anywhere near what she'd pay for her own apartment, and she owed them a lot for all the support they'd given her in the last year.

After lunch, she headed out, opting to take the Red Line all the way downtown to change to the Blue Line. There wasn't an easy way to get from Edgewater to Wicker Park quickly without a car, and even with a car the cross-town traffic could be slow. The long train ride gave her time to listen to an episode of a podcast about meditation Carter had recommended, and by the time it was over, she was heading up the steps at the Division Street stop.

The bakery, which had been run by a Russian family for over forty years, was still thriving, despite the neighborhood's aggressive gentrification. Once full of single-family homes and small shops, Division now boasted a Target, a multi-story parking garage, and the ugliest steel and glass condos Nisha had ever seen. Most of the changes had happened while she and Angie still lived there, but since moving away, Nisha had become aware of just how charmless the neighborhood had become.

Places like the bakery were welcome reminders of what the area had once been. She bought a few pieces of honey cake for Oleg and Nan, her favorite neighbor.

Nan was an eccentric old woman who lived down the hall from Nisha's former apartment. She lived alone and didn't have many visitors, but Nisha didn't understand why. Nan had great stories about queer life in Chicago in the old days. To Nisha, she was a wonderful surrogate queer nani.

"How are you doing today?" She greeted Nan with a hug and stepped inside her apartment. The curtains were all drawn, and the place smelled like sour milk.

Nan's hair had recently been dyed blond, and it made her look younger than her eighty-four years.

"It's very loud today." Nan put her hands over her ears to demonstrate.

Nisha listened for a moment, expecting to hear construction noise or a TV coming from a neighboring apartment. She didn't hear anything other than the usual—and fairly quiet—city sounds filtered through the windows.

"Maybe we should put some music on to drown out the other sounds?" She walked over to the turntable. "What would you like to hear today?"

Nan had a collection of vinyl records, most of which she'd collected in the digital music age by buying them for two dollars at thrift stores. Her original record collection, she'd once explained, had long been tossed out, first replaced by cassettes and then CDs. She refused to switch to iTunes and MP3s and had gone back to vinyl.

"The Bee Gees," Nan instructed.

"You got it."

A moment later, "More than a Woman" was filling the small living room.

"I brought you a treat." Nisha held up the box with the honey cake.

"I'll make some tea to go with it. You'll stay for a bit?"

"Of course. Why else do you think I'm here?"

"To spy on that new girl." Nan peered at her, then shook her head. "No, to talk to Oleg about something. But it's related to that new girl."

"How do you do that?" Nisha asked, breaking their eye contact.

Nan tapped her forefinger to her temple. "I've told you a hundred times. I have the gift." She took the pastry box from Nisha and carried it to the kitchen counter. She opened it, put the slices on small plates, and filled her old-fashioned tea kettle and set it on the stove.

"When are you going to get an electric one? They're much simpler."

"I should get an iPhone, too, and then we don't even have to meet in person. We could just—" Nan gestured holding a phone up and waving at it with an exaggerated smile. Then she mimed throwing the phone down and crushing it with her foot.

Nisha had been trying to get Nan to modernize for a long time, but she also appreciated the way the old woman stuck to her ways. Nan had once said it was the only way to maintain sanity in a world that had gone mad.

She was dispatched to find Oleg while Nan prepared the tea, and a few minutes later the three of them were enjoying the honey cake together. Nan complained to Oleg about some things in her apartment, and Oleg promised to fix them. They all knew it would take him a long time, not because he was lazy or didn't care but because he was one person tending to an entire building that needed repairs, and Nan had a lot more patience than her neighbors.

Finally, when they were out of small talk, Nisha inquired about the new tenant. "I was wondering if you had a chance to ask about my ring?"

Oleg shook his head. "I carry the couch with her. And she accuses me of coming into apartment."

"Wait, what? You carried her couch?"

"Yes, can you believe? Who moves to a new city by herself?"

Someone who'd burned all of her bridges, probably. Nisha could identify with that. At least Suni and Maddie had been kind enough to take her side when she and Angie had split. Without them, she'd have been on her own, too.

Nisha hadn't left the breakup with any furniture, but if she had, she would never have asked Oleg to help move it. That wasn't his job. Of course, he was the kind of guy who would do it without expecting anything in return. He wouldn't have been able to say no to the new tenant.

"Why did she think you came into her apartment? Like, without knocking?"

"At night."

"Are you kidding? Does she think you're some kind of predator?"

The idea was laughable for many reasons, not the least of which was that Oleg had come to the US in the first place because he was gay and wanted to be somewhere safer and happier. Winning the visa lottery had given him a chance to be out. There was no way he'd prey on a female tenant.

"She is no good." Oleg looked to Nan for confirmation.

Nan squinted into the distance. "No, no, I wouldn't say that. That's not how I would describe it at all. I don't think she isn't good. She's carrying her own pain, and that makes it hard for her to think about other people."

"You've met her?" Nisha asked.

"No."

"Then how do you know...." It wasn't worth finishing the question. Nan would just point to her head and say it was the gift. Nisha turned back to Oleg. "I was wondering if I could leave her a note asking about the ring? I'll include my phone number, so she can text me if she finds it. That way, you don't have to be involved."

"Fine with me."

Nisha got up from her chair and crossed the room to her bag. There was some paper in it, she knew, but she rummaged around and couldn't find it. Nan offered some of her stationery instead.

"This will be much nicer." She handed Nisha a piece of pink card stock with a matching envelope. It smelled like pungent roses.

Nisha scribbled out a note and put the card in the envelope. She sealed it shut and gave it to Oleg. "You'll make sure she gets it? I just really want my ring back."

"We know," he teased her. "Everyone know. The ring, the ring, the ring."

"But I know it's in that apartment. That's where it got lost. It has to be there." She sighed. "Every time someone new moves in, it feels more hopeless."

He took the envelope from her. "She will not care, trust me."

Nisha's heart sank. If Oleg was right about what a monster this new tenant was, she'd probably ignore the letter completely.

Nan patted Nisha's hand where it rested on the table. "Give her time."

"Time for what?"

Nan just sipped her tea, her eyes still lost in thought.

CHAPTER THREE

Kara was grateful she'd moved a few days before Horowitz and Stein expected her to start her new position. She needed time to get her bearings in the city and figure out the route for her daily commute and how long it would take. After the exertion of moving and the quasi-intrusion into her apartment the night before, she also needed rest.

Once she'd managed to force the sofa into the living room, Kara returned the moving truck and took a rideshare back to the new apartment. She fell asleep on the couch while streaming a movie on her phone. When she awoke around one, her stomach was rumbling. She had a few groceries, but nothing sounded appetizing. She decided to go out for lunch.

She had concentrated so much on applying to jobs and interviewing that she hadn't spent a lot of time researching the residential neighborhoods of Chicago. And since she'd done her apartment hunting from a distance, she hadn't been able to be picky. Her friend Ana, who had grown up in the Chicago suburbs before they attended law school in Madison together, had suggested Wicker Park. Kara and Hilary had come to Chicago for a weekend getaway once and gone dancing in the gay neighborhood—Boystown, it was called. She had liked how plainly obvious a name that was. But Ana said living in Boystown was a nightmare in the summer because of Cubs games, and Kara had taken her at her word.

So here she was: standing at a six-point intersection in her new neighborhood. Restaurants and clothing boutiques spanned eastward on North Avenue and at a southeasterly angle on Milwaukee. Although it was cold and bleak outside, everyone looked dressed in expensive clothes in styles Kara hadn't really seen before, and she felt out of place in her functional parka. The outfit was rounded out with jeans Hilary had repeatedly told her made her ass look edible, but Kara hadn't worn them so someone would ogle her. They happened to be the only jeans she could find. On her feet were a pair of winter boots, embarrassingly puffy and heavy-soled in contrast to the sleeker flat leather ones everyone on the street was wearing. She'd never cared much about fashion, and she didn't now. But recognizing how different she looked from her new community reminded her how alone she was. It was during times like this that she missed Hilary the most.

You are here to be alone. You are starting a new life. No baggage from the past.

But she didn't want to start a new life with nothing in common with anyone around her. She didn't want to be a complete fish out of water, unable to even make friends. That hadn't been the goal of this move. Why on earth had Ana suggested this place?

This shall pass, and I can do this. This shall pass, and I can do this.

The mantra was kind of stupid, but she'd been using it faithfully since grief counseling. It didn't matter if it made sense in context. It gave her something to think about instead of whatever was upsetting her, and after a few deep breaths, she felt recentered.

Ana wasn't a mean person. She had suggested this neighborhood because she thought Kara would like living here. Kara needed to give it—and Ana—the benefit of the doubt and see what adventures Wicker Park had in store for her.

She ate lunch at a noodle shop and let herself wander up and down the streets. She spied in storefronts, treated herself to an afternoon coffee, and contemplated signing up for a gym membership. The first few times the L train went by, she couldn't help cringing at the noise and turning to look, but eventually, she didn't even flinch.

I've got this city living down. She smiled as she sipped her now tepid flat white and turned onto Winchester to look at some of the houses.

As the sun began to set, she reluctantly headed to the apartment to tackle the rest of the unpacking. It had been an enjoyable afternoon, time to get in touch with herself and this new home, and she had been able to forget the weird events in her apartment. Now, back in the lobby, she checked her mail from the wall of boxes. She was stalling because she dreaded going upstairs, but she knew she had to. There was too much work left to do setting up the apartment, and she couldn't avoid the place where she lived.

She thought about calling the management company and asking politely if they would let her out of her lease. Even if the break-in had only happened in her imagination, she deserved to live somewhere she would feel safe. At least, she was pretty sure that's what her parents and Dr. Warren would say. Maybe this would also give her a chance to move away from the yuppies. Now that she was in Chicago, it would be easier to look at apartments and find some place low-key in a neighborhood that was more her style. Maybe the rent would be cheaper, too.

No one answered the phone number Kara had called to lease the apartment in the first place. There wasn't even a voice mail greeting. What was with this company? Was it run by total flakes? How did it stay afloat with such terrible business practices?

There was a knock on the front door. Kara wove around the boxes strewn about the living room and spied through the peephole. It was the building manager.

Great, here comes round two. She opened the door.

Oleg held out several copies of papers. "Is for you. She say you no have copies. And roofaroof."

"Roofaroof?"

He nodded and walked away.

She looked at the papers. "Rules for Use of the Rooftop Deck," one said at the top. Kara hadn't realized the building had a rooftop deck. It hadn't been in any of the website photos, and it certainly hadn't been mentioned in the two-second tour the manager had given her the day before. Her apartment was on the top floor of the building. If there was a rooftop deck, it might explain how someone had gotten into her unit. She snagged her keys and went to investigate.

The rooftop was accessible by a separate stairwell, guarded behind an unmarked fireproof door. Kara only found it by trying each door handle in the hallway, feeling like a creep and hoping no one would catch her. At the top of the stairs was another heavy door, which locked immediately behind her. Good thing she had brought her keys.

Maybe that was what had happened last night. Maybe someone had gotten stuck on the roof and then leaned over the railing to enter Kara's apartment through the window in desperation. Maybe the orange juice was much-needed rehydration after hours spent trapped outside.

She approached the edge of the deck. It was several feet from the actual edge of the roof. If someone had used it to access the windows below, they'd have had to plan ahead and bring a very long rope. Or they'd have to be an acrobat. Kara imagined whoever it was moving cat-like across the roofline, lowering themselves by tucking their legs over the roof ledge, then turning flips to get inside her window.

She shook her head. There was a slim chance an acrobatic cat burglar had gotten trapped on the roof, reentered the building through her window, and sought sanctuary in her kitchen. If by some wild chance that had happened, why would the person drink orange juice, leave the carton out, and creep toward Kara's bedroom? And how had the person escaped after Kara woke up and turned on all the lights?

A shiver of cold that had nothing to do with the winter weather ran through Kara.

Maybe the person had never left.

She hurried back downstairs. She'd comb her apartment. She'd go through every nook and closet. She'd overturn boxes, check inside every cabinet, turn on every light. No way was she going to let some freak make her apartment their hideout.

When she opened her door, the first thing she saw was the orange juice sitting on the kitchen counter.

❖

"Mom?"

"Hi, sweetheart!" Her mother's voice was bright and cheery, as if she couldn't hear the croak in Kara's throat. "I was wondering when you'd call. Your dad and I wanted to check on you last night, but I got the sense you wanted some time to yourself." For someone so opposed to Kara's plan to move to Chicago, her mom sounded nothing but supportive now.

This was where Kara struggled. On the one hand, she wanted to tell her mom about what had happened last night. Desperately. For all the explanations she had come up with the night before, there was nothing that could explain why the orange juice carton was sitting out again today. And if there wasn't a rational explanation, that meant there was something irrational at play. Like Kara losing her mind. Maybe she had moved away too soon. Maybe the mysterious orange juice was some sign from her subconscious that she wasn't ready to strike out on her own.

On the other hand, she had gone to law school. She was trained to be logical and methodical. As much as she wanted her mom to make it all better, the way she did when Kara was little, she also didn't want to burden her with things her mother couldn't change. Mom had already tried hard enough to help her through the last year and a half until Kara had pushed her away and moved to a different state. She owed it to her family to act as if she was okay. To be okay.

"My neighborhood seems cool," she lied. "Lots of shops and stuff. It's nice, I guess."

"I'm sure you'll make plenty of friends. You just need to give it time. How's your apartment? Levi's already asked when he can come visit."

Kara's mouth went dry at the thought of her nephew in this strange land, but that was normal. She knew from the endless sessions with Dr. Warren that it was common for people experiencing grief to worry about something bad happening to their other loved ones.

"Honey? Are you okay?"

She never had been any good at lying to people she was close to, and now was no exception. "I think—I think maybe there's an intruder in my building."

"Right now? I want you to hang up and call the police."

"No." Kara squeezed her eyes closed. Why was it always so hard to get her mother to understand what she meant? "Last night. I think someone tried to come into my bedroom last night."

"You saw them?"

"No, my door opened. And then there was the orange juice."

"What orange juice?"

"On the counter. I think they drank some of it."

"Kara..." Mom's tone of voice said everything. "Honey, remember, the nightmares—"

"It wasn't a nightmare. It was real."

"We talked about this with Dr. Warren. This is why we didn't think you should take a job so far from home. Honey, it hasn't been that long since Hilary—"

"This isn't about that!"

"Kara." Mom said it softly, in contrast to her curtness, but with all the air of authority only a mother could manage, no matter how old her child might be. *Kara, you haven't fully processed your grief yet. You need to be around your support network.* She knew that's what her mom wanted to say.

Kara had processed her grief. It was all she had done for almost two years. That's why she needed a fresh start. It didn't mean she was done grieving. She'd always miss Hilary, always love her, and always be in pain that she had died so young. But stewing in the endless counseling and support groups with her family looking over her shoulder in concern every five minutes had become unhelpful to that process. It had started suffocating her, and she had felt prohibited from moving forward.

She squeezed her eyes closed again. "I'll be fine. I'm sure it was nothing."

"Your doors were locked?"

Oh, now you act like you believe me. "Yup, and the windows. It seems like a safe neighborhood."

"Just remind yourself of that before you go to bed tonight. And tell yourself that you're here, that you're healthy, that nothing's going to happen to you. And, honey, it might not hurt to give Dr. Warren a call."

Prolonging her professional relationship with Dr. Warren sounded like absolute torture.

Death is an inevitable part of life, the doctor had said once. Kara would never forgive her for that, for making it seem as if what had happened to Hilary was mundane. Of course every life eventually ended in death. Kara knew that intellectually and had worked hard to understand it emotionally. But there was nothing inevitable about dying of cancer at thirty. It was way too young. When Kara tried to express that it wasn't death itself but rather Hilary's particular circumstances that bothered her, Dr. Warren had plowed over her to say that Kara was in denial of reality and needed more time to work through her feelings.

The next day, Kara had started thinking about moving to Chicago.

Besides, she didn't need a therapist right now. She needed a security alarm.

"I'm fine, Mom. I need to think about my job and the future."

She responded in that condescending way only mothers can— saying something to the effect of "Whatever you say, dear"—but Kara wasn't too annoyed. Mom was right that she needed to ground herself, even if she refused to do it through Dr. Warren's help. It might take a few days to get used to the bustle and lights of the city, but she would eventually. And, until that happened, she could throw herself into her new job.

❖

At 8:20 a.m. on Wednesday morning, Kara arrived in the lobby of a skyscraper in the Loop. She checked in with the security guard, who phoned up to the office to ensure she was allowed past the lobby, and after he received approval, he let her through the electronic gate. The elevators were crowded, wall to wall with bodies and smelling of espresso, men's aftershave, and women's perfume all at once. Kara shouldered her way out when the elevator reached the tenth floor, and she paused in front of a frosted glass door bearing the name Horowitz and Stein.

She smiled to herself. This was it, the big moment she'd been working toward for a long time. Freedom. Upward mobility. Big challenges and a fat paycheck to match.

The receptionist met her in the lobby. She carried herself with the neat efficiency of someone used to doing forty tasks at once. She was plump, with red hair, and she wore a pink sweater set with a purple pencil skirt that hugged the curves of her hips. Though she wasn't exactly Kara's type, Kara couldn't help but admire how attractive and put-together she looked.

By contrast, Kara was wearing a boxy suit jacket and loose pants with an embarrassing crease down the front. She was clearly going to need a new wardrobe to go along with the new job.

The receptionist said her name was Ruthie, but as soon as they were introduced, Kara was passed to the HR manager. The HR manager sent Kara down to the lobby to get an ID badge that would allow her to swipe herself into the elevators. Once her picture was taken and the badge printed, the security guard sent her back upstairs to HR, where she was handed a folder of tax forms and insurance paperwork to fill out in an empty conference room. When she finished, she hovered awkwardly in the corridor, wondering who she'd be pawned off on next. At last, Ruthie hung up the main phone and took off her headset.

"All set?" She took the folder from Kara. "Why don't I show you around?" She rushed into the bowels of the office, whizzing past spaces and calling out their functions before Kara could see inside. "Bathroom there, kitchen there, copier there, don't try to fix it yourself if it jams, call me, and here's your office."

She paused in front of the doorway to a tiny but tidy room. "IT will be around shortly to help you set up the phone and computer. Anything else you need?" She didn't wait for an answer before teetering back to her desk in her pink heels.

Kara surveyed her new office. There was a shiny wooden desk. Someone had thoughtfully stocked it with ballpoint pens, Post-It notes, paper clips, even a letter opener still in its packaging. As promised, someone else came around before she could sit down, and within a few minutes, she had a computer ID and password and a new voice mail greeting. Once she logged onto the company network, she was inundated with things to do until the ten o'clock meeting, after which she had a new list of things to do. At the top was reading the case file for a client handled by one of the partners; she had been notified she'd be attending their 8:30 a.m. breakfast meeting the following day and serving as additional counsel. Horowitz and Stein were going to make her earn every cent of her ridiculously large paycheck.

Being absorbed in work felt good. It made Kara feel useful and confident in a way she often didn't feel during her off-hours. The morning passed in a blur as she worked at her desk alone. At lunchtime she rode a crowded elevator to the first floor, where she stood in line for fifteen minutes to buy a sandwich from the convenience stand in the lobby. Then she rode the elevator back up, surprised at how long the endeavor had taken. She ate her sandwich while poring over a file and trying not to drip mustard on it.

At six thirty, she left her first day at Horowitz. Because she'd been so busy, she'd managed to go for a few hours without thinking about Hilary, and she'd forgotten all about the orange juice by the time she descended the steps to the train at Daley Plaza. She rode the Blue Line with confidence, exited at the Damen stop, and only for a brief moment had to think about which direction to walk toward her apartment.

While she retrieved her mail in the building's vestibule, the building manager came up to her with a starchy pink envelope. Kara wondered if it was a note of apology from the drunken intruder, or perhaps Hilary's sister had sent her an invitation to her upcoming baby shower. The envelope had only her apartment number on it, no name and no return address. It smelled like old lady perfume. She opened it with caution.

Dear new resident,

I'm sorry to bother you while you're settling in. I used to live in your apartment, and I lost a ring. If you happen to find it, would you call me at 773-555-9786? It has a lot of sentimental value.

Thanking you in advance,

Nisha

As she rode the tortoise-paced elevator to the fifth floor, Kara wondered how much value Nisha's ring actually had. Maybe in desperation to find the ring, Nisha had returned to the apartment. The lock probably hadn't been changed. Maybe Nisha had let herself in and out with her old key, and that explained why everything was still locked when Kara had checked after hearing the noises.

Nisha coming around to snoop made a lot more sense than the theory of the acrobatic, thirsty thief. Maybe Nisha hadn't known there was a new tenant, and when she'd opened the bedroom door and spotted Kara, she'd beat a hasty retreat and sent the note instead.

Yeah, that sounded like the most reasonable explanation.

As she waited for her dinner to microwave, Kara reflected on her day and how good it had felt to be away from the confusion of the apartment and the experience of being in a new place. But, as she reviewed the day's events in her mind, she realized she had spent most of her time alone, silent, reading files and answering emails. Had she spoken to anyone?

On a lark, she decided to get in touch with Nisha. Maybe she could find out more about the missing ring and determine whether Nisha had been the intruder. At the very least, it would be a break from the solitude. She entered the number on the pink stationery into her phone.

Hi, my name is Kara. I live in your old apartment. You left the note for me.

The three dots appeared, indicating Nisha was already replying. After a moment, Kara read: *You found my ring?!*

She felt a little bad for getting Nisha's hopes up. *No, sorry. Do you want to tell me more about what I'm looking for?*

Thanks. I'm sorry to bother you. It's probably gone forever.

If Nisha gave up hope, Kara would never learn what had really happened the night of the seeming break-in.

Is there anything else I can do for you?

If you happen to find it, you have my number.

She decided to move in for the kill before their text conversation ended. *Yeah, and you have a key to my apartment.*

A series of short messages arrived, one after the other.

What?

Oh, sorry, did Oleg tell you that?

I guess I never took it off my key ring.

The three dots appeared again, but that was enough proof for Kara. She pushed the button for a phone call, and to her surprise Nisha answered.

"Do you really think it's appropriate to barge into people's houses and scare them to death in the middle of the night?"

"What?"

"We both know it couldn't have been anyone else."

"I don't know what you're talking about."

So that was how Nisha wanted to play it. "Okay."

"Look, why would I bother leaving you a note if I was going to let myself in anyway?"

That was a good question. "This ring," Kara asked out of sheer curiosity, "tell me more about it. Was it worth a lot?"

"Do you want a reward or something? I don't have much money, but—"

"No, no, that's not what I meant." The microwave beeped. Kara removed the plastic tray of food with her bare hands and dropped it on the counter. She shook the heat out of her fingers. "Were you in my apartment yesterday? Or the day before?"

"No!"

"Are you sure? Because the way I see it, if you lost something that's important to you, maybe you were so desperate to find it that you came back over. Maybe you didn't know I had moved in. But I had, Nisha. And I could sue you and the building manager if he helped you get in." Most people were so ignorant of the law that simple threats of being sued worked on them. "Do you like orange juice, Nisha?"

"Orange juice? What does that have to do with anything?"

"Why did you leave the orange juice on the counter?"

"Honestly, you're as awful as Oleg said you were. I just left you a note asking for some help, and you're yelling at me."

Outside of work, Kara had met one person in Chicago, and he already hated her. This Nisha, assuming she wasn't a burglar, was about two seconds away from hating her, too. She took a breath.

This shall pass, and I can do this.

"You really don't know what I'm talking about?"

"I really don't," Nisha said. "I came to visit a friend in the building and left the note with Oleg. That's it. I haven't been in your apartment."

Kara took another deep breath to encourage her racing heart to slow down. "I'm sorry. I've had a rough few days. There are some weird things going on, and the most logical explanation—what I hoped you'd tell me—was that it was you. Then I could be angry at you, but at least I'd know what had happened."

"I didn't break into your apartment. I'm not that kind of person."

"Do you know the building guy—what's his name? Do you know him very well? I was wondering if he—"

"Oleg did not break into your apartment. How do you know it wasn't one of your friends pulling a prank on you or something?"

"Because I just moved here from Wisconsin. I don't know anybody yet."

They exchanged a few more words, neither able to help the other. Kara said she'd keep an eye out for the ring, apologized for her rudeness, and hung up.

The frozen dinner wasn't fully cooked. She choked down a few mouthfuls of half-scalding, half-icy lasagna before throwing the whole thing away and collapsing onto the air mattress.

CHAPTER FOUR

W̶ho was that?" Maddie asked.

As she weaved around Nisha to get to the refrigerator, Nisha had the all-too-common feeling of being in the way. She moved to the other end of the kitchen, near the opening that led to the hallway.

"The person who lives in my old apartment."

"Is Nish making friends?" Suni put her hands on Nisha's shoulders to move her aside as she squeezed into the kitchen. She kissed Maddie's cheek and went to the sink to wash her hands. "What are we doing for dinner tonight, team?"

Nisha gave a quiet sigh. She loved them dearly, and she appreciated that it was always "we" and "team." She'd needed that at first, but these days she, Suni, and Maddie felt less like the three Musketeers and more like two newlyweds and the barnacle of a friend they couldn't shake. The more they tried to include Nisha, the more obvious it was that she was an obligation.

"Actually, I have plans tonight."

Suni's carefully brushed and threaded eyebrows raised to her forehead. "Our little Nish has friends?"

"Stop that," Maddie chided her. "She's always had friends. Don't be mean." She set a pan on the stove and turned on the burner. "I was going to make sweet potato and cauliflower curry. We had that cauliflower head that needed to be used up."

Suni and Nisha exchanged a look. Maddie was always looking up recipes on food blogs, mostly written by white ladies who thought they had good taste. And bless her for the effort, but her food was always flavorless.

Maddie drizzled some oil in the pan and turned to Nisha. "So where are you going?"

"Um…I have an extra yoga class tonight, and we might get some dinner afterward."

"Okay, have fun."

"Yoga class, hmm?" Unlike Maddie, who was too nice to question whether someone was telling her the truth, Sunita didn't believe her. "Isn't that usually on Mondays?"

"She said it was an extra one," Maddie said.

"Okay, I guess she wants to get extra limber or something."

"Or something," Nisha agreed, fleeing the kitchen before Suni could press her any further.

Despite how long Nisha had lived there, the guest bedroom didn't look like her space. Or feel like it. It still had the modern yet neutral decor Suni and Maddie had selected when they'd moved in. She took her phone off the nightstand and scrolled through her contacts. What was she going to do tonight? She thought about taking herself to dinner, but that sounded depressing. There probably was a yoga class somewhere, but she had just made it up.

She looked at the texts the woman—Kara—had sent. She'd said she was alone in Chicago. Her cranky attitude was probably just loneliness.

Nisha hit the call button before she could think twice.

"Hello?"

"Hello, Kara, this is Nisha Rajchandra. We spoke a little while ago. I hope you don't mind me calling you."

"Hello, Nisha Rajchandra," Kara said, sounding amused instead of angry. "I didn't expect to talk to you again."

"You said you'd just moved here and didn't know anyone. I wanted to check on you, but first I have something to say. What you said about Oleg was completely out of line."

"Who's Oleg?"

"He was nothing but nice to me when I lived there, and I still consider him my friend. Just because he's Ukrainian doesn't mean—"

"Are you talking about the maintenance guy?"

"Oleg is a sweetheart. He called me to tell me you'd moved in, and he and I talked for an hour when I came over the other day to leave that note for you. As someone whose grandparents often get discriminated against for being immigrants, I don't appreciate you making accusations about Oleg just because he's Ukrainian."

"Whoa, wait a second! I don't care where he's from as long as he stays out of my apartment. I'm sorry if I falsely accused him. I just couldn't think who else would have a key besides him and you."

Nisha took a beat to evaluate if Kara was telling the truth. "Okay."

"It's not my style to think anything about someone because of their immigration status or national origin." Kara sounded sincere.

"I'm sorry if I assumed. Oleg told me you're from Wisconsin."

"Hey, people from Wisconsin aren't so bad. We're mostly too busy drinking beer to cause trouble. Anyway, now who's stereotyping?"

"Fair enough."

"Did you just call to yell at me?"

"No, now that that's settled, I'm hoping we can move on from it. I just couldn't leave it like that."

"Okay." Kara gave a slight chuckle, but Nisha didn't know what was so funny.

"Anyway, I was wondering if you'd like to get some dinner or a drink or something tonight?"

"You're inviting me to dinner two seconds after accusing me of being prejudiced against immigrants?"

"You said you'd moved here and didn't have any friends yet. I know it can be hard to meet people, so I thought I'd be neighborly and offer you some company."

"Actually, maybe you could help me figure out where's a good place to go. Like, with women." Kara sighed. "Look, I'm gay, and I want to figure out how to meet other people like me. Do you know where they hang out?"

Nisha laughed out loud at what Kara must have thought was a big declaration. Maybe where she was from it was. But Nisha worked in theater and volunteered at the LGBTQ community center. In her world, people only had to come out as straight.

"If that's offensive to you or not your scene—"

"No, it's just that I'm gay, too. Everyone I know is gay or bi or trans or something queer."

"Really?" Kara sounded hopeful now.

"There isn't one special bar where we all hang out. I mean, queer people are all over this city." She thought for a moment. If Kara wanted to make friends, where was the best place to take her? Somewhere quiet, where people made conversation, and she had a better chance of getting to know someone. "All right, I have an idea. I think I know a place you might like."

"Okay, text me an address. Should I take the train? I've only taken the train to the Loop for work. I'm not sure I've figured out how to get around yet."

"Take a cab. It'll be much faster."

"What do I wear?" For someone who had seemed so brash during their first phone call, Kara sounded self-conscious now. "My hangout clothes are usually sweatshirts and jeans, but I get the sense that's not the best way to make an impression here."

If she needed fashion advice, she had met the right person. Nisha understood why the universe had brought them together. She'd help Kara make herself over—not to be someone different, but to bring out the best parts of herself—and introduce her to Chicago. She'd help Kara feel more at home here.

"I got you," she promised.

She texted the address to a lesbian-owned wine bar in Ravenswood where she'd been a few times. It was dark and quiet, and the bartenders never made anyone feel embarrassed if they didn't know much about wine. A really welcoming, unpretentious place, frequented by women. Kara was bound to make a friend or get a phone number.

A few minutes later, she texted a picture of the outfit she planned to wear, laid out on her bed, as guidance for Kara. She paired a white cable-knit sweater with cropped maroon velvet pants and a pair of strappy black suede heels. Without tights, her feet would be cold, but the shoes were sexy and had a chunky heel that made them appropriate for fall. To complete the look, she opted for her turquoise peacoat and a cream pashmina.

Oleg had described Kara as skinny and blonde, but he either hadn't noticed or wasn't able to describe anything more than that. Nisha had no idea what kind of style Kara might have, but her own outfit was dressy enough for a night out and versatile enough to go with anything from a dress to jeans.

Although she'd told Kara to take a cab, Nisha wasn't going to waste the money doing the same. The bar was only a mile from Suni and Maddie's, so she put on a pair of ballet flats, carrying her heels, and walked the distance. Around the corner from the bar, she switched shoes and tucked the flats into her purse.

The place was dimly lit and had low modern jazz playing. People, mostly women but some men and genderqueer folks, sat at small tables decorated with tea lights and drank wine as they quietly conversed.

Nisha took a seat at the bar and waited. She wasn't entirely sure how she'd spot Kara, but soon enough a tall blonde in a ponytail entered and was waving at her.

"I recognized the shoes from the picture you sent," she explained.

Nisha extended one leg from the barstool to look at her heels. They were one of her favorite pairs, and it was nice they'd been so attention-grabbing.

Kara took off a puffy coat to reveal a pair of straight-legged jeans with a plain white button-down shirt and a green vest over it. Her shoes were brown leather oxfords. It was fine overall as an outfit, but it didn't really say much about Kara's personality.

"It's nice to meet you." She held out her hand for a shake.

Nisha was surprised by the formality. "I feel like we should hug!" She hopped down from the stool and gave Kara a quick squeeze. She didn't miss the fact that Kara only reciprocated with one wimpy pat to the back.

"So what's the deal with this ring?" Kara asked.

"Thank you for looking for it," Nisha said as she settled back onto her barstool. "You're the second person to move in after me, and the other guy wouldn't even talk to me."

"Oh, so you didn't just move out?"

"No, it was about a year ago. There was a single guy living there between us."

"Oh, I thought…Never mind."

"Thought what?"

"It was kind of dirty when I moved in, and you said you still had a key, and I—"

"You jumped to the conclusion that I left it a mess? Hardly. Besides, they charged us two hundred dollars in cleaning fees when we moved out, even though we'd paid for professional cleaners to get our deposit back. Such a scam."

"Who's 'we'?"

Oops. Nisha was usually careful about choosing "I" over "we." She wasn't a "we" anymore, unless being part of Suni and Maddie's team counted.

"My ex Angie. We lived there together."

She didn't want to get into the whole story, and she doubted Kara wanted to hear it anyway. She picked up the menu the bartender had put in front of her. "Do you prefer white or red? Or sparkling?" Kara hesitated. "I didn't even ask if you're a wine drinker, but if you're not, they have some really nice cocktails here."

"Red, I guess."

"Do you have a varietal preference? They also have great flights here if you can't settle on just one."

"Honestly," Kara said, "I don't know much about wine, and it always seemed too overwhelming to learn when beer is really easy to figure out."

"They might have beer bottles if you'd prefer."

"If you'd be willing to teach me about wine, I'd be up for learning."

Nisha nodded and pushed the menu away. "I've got you covered."

When the bartender came, she ordered two different flights, and a neat row of eight wine glasses with liquid ranging from pinkish red and translucent to nearly black and opaque was placed in front of them. Nisha explained what each was before Kara tasted, and soon they were trying each other's. Kara said she liked the fruitier varieties better than the dark chocolate-tasting ones.

"How do you know all this?" Kara asked.

"I learned it from coming here. They're really nice about explaining, especially on weeknights like this when it's not crowded."

"Do you usually go out on weeknights?"

She didn't usually go out at all. "I work in theater, so Thursday, Friday, and Saturday nights I work. It's easier to get drinks on a Wednesday. What do you do?"

"I'm an attorney. But not the cool kind on TV. The boring kind who looks at contracts all day."

When they finished their flights, Kara offered to buy a second round. Nisha accepted and once again did the ordering, this time getting each of them one full glass. Kara's was a valpolicella she had liked in her wine flight, but Nisha let her try the tempranillo she'd ordered for herself. It tasted like black cherry and smoky vanilla, warm and comforting.

"There's an aftertaste, though. It's something." Kara smacked her lips. "It makes your tongue feel dry."

"It's the tannins." She liked that Kara was being a good sport about learning.

Somehow their conversation drifted from wine and to the personal.

"You said you just moved here from Wisconsin. What prompted that? May I ask?"

"There are more opportunities to get ahead here. I had a job at home, but a bigger city means bigger clients and more career paths. Even if there are a thousand more attorneys."

"I guess we're a litigious city."

"Nah, you just have five law schools." Kara took another sip of the wine. "I also have an ex, and that was part of the reason I moved."

Nisha's wine warmed her body to the core. She took another sip and could feel its effects on her hot cheeks. The muscles she usually held so tight were slowly beginning to relax.

She didn't want to talk about Angie, and she wasn't going to push Kara to talk about her ex if she wasn't willing to share her own breakup story. She tried to figure out where to steer the conversation next, but Kara was more forthcoming than she expected.

"She's not an ex. She's a former." Kara reached behind her head and tightened her ponytail. "My partner Hilary died."

"Oh, Kara, I'm so sorry!" The words sounded useless in the face of something so terrible. No wonder Nan had said Kara was in pain.

Kara stared at her wineglass as she twirled the stem back and forth. "I've spent a long time grieving, and I couldn't move forward without a new start somewhere else."

"I can't understand going through that kind of loss."

"I wouldn't wish it on my worst enemy." Kara turned to Nisha, a wan smile on her face. "It's taken a long time and a lot of counseling and meditating to get this point, where I can talk about Hilary like this. I'm not trying to ignore what happened by moving here, but have you ever felt like you needed to break away from things to really be yourself?"

Nisha hadn't lost a loved one like that, but she had broken away from her parents when she'd come out. She'd moved to a new part of town and starting hanging out with new friends, people who accepted her as herself instead of pushing their expectations onto her.

"I can understand wanting to move for a fresh start."

"Is that why you moved out of the apartment? Were you trying to get a fresh start, too?"

It seemed only fair to be equally forthcoming.

"Angie and I were in the process of buying a condo together when she dumped me. They had accepted our offer, and the mortgage was being processed, but we hadn't closed yet." Nisha sighed and shook her head. "Then Angie said she was leaving me and Chicago. I called the mortgage broker and resubmitted everything in just my name, but without Angie's income and credit rating, they couldn't approve me. I told Oleg what happened and tried to renew the lease on the apartment, but by then the management company had already rented it to someone else, and there weren't any other vacancies."

"You basically got kicked out of your own house."

No one had ever put it that way before. Her parents had blamed her for being dumb enough to buy a house with another woman, and even Suni had made it clear she thought Nisha should have been less financially reliant on Angie if they weren't married.

"I guess so."

"Where are you living now? If you didn't get the place you were trying to buy?"

"I've been staying with some friends. I rent their extra bedroom. Actually, it's not too far from here."

"Is that why you suggested this place?"

"No, I thought you'd be able to talk to someone here, make some friends. Isn't that what you wanted?"

Kara covered her face with her hand and stifled a laugh. "I think there was a misunderstanding. I thought you'd tell me where there was a club where I could dance and let loose and maybe…" She made a vague gesture with her hand.

"You wanted a hookup," Nisha realized.

"Yeah, and then I walked in here, and it's kind of…slow and quiet, and it matched your stationery."

"My stationery?"

"From the note you left. It was pink and smelled like—"

"Oh, that's Nan's! She's in her eighties."

"Oh, wow. I thought you had some pretty old-fashioned perfume."

Nisha shook her head with a smile. "We both keep making false assumptions, don't we?"

"You don't dress old-fashioned."

Nisha noticed the way Kara tugged self-consciously on her vest, but they hadn't known each other quite long enough for Nisha to offer fashion tips. Hookup advice, though, that was a different story.

"If you're trying to meet people, why don't you just use Tindr like everyone else?"

Kara looked at her open-mouthed. "That never even occurred to me!" She shook her head. "Honestly, I guess Hilary and I were together so long I missed that whole era."

"It's still an era."

"We used to go to the Twin Cities for Pride, and they had this dance pavilion where there would be hundreds of people, just wall to wall bodies, everyone dancing and having a good time. Every spectrum of the rainbow you can imagine. I guess I was hoping to find that here."

"Are the Twin Cities close to where you lived?"

"Really close. Eau Claire's in Wisconsin, but it's only a little more than an hour to Saint Paul."

"Why didn't you move there instead of all the way down here?"

Kara shook her head. "Way too close to home. I needed some distance from my family after the last two years."

Nisha's parents only lived a few miles away. As infrequently as they talked and saw each other, they may as well have lived in a different city.

"I've told you a lot about myself, given that we just met," Kara said.

Nisha offered what she hoped was a disarming smile. "Well, you don't know anybody else in Chicago, right? That makes me your best friend here."

For a second, Kara looked terrified at the idea. Then she smiled back and said, "I guess you are."

Nisha could see she was pretending. Maybe Kara didn't want to continue being friends after tonight, and that was fine. But Nisha was at least going to make sure Kara was set up for success in her new city first.

She drained her wine glass. "All right, you want to go dancing. I know a place. We can take a cab there."

"Cool. Lead the way."

CHAPTER FIVE

Two hours later, Kara had lost track of Nisha in a throng of sweaty bodies and artificial smoke. She'd had two drinks, and she'd danced surrounded by people without feeling self-conscious about what she was wearing or how badly she was dancing. She'd even spent a few seconds grinding with a random woman in a sequin mini dress before another woman had yanked the dancer off the floor. Kara had died and gone to gay heaven.

The DJ put on a hip-hop song she hadn't heard before, one that seemed hard to dance to, and she took it as her cue to take a break. She pushed her way to the bar and asked for a glass of water. The bartender returned with a plastic bottle, its cap missing, and declared she owed him three dollars. Before she could complain, the next group of patrons had pushed in front of her to place their order. She left a five-dollar bill on the bar and looked for a spot to linger while she drank the precious water. She spotted Nisha near a window talking to two people and made her way over.

Nisha had taken off her sweater to reveal a form-fitting white bodysuit. In the black light, her bra glowed hot pink underneath the thin fabric. Kara wondered if Nisha knew it was showing and drawing attention to her perfectly rounded, perfectly sized chest. Was this her normal bra and shirt combo, or had she dressed this way for her wine bar date with Kara?

Not that it was a date. It was really a pity invitation.

Kara quickly looked away, but in the second she'd looked at Nisha's breasts, one of the other women had caught her. She stared at Kara, her lips pursed, and Kara's cheeks flushed with embarrassment.

"I hope I'm not interrupting!" she shouted over the music.

"You looked like you were having a good time!" Nisha replied. "These are my friends, Madeline and Sunita! They just happened to be here tonight!"

They gave their hellos, but Kara doubted Nisha's claim that they just happened to be at the same club at the same time on a Wednesday night. More likely, this was a friend intervention.

"Thank you so much for bringing me here! This is awesome!"

"Will you be okay getting home on your own?"

"Where are you going?"

Nisha's hand came up to Kara's waist, and she leaned close to Kara's ear to be heard. "Bed." Kara felt a shiver run through her body at the word and the sensuous way Nisha said it. "It's getting late."

Kara looked at Nisha's friends. They were actively listening, not even pretending to give them privacy. "It's only ten."

"I'm done, and my shoes are done." She raised a hand to show her heels dangling from a finger. On her feet, as if by femme girl magic, were a different pair of shoes that looked far more comfortable. "We already called a rideshare."

Madeline said, "It was nice to meet you." Sunita, the one who had seen Kara momentarily glance at Nisha's breasts, just glared. The two of them turned toward the exit.

Nisha gave Kara a hug, and unlike the one they'd shared at the wine bar, this one was long and tight. Kara could feel every curve of Nisha's warm body.

"I hope you have a really good night tonight," Nisha said in her ear. "I hope you get everything you're looking for." She turned to follow her friends.

A feeling Kara couldn't identify bubbled up inside, and she yelled, "Wait!" But Nisha couldn't hear her over the music and the space between them. She followed the trio all the way to the exit, which was bright and quiet and incongruous with the dark noise inside the club. She reached past Sunita to touch Nisha's elbow, and Nisha turned in surprise.

"Could we maybe talk privately before you leave?" Kara asked. "Is your car here already?"

Madeline seemed to like Kara better than Sunita, who folded her arms over chest. "We have two minutes if you guys want to talk. Come on, Suni."

"Nish, you okay?" Sunita asked without moving.

"I'm fine. I'll meet you guys outside in a second."

Yeah, she's fine, Kara wanted to say, but she didn't want Nisha's friends to be more off-put by her than they already were. In truth, Kara didn't know why she'd run after Nisha.

"I didn't mean to freak Sunita out. I don't think she likes me very much."

Nisha gave her coat to Kara while she pulled her sweater back on. "Suni thinks she's everyone's bodyguard." Kara held out the coat as Nisha slipped her arms into it. Then Nisha flipped her long black hair back into place. "Was that all you wanted to say?"

"No, I..." Kara stuck her hands in the back pockets of her jeans. "I just wondered why you were leaving so abruptly."

"What more do you want? You want me to pick out your hookup for you?"

"What?"

"That's what you wanted, isn't it?" Nisha said, walking backward toward the door. "You wanted me to be your wing man. I brought you here, and you can have your pick of people. You don't need me anymore." She pushed the door open and called over her shoulder, "Have a good night, Kara."

Kara had indeed asked Nisha to be a tour guide and wing man, and Nisha had agreed. So why was Nisha being weird about it? And why did Kara feel so awful?

She waited until Nisha and her friends climbed into an SUV, and then she walked out of the club to figure out her own way home.

❖

The next morning, there was a glass lying sideways on the counter and a sticky orange mess congealing beside it. Still only half-awake and slightly hungover from too much alcohol and not enough water, Kara was more angry than freaked out.

Nisha had testified on the building manager's behalf and had said they were friends. Maybe Nisha had told him about the sour end to their night out together, and he'd left the orange juice as a message to Kara not to hurt Nisha's feelings.

Kara hadn't done anything wrong. Nisha didn't have a valid reason for being upset. Even if she did, Kara didn't deserve to have her home and privacy violated because of it. The situation was unacceptable, and it was time to stop it. Either the building manager was going to tell her what was going on, or, if he continued to assert he wasn't involved, she was going to insist to the management company that they break her lease.

She slid a bra underneath her T-shirt and hooked it, grabbed her keys, and headed to the basement to the custodial office. It was shut and locked. She walked the first floor corridor until she found the apartment where Oleg lived and knocked on the door. Nothing. She banged harder and faster. Still nothing.

"Open up! I'm not playing around!"

A man carrying a laundry basket of folded clothes came out of the back stairwell. "You looking for Oleg?" Kara nodded. "He's out of town the rest of this week. There should be a note on his door to call the emergency number if there's a problem in your apartment."

Kara saw a handwritten note with blocky lettering pinned to the bulletin board next to the door. She turned back to the guy with the laundry, who was now balancing the basket on one hip while he fumbled with the lock to his apartment door. "Do you know when he left?"

"Yesterday afternoon, I think." He opened his door and went inside.

If Oleg had been gone since the afternoon, he couldn't have been the one who broke into Kara's apartment.

She trudged up the five flights of stairs to her own apartment. She found the copy of her lease and called the number to the main office.

The call disconnected.

Kara looked at her phone to make sure there were enough reception bars and the battery was fully charged. She dialed again, confirming the number before she hit the green button, and waited. It rang once, twice, and then—

It disconnected. No answer, no voice mail. She slammed her phone down on the newly scrubbed kitchen counter in frustration.

She didn't have time for this nonsense. She had to get ready for work. She took a shower to shake off her bad mood. The hot water felt soothing on her bone-weary body, and it was only with reluctance that she finally made herself shut it off. She pushed the shower curtain back and reached across the small space for the towel.

The mirror opposite the tub was fogged up, but as she approached it to brush her teeth, she could see something written in the fog.

LOVE

She threw the towel around her body. She looked around the bathroom, but there was no one else. Her heart was pounding as she turned the doorknob, and the floor creaked as she stepped into the hall.

"Hello?" She waited, then called out again a few times.

The apartment was eerily quiet. She couldn't even hear the radiators or the buses outside.

She retrieved her slippers—because the floors were still sticky and gross—and then she did a full inspection. The kitchen and living room were empty, and the door was still bolted shut. No one was in the bedroom, and the closet was empty.

This was beyond creepy. It was one thing to drink someone's orange juice, but it was another to come into a bathroom while she was in the shower. And what the hell did "LOVE" mean, anyway?

Maybe she should have called the police after the first night instead of wasting time asking Oleg and Nisha about it. But the police would ask if anything was stolen, and as far as she could tell, nothing was. They'd look around as she had done and tell her there were no signs of forced entry. Then they'd look at her differently, and she'd lived through that before. She didn't need them making her feel as if she was seeing imaginary things when she knew for certain she wasn't.

She got dressed and decided to get the hell out of there. She could spend her lunch break trying to find an Airbnb or hotel room for the night.

The morning was rushed with meetings and phone calls and mounds of files that were starting to take over her office, and she was so lost in work she forgot about everything else—the apartment stalker, Nisha, all of it was blotted out of her mind through the cleansing power of drudge work.

When it was finally time to take a lunch break, Kara wasn't hungry. She opted for coffee from the café on the ground floor. As she drank her flat white, she sat at a counter facing the sidewalk. She pulled out her phone to begin a search for a place to stay but got distracted by a text message from Nisha.

Hope you made it home safely last night. :)

She nearly rolled her eyes. They barely knew each other, and Nisha worried about Kara getting home—yet not enough to stay at the club until Kara left. The person Nisha was in written messages was totally different from the person she'd been at the club. Kara debated whether she should respond and, if so, what to say.

She didn't really want to cultivate a friendship. They didn't have much in common, except that they both lived in apartment 503. Nisha clearly wasn't over her breakup. Listening to her wallow in pain would make Kara constantly think about her own pain, and that was something Kara didn't want to do. She was actively working to heal and move forward, but Nisha didn't seem interested in doing the same.

But Nisha had been respectful when Kara said she didn't want to talk about Hilary. She hadn't asked how long they'd been together or how Hilary had died, the things people usually asked, right before they asked when. As if the date of Hilary's death could somehow determine their appropriate level of sympathy for Kara's grief.

It's been six months, and her shoes are still lying in the middle of the hall, her sister Becca had once scolded her. That was right after Kara had been sent home from work early with a clear message that if she didn't pull herself together, she'd lose her job. Six months, and Kara could still hear Hilary breathing beside her at night as she lay in the dark. At eight months, Hilary's pillowcase no longer smelled like her shampoo. At nine, the remaining traces of Hilary all over the house stopped feeling comforting, and Kara had slowly started to clean and box up Hilary's things.

She wondered how Nisha managed to stay in Chicago, where every street corner must have reminded her of her relationship with Angie. She seemed to enjoy that. Maybe she and Oleg cooked up a plan to scare Kara out of the apartment. Maybe Nisha wanted to move back in.

It didn't seem likely. The person Kara had met was kind—maybe too kind—and it didn't seem forced or artificial. What had she said? That she was Kara's best friend in Chicago? Seriously weird.

Missing ring or not, Kara didn't have to talk to Nisha again. She wasn't under any obligation.

Her fingers didn't seem to realize that. They pushed the call button of their own free will.

Nisha answered on the third ring. "Hi." Her voice was flat. "I didn't think I'd hear from you after yesterday."

"You texted me."

"I didn't think you'd text back. I definitely didn't think you'd call."

"I'm not sure why I did."

"I'm sorry about last night. I was pissy, and I shouldn't have asked Maddie and Suni to come rescue me."

"I knew you didn't run into them by chance!"

"Yeah, well...I was getting bored, and they kept texting me to find out who I was with and what we were doing. I guess they were worried. Anyway, I'm sorry if I ruined your night. I hope you had a better time after I left."

I wished you had stayed.

The thought made Kara choke on a sip of coffee, and coughing into a napkin gave her time to figure out what to say aloud.

They could just talk about Nisha's feelings.

"You were miserable last night, weren't you?" Kara asked.

"Honestly? I've always hated that place. But you said you wanted to dance, and the wine bar didn't really seem like your scene."

"I didn't mean for you to spend your night having a bad time on my account."

"It's not a big deal. It's just that Angie was always dragging me there."

"Then why on earth did you suggest it?"

"I don't really know many clubs," Nisha admitted. "That's not really my scene."

She had gone to a club that reminded her of her ex to make Kara happy. "That was really generous of you. I wish I had known. We could have stayed at the wine bar."

"It's probably time I stop being afraid of going certain places anyway."

"Give yourself time, Nisha. Revisiting places is hard. Hell," she said with a scoff, "it's all hard, and it hits you at times you least expect. One minute you're fine, and then suddenly—"

"Suddenly you're in the middle of the dance floor, and all you can think about is the last time you danced together. And you're with someone desperately hunting for a hookup, and it just reminds you of how people don't want to commit. How fleeting most relationships are." There was a pause. "Do you think I'm pathetic?"

"Noooo?" Kara hoped it sounded more convincing to Nisha.

She took another drink of her coffee. Her stomach protested the lack of nourishment, and she regretted that she hadn't made time for food with her lunch break nearly over. No one would give her any trouble if she was late coming back. They probably wouldn't even notice, since people were always rushing out to meetings and to court, but as the new person in the office, she wanted to show herself as a model employee. She'd have to make a point to eat after work, maybe before she took the train home.

"Do you want to get dinner tonight?" she asked.

"Oh, that's really sweet, but I have to be at the theater at five. Maybe we could meet this weekend for brunch instead?"

"How about coming over to look for the ring?"

"Really?"

"Yeah."

"I'd really like to see the space again. I haven't been inside since I moved out. Thank you."

That settled two really important things. First, Nisha wasn't breaking in and playing mind games. She said she hadn't been in the apartment, and Kara believed her.

Second, despite saying she didn't want to, Kara was definitely cultivating a friendship.

CHAPTER SIX

K ara texted that she was on her way back from the grocery store and running a few minutes late. With Oleg out of town, it didn't seem right for Nisha to let herself into the building. Although the weather was crisp, the sun was shining, so she took a seat on the cement steps leading up to the building to wait.

She was wearing a waist-length wool jacket over a burnt orange dress with a pair of black motorcycle boots and black leggings. Her hair was tucked up into a low side bun, and she wore a pair of dangly jade earrings she'd had since her twenty-first birthday. It was a look she hoped said casual but still fashionable, comfortable enough for brunch at home but put-together enough in case they decided to go somewhere afterward if Kara was up for hanging out.

"I hope you weren't waiting long." From down the sidewalk, Kara raised two shopping bags in explanation. She was wearing a Packers hoodie with jeans and sneakers, and Nisha felt self-conscious about how much more effort she'd put into getting ready by comparison.

When Kara reached her, Nisha took one of the bags. "Only a few minutes. I thought it might be weird if I used my key, and it's a nice day."

They rode the tiny elevator to the top floor. When they stepped into the hall, Nisha pointed at the door to 505. "Have you met her yet? She's lovely."

"The old lady? She always stares at me in the mail room. It creeps me out."

"That's just Nan being Nan. She's probably trying to read your mind."

They were talking so comfortably that when Kara opened the door to 503, Nisha was hit with a punch to the gut that made her gasp. She and Angie had lived here together. They'd been happy here. And now someone else lived inside, and everything looked and smelled different, and they weren't happy together anymore.

The living room in front of them was where Angie had broken Nisha's heart and Nisha's world had come crashing down.

Her feet were stuck in place, but her heart was breaking world records for speed.

"Oh, shit, maybe this wasn't a good idea." Kara took the bag from her and brought the groceries inside. "Come sit down."

Each footstep into the apartment was a march deeper into agony. "I'm fine."

Kara handed her a Kleenex. Nisha hadn't realized she was crying, but when she dabbed her eyes and nose, her face was wet. She tried to shake off the feeling. "I'm sorry. I didn't expect that to happen."

"Guess you really aren't the one who's been breaking in."

"What?"

"Do you want to go somewhere else? We could eat out instead."

"No." Nisha said it automatically, without thinking, but after a second she knew it was the right thing to say. "I don't want to be so haunted by a breakup that I have to avoid an apartment."

"Would you like a hug?"

It was a gracious offer, given how awkward Kara had seemed when they hugged at the wine bar. That was a hello hug, though, and now they knew each other a little bit better. Nisha nodded.

They fit together well with Kara's arms around Nisha's waist and Nisha's chin resting on Kara's shoulder.

She took a deep breath and let go. "Thank for you that."

"Do you want to take a look around?"

"I think I just want to get used to being in this space. Maybe after we eat, you can give me a tour and we can start looking for the ring? If you don't mind?"

"Make yourself comfortable."

Kara unloaded an assorted box of prefilled coffee cups and read off the options. Nisha picked frosted donut because it sounded like a low-calorie way to taste something yummy. In a few short minutes, Kara delivered a steaming cup to her.

"Listen, I don't know how to ask this, but when you lived here, did anybody ever do anything?"

"Do anything?"

"Like, try to screw with your head?"

Nisha shook her head, but she wasn't really sure what Kara was asking.

"Did anybody ever come in here without permission or anything like that?"

"No, of course not."

Kara sighed and settled on the sofa beside her. "Remember that weird stuff I told you was going on? How I found orange juice on the counter? The morning after we went out, I was taking a shower, and when I came out, someone had written in the fog on the mirror."

"That's terrifying."

"I know. I spent the last two nights sleeping in a hotel room."

"Why didn't you text me? We could have let you crash on the sofa." Nisha didn't actually know if Suni and Maddie would have been okay with that, and Kara didn't seem like the sofa-crashing type, but she didn't like the idea of someone being afraid of their own home. "Did you call the police?"

Kara went to the kitchen to retrieve her own coffee. "I should, but I can't."

"What do you mean, you can't?"

Kara looked fidgety and uncomfortable.

"What is it?"

"After Hilary died, I was seeing and hearing things for a while, and the way people looked at me…First it was sympathetic, but at a certain point I realized they didn't think they could believe me even when I was stating fact anymore. Even when I was better, people didn't seem to trust my judgment, and it affected my work. I guess I talked myself out of calling the police because I couldn't handle having people look at me that way, thinking I was losing my mind."

What a terrible experience, Nisha thought. Kara must have been so frightened to think she was losing her mind, but it must have been worse when she knew she wasn't and no one believed her. Of course

she was worried about saying something about the weird things that
had happened in the apartment. But if she didn't, and it escalated...

"If you're afraid to be in your own apartment because of
someone—"

"I tried to get the building manager to replace the locks, but he's
out of town. So I thought I'd file a complaint with the management
company, but every time I call, there's no answer and no voice mail.
So here we are." She sat on the couch again. "Can you imagine coming
out of the shower and there's stuff written on the mirror in fog?"

A memory scratched at the back of Nisha's mind. "Wait a second,
what was written on the mirror?"

"The word 'love.'"

She blinked a few times, processing the coincidence. "Angie
used do that in the morning while I was in the shower."

"Could it be Angie? Maybe she thinks you still live here?"

Even if Angie hadn't taken a job in Seattle, there was no way
she'd come back to profess her love for Nisha. No way.

"It wasn't Angie."

"Are you sure? Seems weird that someone else would do the
exact same thing."

"She just posted a photo of her new townhouse in Seattle, where
she lives with her new girlfriend." The same stupid photo of Angie
and what's-her-name, who was only ever acknowledged as "my baby"
in Angie's social media posts, had been on Facebook and Instagram.

"You should probably unfollow her."

It wasn't the first time someone had told Nisha that. "It's not that
easy."

"I know." Kara leaned forward to set her empty mug on a
cardboard box that was serving as a coffee table. "That's why I moved.
Fresh start. No connection to the past." She rose to her feet. "I'll get
the food ready. Make yourself at home. I don't have much here."

"The cardboard aesthetic is a really bold design choice."

"Furniture has been bought, but it's all on backorder. Supply
chain issues."

Nisha walked down the hall to the bathroom to look at the mirror
in question. As she took a step across the open doorway, a shiver
ran down her spine. She stepped fully in, expecting an open window

to be the cause, but the bathroom was still warm and humid from Kara's shower that morning. She looked at the mirror. Who would do something like that to Kara?

Maybe the word in the fog had been a lingering trace from one of the times Angie had written it to Nisha. Sometimes if you wiped a foggy mirror, the streaks showed the next time the mirror fogged over. Maybe the word "love" had been an echo from the past.

Nisha stepped back into the hall, and again when she crossed the threshold a finger of ice traced down the center of her back.

The experience was freaky, and it made Nisha crave the warmth of someone who took freaky things in stride and made everything seem so pleasant and normal.

"How much longer will you be cooking?"

"Really just chopping some fruit and heating some stuff up. I'm not much of a cook."

"That's no bother, I'm grateful for anything you make. I just wondered if I have time to go to the neighbor's—Nan, the lady I told you about. I visit her every few weeks, and I thought I'd say hi while I was here."

Kara nodded her approval at the plan, and Nisha made her way down the hall. It took three rounds of knocking, each time a little louder, before Nan answered.

She was wearing a fluorescent yellow house dress that zipped up the front and a pair of ratty slippers. Her hair was an uncombed tangle of hairspray. She smiled and gave Nisha a kiss hello.

"I thought I'd check on you."

"That's not why you're here."

"Fine. I'm having brunch with Kara, the woman who lives in my old apartment."

"About time you made some friends."

Nisha chose to ignore the jab. "Would you like to meet her?"

"Why would I want to do that?"

"Nan!"

Nan just shrugged. "Are you offering an old woman breakfast?"

"Is there an old woman around somewhere?" Nisha pretended to look over Nan's shoulder into the apartment.

"Don't be cute." Nan opened her door to let Nisha in. "I don't suppose I'm dressed for brunch."

She looked like a hot mess, but she was in her eighties. She was allowed to look however she wanted.

"Where's your brush? I can do your hair."

Nisha tried to put Nan's hair into some semblance of order without brushing out all the product and killing the volume. When she was done, it looked a little less like a bird's nest and more like a fluffy helmet. Nan changed out of the house dress and into a pair of polyester pants with a stretchy waistband and a hideous sweatshirt with a cat made out of sequins on the front. In truth, it wasn't much of an improvement.

Nisha hadn't meant to imply Nan was invited to eat with them, since it wasn't her decision to make. It was Kara's house and Kara's food. But Nan assumed, and now it would be a litmus test to see if Kara really was "no good," as Oleg had said. A nice person wouldn't refuse to share with a lonely, elderly neighbor.

"One more thing." Nisha pulled a plum-colored lipstick from the pocket of her jacket and applied it to Nan's lips in a few gentle strokes. It was too dark, given how thin her lips were, and it only accentuated the wrinkles around her mouth. But it made her look polished, as if she was ready to be seen at some formal event instead of just a casual meeting with her neighbor.

"Perfect. You look great."

"I look like an old lady wearing makeup."

"Don't say that," Nisha teased her. "You look like an old lady in a cat shirt wearing makeup."

She took Nan's hand, and as they stepped into the hall, Nan said, "I knew you'd hate this shirt. Why do you think I picked it?"

Nisha knocked on the door to 503 once before opening it. "Hey, Kara, I brought my friend Nan, who says she—"

Nan yanked her hand from Nisha's and took two steps back into the hall. "There's a ghost in there!"

❖

In the hallway, the old woman was ranting, and Kara could make out that it had something to do with spirits. Clearly, the woman was senile, but Nisha's voice, floating through the open doorway, was patient and loving as she tried to calm her down.

Kara thought it was best to leave them alone, so she continued spearing cornichons, olives, and cheese cubes for the Bloody Mary garnishes.

Finally, the noise in the hall subsided, and Nisha entered, leading the woman by the elbow. Kara came out from the kitchen to greet them.

Nisha pretended nothing had happened. "Kara, this is my friend Nan."

Kara decided to go along with it. "Hello, Nan, it's nice to meet you. Would you like to join us? We're just about to eat."

"I...I can't remember if I ate today."

"You said you were hungry," Nisha reminded her. Then to Kara, she said, "Anything I can help you with?"

"Is Nan able to drink alcohol?"

"I'm standing right here."

"Sorry, can you drink? Do you take any medications that make it prohibited? I was going to introduce Nisha to a real Wisconsin Bloody Mary breakfast, and I'll make you one, too, if you'd like."

"I'd like."

"Spicy okay?"

"Do I look like I'm in a home eating baby food and shitting in a diaper? Give me the whole enchilada!"

Nisha gave Kara an apologetic look, but she didn't have anything to be sorry about. Nan had sass, and Kara respected that. Not everyone aged into the fluffy grandmotherly type.

In the kitchen, she got out a third glass and rimmed it with her special mix of celery salt, chili powder, and a little habanero salt. Then she neatly poured in a bit from each of the other two drinks until all three glasses had more or less the same amount. Once she added ice and celery sticks, they looked like full pints. She sprinkled a little more celery salt and a dash of Worcestershire sauce on top of each drink before adding the skewers of cornichons, olives, and cheese cubes. She would have included bacon-wrapped shrimp, but she'd forgotten to ask Nisha if she had any food allergies or restrictions. Plus, for a first-timer, this was probably already a lot. She'd have to work Nisha up to the kind of outlandish garnishes her home state took pride in. Brats, chicken sliders—nothing was too big or too elaborate for a good Bloody topping.

She cracked open one of the precious bottles of Spotted Cow she'd brought from home, knowing the beer wasn't sold outside Wisconsin. She poured three small chasers and put the six glasses on a tray to take to the living room.

"What on earth is that?" Nisha asked with a laugh.

"You introduced me to wine. Now I'm introducing you to a real Wisconsin Bloody brunch."

"We used to go to Milwaukee all the time for the weekend," Nan said.

"Who's 'we'?" Nisha asked.

Nan didn't answer. She accepted a glass and, before Kara could warn her about the habanero salt, took a sip. "Excellent." She didn't even flinch from the spice. She set the glass on the cardboard box coffee table and picked up a beer. She took a quick drink, foam clinging to her upper lip, and gave an unashamed belch. "That's good stuff."

Nisha made the apologetic face again, but Kara thought it was funny. Nan was definitely tougher than she looked.

"Kara, I'm not sure what you'll think of this." Nisha set her glass down and sat up a little straighter. "Nan was telling me she might have an explanation for what's been going on here. In fact, she was a little frightened to enter at first because it hit her so hard, but you're all right now, aren't you, Nan?"

Nan took another gulp of Bloody Mary, followed by a chug of beer.

"Will you tell Kara what you were saying to me?"

Nan put her glasses beside Nisha's on the table. She extended her arms in front of her body, palms turned up, and closed her eyes. She wiggled her fingers as she breathed in and out. She opened her eyes.

"There's a spirit in this house." Then she hiccupped.

"What do you mean by 'spirit'?"

The eyes Nan turned on Kara were lucid and bright. "A ghost." She extended her arm, pointing at Nisha. "You lived here." She turned the pointing finger at Kara. "Now you live here. But the spirit—it lived here before."

It had to be the most ridiculous thing Kara had ever heard, the ravings of a senile old woman. It wasn't logical. It wasn't possible.

"Maybe it's an angry ghost," Nisha said. "That's why it's still here."

"A ghost who likes orange juice?" Kara looked between them to see if this was a joke. "Oh, come on, either you two are trying to play me, or you're actually nutty enough to believe what she's selling? There's no such things as ghosts."

Right as she said it, the lights went out, and the bathroom door slammed shut.

In the darkness, Nisha reached for Kara's hand. Kara squeezed back reflexively. Nan mumbled something too quietly for Kara to hear and hiccupped again.

A second later, the lights came up again, and the orange juice carton was on the coffee table. And sitting next to it was a diamond ring.

CHAPTER SEVEN

Nisha couldn't see anything but the ring. The missing ring. The ring that had been lost the day Angie moved out, the ring she'd been trying to find for a year. Suddenly it was sitting on a cardboard box next to some horrible tomato drink topped with cheese.

"Did the ghost do that?" she asked.

"It's a message for you," Nan said.

Kara reverently lifted the ring and presented it to Nisha. She took it, stared at it for a minute, and then put it on her middle finger, because Angie's fingers were bigger than hers. Her own matching ring was in Suni and Maddie's guest bedroom, safely tucked in a jewelry box after Suni had forbade her from wearing it anymore.

"Are you okay?" Kara asked.

Nisha couldn't answer. Having the ring back was a huge relief, closure to her year-long quest, but she also felt confused as to how it had reappeared and crushed at the reminder she and Angie were totally over.

"Nan, not that I believe in ghosts," Kara said, "but if a ghost did this, why?"

"Ghosts exist when people have unfinished business."

"I have my ring back now," Nisha said. "So maybe the ghost's work is done?"

Nan closed her eyes and did the finger wiggles again. She got up from the couch and paced around the living room. She spun in two slow circles, her arms stretched out on either side, and then walked back to the couch and collapsed.

"Let me get you some water," Kara said. "And food. You had a lot to drink."

Nan hiccupped again. Her face was flush. Nisha took her hand, which was clammy, and felt for a pulse on her wrist, but it seemed normal.

"I don't think she's reacting to the alcohol."

"It's still here," Nan said.

"What is?" Nisha asked.

"The spirit. It's not gone yet. Its business isn't over."

"What is its business?"

Nan looked at her. "How would I know? It's not like I can have conversations with dead people."

"But you just…"

Kara returned with a glass of water and a bowl of fruit salad. "So, uh, the idea of a ghost is a little—how should I say it? I'm not sure I can get on board with that."

"You said yourself you were home alone every time something happened, and the doors and windows were all locked."

"Therefore the most reasonable explanation is that there's a ghost living with me?"

Nisha had never thought much about whether she believed in ghosts, but she did believe in Nan. And if the past year of spiritual examination and self-growth had taught her anything, it was that the universe was more complex and mysterious than she had previously recognized.

She touched Angie's ring on her finger. What else could explain how it had suddenly appeared?

"I wonder why I got the ring back now."

"Maybe the ghost was waiting for you to come here."

"So you do believe."

"I didn't say that," Kara said. "*If* there's a ghost and *if* the ghost put your ring out, then maybe it's because the ghost was waiting for you. *If.*"

"If," Nisha echoed. "What else could it be?"

"I'm not saying I have an explanation that is more reasonable, but whatever it is, I'd like my privacy back."

Nan put the now empty bowl on the cardboard coffee table. "Miss Pythia can help you with that."

"Who's Miss Pythia?" Nisha asked.

"She has a shop on Damen."

As if that explained everything. Nisha and Kara exchanged a look.

"What does she do at her shop?" Kara asked.

"Tarot card readings."

"How will that help me?"

"It won't."

Kara threw her hands up.

"Nan," Nisha said, "is there a connection between someone who does tarot card readings and helping Kara with a ghost?"

"You asked what she does at her shop. She does tarot card readings there. You didn't ask me how she'll help you with the spirit. Obviously not with a deck of tarot cards."

Kara bit her lip and turned her face away from them. Nisha couldn't tell if she was going to laugh or scream.

"Maybe we can talk to the ghost ourselves," Nisha suggested. "If it tried to communicate with you in the mirror fog, maybe we can do the same."

"Not that I believe there's a ghost, but that's a good idea."

They went to the bathroom. Kara turned the shower on and let it run hot for a few minutes until the small room was humid and warm. When the mirror had fogged over, Nisha wrote with her index finger: *WHAT DO YOU WANT*

They waited with the water still running. Kara sat on the closed toilet lid while Nisha perched on the edge of the tub, the shower curtain behind her to keep her from getting wet. They watched the mirror with anticipation to see if the ghost would respond.

A few more minutes passed, and Nisha was starting to feel anxious about how much water was being wasted. Kara moved in front of the sink, gripping its edges as she faced the mirror, willing something to happen.

"Hello? Ghost? Are you here? I'm Kara. I'm the one who just moved in here. We saw the ring. Nisha got the ring. Thank you. She's relieved to have it back."

They waited another minute.

"Is there a reason you gave the ring back today?" Kara continued. "Is there anything else we should know?"

"Were you waiting for me to come over?"

"The message in the fog," Kara said. "Was that a message for her?"

Nothing happened except that the room was full of steam and uncomfortably hot. Kara shut off the shower, and they opened the door to a gust of cool, dry air from the hallway.

Nan was right. They needed a professional.

❖

After they ate Kara's hastily made brunch of toast and fruit, Nisha escorted Nan home with the promise of visiting again soon. She returned to Kara's apartment with the address of Miss Pythia's shop. They set out on foot to find the storefront, moving south on Damen until they arrived at an old three-flat with no visible address markings. The only indication they were at the right place was a sign on the sidewalk suggesting that Miss Pythia could perform "honest readings to help you get in touch with dead loved ones."

Nisha had had her cards read a few times at street festivals. Coincidentally, each time, it had been the same reader. Twice she was told to go to Lake Michigan and make friends with a rock on the shoreline. She'd thought the advice sounded silly, but standing in front of Miss Pythia's shop now, she realized that, in a way, that's what she did during her early morning runs.

"Have you ever had a tarot card reading?" she asked Kara.

"Of course not. That stuff is such a silly waste of money."

Nisha tried not to take the comment personally. "I don't know. I've done it, and it seemed like good advice."

"They just say the vaguest possible things, so their predictions apply to everyone. It's not real. None of this is real."

"Then why did you agree to come here?"

"Because if I believed there's a ghost in my apartment—and I still don't—then I guess it would make sense to get help from someone who knows more about these things." Kara stuffed her hands in the pockets of her hoodie and shrugged. "Worst-case scenario, it'll be good for a laugh."

They descended the stairs to the basement-level storefront and rang the bell.

A very round woman with olive skin and a mangle of curly black hair answered the door. She ushered them in with her long ruby talons.

"You want a reading." It wasn't a question. "Twenty-five dollars for twenty minutes. I won't talk about your death. It wears me out."

"People ask you about their own deaths?" Nisha asked.

"It's all they ever want to know," Miss Pythia said with a weary sigh.

"We're not here to ask about ourselves," Kara explained. "Someone told us you know a lot about ghosts."

"Please! Spirits!" She held an index finger with a long red nail to her mouth like a fake moustache and spat under it. "'Ghosts' sounds like something from sensational television. What is your name?"

Nisha half expected her to say, *No, don't tell me, let me guess.* "I'm Nisha. This is Kara." She offered her hand.

Miss Pythia's grip was warm and firm, though she nearly missed grazing Nisha with her claws as their hands slid apart.

"Mmm," Miss Pythia said, "you have good energy."

"Um, thank you?"

Miss Pythia shook Kara's hand and held it for a few seconds, but she didn't tell Kara whether her energy was good.

"You want to talk to a spirit? Fifty dollars for thirty minutes. I need advance notice and an object that was meaningful to the dearly departed."

How were they supposed to get an object meaningful to someone they'd never met?

"We don't know the spirit. Kara just moved into an apartment, and we think it's haunted by someone who lived there before."

"I don't have any of the gho—the spirit's things," Kara added. "I just want to know how to get rid of it."

Miss Pythia frowned. "You don't 'get rid' of spirits. You find out what their unfinished business is and help them take care of it. If a spirit is staying in your apartment, it has a reason for being there."

"Right, that's what the old lady said."

"Old lady? Who is this 'old lady'?"

"Nan Galt," Nisha said. "She recognized the presence of the spirit when she came to the apartment, and she said you could help us."

"Nan!" Miss Pythia clapped her hands once as her eyes grew considerably friendlier. "Special discount for friends. Forty dollars for thirty minutes, and I'll throw in an aura reading. Now, tell me what this spirit's been doing."

"You know what?" Kara took a few steps toward the door. "I'm sure I've just been hallucinating. I'm sorry I bothered you." She hurried out of the store, up the steps, and out onto the sidewalk.

Nisha frowned. "I'm sorry. She's not sure she believes in all this."

"You'd better go after her."

Nisha trotted up the stairs to the sidewalk. The sky had clouded over, and it was starting to snow. A flake landed in her eyelashes, and when she brushed it away, she could feel a streak of wetness across her cheek.

Kara was speed-walking down the sidewalk in the wrong direction from home. "Kara! Wait up!" When she didn't stop, Nisha jogged to catch up with her. "Hey, what was all that about?"

"Ghosts aren't real. I told you I don't believe in them."

"Could it really hurt to hear what Miss Pythia had to say?"

"She's friends with Nan, Nisha. Clue in. They probably concocted the idea that Nan would tell people their apartments are haunted and send them to Miss Pythia, and for a fee she'll get rid of your ghost for you. And the two of them split the profits and laugh all the way to the bank."

"Could you stop?" Nisha tapped Kara's elbow, and she finally stopped speed-walking away. They turned to face each other, the light snow sprinkling down on them. "You have a really pessimistic view of people. First you think Oleg and I are out to get you. Now it's Nan and Miss Pythia."

"The world isn't all sunshine and roses, Nisha. There are a lot of shitty people out there, and shitty things happen to good people when they least expect it."

This wasn't about Miss Pythia. It was about Hilary. Nisha wondered what kind of person Kara had been before Hilary's death had given her such a cynical outlook.

"I don't know why you stopped me," Kara continued. "I'm not going back to that woman."

"Okay, we don't have to, but you were going the wrong way. You live that way." She pointed north on Damen.

"What? Oh."

They started walking in the right direction. As they approached Miss Pythia's shop, Nisha could see her standing on the sidewalk, waiting for them.

"It's very cold out here," Miss Pythia said. "You won't find the answers you're looking for out there."

"Why on earth should I listen to you?"

Miss Pythia took Kara's hand between hers and closed her eyes. After a few seconds, she opened them to look intently at Kara.

"Sometimes I hate this job. I hate every minute I have to connect with the spirit realm—it's draining, you know—and I hate seeing good people fall apart when the spirit realm reaches out to them. Come back inside, Kara. I can make some tea, and we can talk."

To Nisha's surprise, Kara nodded.

Miss Pythia escorted them past the front room with its table for readings, through a beaded curtain and into a living room. The front room was decorated with every cliche of a psychic medium, but this room looked like it had been put together at IKEA. She left them on a plain navy sofa while she disappeared to make tea.

"Is this weird?" Kara asked quietly. "Tell me this isn't normal."

Past the arched doorway through which Miss Pythia had gone, there was a lot of banging and drawers slamming, and then the microwave ran.

"Definitely one of the weirder experiences I've had," Nisha agreed.

The microwave beeped, and shortly after Miss Pythia came back with two ceramic mugs sloshing tea on the hardwood floor.

"Ginger tea," she said. "It soothes the nerves." A paper Lipton tag was hanging over the side of the mug she handed Nisha. "The tea's on me, but the conversation isn't free. Twenty-five dollars for a consultation, thirty minutes."

Given how supportive and understanding she'd been outside, this seemed mercenary of her. Nisha expected Kara to change her mind and walk out again.

Instead she said, "What the hell? Cheaper than my therapist."

Miss Pythia slid a cube ottoman closer to the couch and sat facing them. She clasped her hands and let them rest between her knees.

"Now, tell me what you know about this spirit."

"Well," Nisha explained, "I couldn't find my partner's ring. Then today, out of nowhere, the lights went out, and when they came back on, the ring was sitting in front of me. I kind of wonder if the spirit had it the whole time and decided to give it back today?"

"What was special about today?"

"It was the first time I've been back in that apartment since I moved out."

Miss Pythia nodded sagely, as if she'd anticipated this answer.

"Wait a second," Kara said, turning to Nisha. "The ring you've been looking for all this time was Angie's? Not yours?"

Nisha felt a little hot in the face. "Is that important?"

"You didn't tell me it was Angie's. You made it sound like it was your ring."

"Can we talk about this later?" Preferably in private, away from a stranger who didn't need to know about Nisha's embarrassing breakup.

"No, no," Miss Pythia said. "This is important."

"Yes, it's Angie's ring, okay? We had matching engagement rings, and when we broke up, she took it off and threw it, and I couldn't find it before I had to move out."

"Why on earth do you want Angie's ring?" Kara asked. "She broke up with you."

"Because." Nisha faltered. Because it was a sign of what their relationship had been before it fell apart. Because she loved and respected Angie, even if Angie didn't care about her anymore, and she treasured the memories of what their relationship had been. Because holding on to it meant holding on to those memories. "Because it was expensive."

Kara snorted.

"Tell me what else happened," Miss Pythia said. "Was today your first encounter?"

Kara told her about the noises she'd heard and about how the orange juice had been left on the counter. She recounted the incident with the mirror fog and their attempt to re-create it that day.

Miss Pythia nodded and said, "Wow," at the appropriate places, even adding one or two expressions like "I hear that so often..." as if to reinforce her expertise.

"And then I tried talking to the spirit," Kara said. "But it didn't respond."

"What did you say?"

"I think I introduced myself." Kara looked to Nisha for confirmation.

"You said I was grateful to get the ring back, remember?" She fidgeted with Angie's ring. "Nan said it might be the spirit of someone else who lived in the apartment before either of us."

"But you never saw signs of a spirit when you lived there?" Miss Pythia asked.

Nisha shook her head. She'd thought about it since Kara told her about the unexplained noises and signs, but she and Angie had never experienced anything out of the ordinary. "Does that mean the spirit wasn't around when I lived there?"

"More likely it didn't have business with you," Miss Pythia said. "It was laying low."

"So you mean it was there the whole time, and we didn't even know it? That's creepy."

"It's creepier when it's writing on your bathroom mirror while you're in the shower," Kara said hotly. "What business does it have with me? I just want to be left alone."

"What do you think you have in common with it?" Miss Pythia asked. "We know it shared a bond with Nisha over the ring."

Nisha opened her mouth to protest that the spirit had never drank her orange juice, but Miss Pythia added, "It made a conscious choice to give you the ring today. There was something significant."

Nisha had been with Kara and Nan when she got the ring back. She'd have to think a little on why that was significant.

Miss Pythia turned to Kara. "But the spirit didn't show itself until you moved in. Why do you think that is?"

Kara stared at her tea for a bit, mulling it over. Finally, she mumbled, "Because I miss Hilary."

It was the first time she'd admitted it so plainly instead of acting so ready to move on. Nisha set her mug down on the coffee table and put a hand on Kara's knee. Kara looked up at her and gave a sad smile.

When the first thirty minutes expired, Miss Pythia was quick to tell them that she'd require additional payment if they wanted to continue their session. Her calling it that, as well as the turn the conversation had taken toward Hilary, made it feel more like therapy than a consultation over a ghost. That's what Nisha's previous tarot card readings had felt like, too. The second time, the reader had held Nisha's hand while she cried over the six-month anniversary of the breakup, and after hearing about it, she'd told Nisha that she had a beautiful smile and that the world needed to see it instead of her tears.

"I moved here to try to get some distance from all the memories," Kara admitted. "And then this person contacts me, and she's desperate to keep memories of her ex. It felt coincidental, but in a backward way."

"There's more," Miss Pythia said matter-of-factly.

"What else?" Nisha looked at Kara.

"I want to know if the spirit can talk to Hilary."

And she'd said she didn't believe in ghosts.

Miss Pythia told them that for seventy-five dollars she could give Kara the appropriate herbs and an incantation to enable easier communication with the spirt. For one fifty, she'd come to the apartment and do it herself.

Nisha wondered if she was leading Kara into false hope. Taking advantage of Kara's grief that way would be grotesque.

If Miss Pythia was telling the truth, though, it would be useful to be able to communicate with the spirit. Both Nan and Miss Pythia had said it couldn't leave until its business was resolved, and if they didn't know what that business was, how could they help?

"You can't keep living like this," Nisha said to Kara. "We need to know what the business keeping the ghost here is."

"Please!" Miss Pythia said. "Spirit."

"Can you give us a second to talk privately?" Kara asked her.

Miss Pythia took their empty tea mugs back to the kitchen.

"Nish, seventy-five dollars is a lot of money to waste on mumbo-jumbo."

It was a lot of money for Nisha to waste, especially right now, but this was a special circumstance. What was the alternative? Doing a price comparison with another medium?

"It's the same as a week of Starbucks."

"What on earth do you order at Starbucks that costs that much?"

"My point is, think about Nan. The lights going out, the ring. We were wrong about the line between life and death, and, like you said, if we can communicate with the spirit, maybe you can communicate with Hilary. Isn't it worth some money to find out?"

"It's a long shot. And she's probably selling bullshit."

As it turned out, Miss Pythia accepted credit cards.

CHAPTER EIGHT

When they got back to the apartment, they cleared a space to work in the living room. Nisha placed the candles that had come in their "contacting spirits" starter kit on the floor. They were not, Miss Pythia had sworn, the same votives that were sold at every big box store. She'd also given them a few plastic baggies of dried flowers and herbs, which looked like regular old lavender and oregano to Kara, but Miss Pythia had insisted it was a "potent mix of rare plants used for centuries in white magic." She'd asked Kara if she had a mortar and pestle, and when Kara said she did not, Miss Pythia had added a small stone bowl and grinder to the package for an additional twelve dollars.

"Does this look right?" Nisha said, holding up the chart for the candle placement Miss Pythia had drawn by hand. She'd seemed to be freestyling when she made it, further convincing Kara that this whole thing was a hoax being made up on the fly.

"I think so. I guess I'll work on the 'potent mix.'" Kara crushed dried herbs and plants in the mortar one bag at a time. Then Nisha read the magic recipe aloud as Kara put the herbs one by one into a stainless steel mixing bowl. Finally, Kara struck a match and dropped it into the bowl. The herbs crackled, sending up fumes that smelled like diarrhea. The smoke detector started shrieking.

"Help me open the windows!"

"No, you can't!" Nisha said. "The ghost might escape!"

Kara dragged a chair into the hall, climbed up, and removed the battery from the smoke detector.

Miss Pythia had given them an incantation, which Nisha recited, and she'd recommended that afterward they make a noise that sounded like Tibetan throat-singing. Kara couldn't bring herself to do it. Nisha did, without hesitation, and she was able to sustain a note for an impressive amount of time.

"Now what?"

"Now we count to ten." Nisha reached for Kara's left hand and moved around the coffee table so they were facing each other. Then she reached for Kara's right, the circle around the herb bowl complete.

They counted aloud together.

Then Kara asked, "Spirit, are you still here? We want to talk to you."

They waited another moment.

Nothing happened. Kara let go of Nisha's hands. Not that she'd expected it to work, but it appeared the foul-smelling plants really were nothing more than yesterday's compost. She blew gently on the bowl, sending a few stray bits of burnt herbs into the air. She pinched her fingers over the wicks of the votives to snuff out the flames, and then she climbed back on the chair to replace the smoke detector battery.

At once several things happened: the smoke detector began to beep again, the temperature in the room plummeted, and the lights went out. After a few seconds, all was quiet and bright again.

Except there was a woman sitting on the couch.

Kara and Nisha screamed and grabbed each other.

The woman looked equally startled. "You can see me?"

"Of course we can see you!" Kara said. "You're sitting right there! Who the hell are you?"

"Now do you believe in ghosts?" Nisha said to Kara.

The woman looked down at herself. Her skin was somewhere between Kara's pasty porcelain and Nisha's bronze. From the crinkles around her eyes and the sagging lines around her mouth, she looked older than either of them. Her hair and clothing were dated, as if she had died a while ago and not been able to update her wardrobe. She was wearing white Reebok high-tops and pleated jeans into which her short-sleeved blue silk shirt was tucked. The shirt had shoulder pads that gave her torso a V-shape, and her brown hair, streaked with gray, was parted in the middle and feathered away from her face to her shoulders.

The ghost raised her hand and flipped it over to inspect the palm. She reached toward the cardboard box coffee table, and her arm went right through it. Not in the way of masters at karate or those with anger management problems. Her arm was actually sticking out the other side, but the table was undamaged. She withdrew her arm and reached for one of the candles. This time she picked it up.

"How did you do that?" Kara asked.

"I don't know. Sometimes if I concentrate, I can touch things. Mostly I go through them."

"Mostly? How long has this been going on?"

The ghost shrugged. "How long have I been dead?"

She rose from the couch. She didn't sink through the floor. That had to mean something, right? She also didn't float. She walked with regular human steps toward the kitchen.

"I'm thirsty."

Kara followed the ghost into the kitchen and watched as she opened the refrigerator, pulled out the orange juice, and poured herself a glass. She offered the carton to Kara.

"You want some?"

"Do you mind? This is *my* house."

"It's my house, too, babe. Been my house a lot longer than it's been yours."

"But you're dead!"

"I know I'm dead, but I'm obviously still also here. In this space. Where I lived long before you came around. I wonder why you can see me now."

Nisha rushed in, waving the paper with the instructions Miss Pythia had given them. "We screwed up!"

"What do you mean?" Kara asked.

"It says if you use Chinese mugwort instead of Korean mugwort, you have to put the thyme in first."

"Are you making this up?" Kara took the paper from her and saw the small asterisk next to the mugwort. At the bottom of the page was the note. "Which mugwort was in the kit?"

"Clearly not the right one!"

"You guys did some kind of spell or something?" the ghost asked.

"We have to call Miss Pythia," Kara said. "I don't care what she wants to charge us. This is a disaster."

"We said we wanted to be able to communicate." Nisha gestured at the ghost.

"Communicate! We were supposed to get her to write in the mirror fog, not come back to life!"

"You summoned me without even knowing what you were getting into? Boy, are you guys dumb." The ghost went back to the living room, with Kara and Nisha trailing behind. She scrunched her eyes and face as she concentrated on being able to sit on the sofa. She picked up the remote and turned the TV on.

"What are you doing?" Kara demanded.

"Seeing if there's anything good on. Do you know how lucky you are to live in a time with so many channels? When I was alive, we only had five."

"You cannot watch my TV." Kara snatched the remote and turned the TV off. "You have to go back to wherever you came from. You can't live with me."

"I don't know how to tell you this, sister, but we've been living together since you moved in. And by the way, next time you clip your toenails, would you mind closing the door? I can't stand the sound."

Kara had no idea why they'd ever thought communicating with the spirit was a good idea. "I was only trying to talk to you, not make you—" She gestured at the spirit's feet, which were half resting on the coffee table and half hovering inside it.

"Well, you got me in all my splendid glory." The ghost patted the sofa next to her. "Come on, let's order a pizza and do this right. Girls' night in."

Kara threw up her hands. "Nisha?"

Nisha shrugged. "She's more bewildering than scary, isn't she? I'm not sure what I expected, but it wasn't this." She turned to the ghost. "What's your name?"

The ghost looked away from the television she'd turned back on. "It's about time one of you asked me that, geez. I'm Barb."

"Do you know what year you died?" Nisha perched gently on the sofa beside her.

"It was a cold night in 1910 when my grandpappy ran out of coal for the fire. Mama had us ten children to care for, and Papa had just died of consumption."

"Barb, be serious. What's the last thing you remember about being alive?"

Barb closed her eyes. "Pain." She tapped her chest. "Burning and squeezing for several days and then finally a hot flash of pain and nothing else." She opened her eyes. "I think I had a heart attack. It was 1986. It was a Sunday. I had just eaten lunch, and they were playing 'We Are the World' on the radio."

"Did you die in this apartment?" Kara sank to the sofa on the other side of Barb.

"In this room."

"And you've been...haunting ever since?"

Barb shrugged. "I didn't know that's what I was doing. I was waiting for the instruction manual to come out as a book on tape."

"But I mean—" Kara looked to Nisha for inspiration to say the words more sensitively. "You never went to heaven or the afterlife or whatever?"

"Honey, you'd have to believe in heaven to get there."

"Miss Pythia said you must be trapped between realms because you had unfinished business."

"Miss Pythia? You talked to her?"

"Yes," Nisha chimed in. "Do you know her?"

Barb smirked. "Back in my day, she was just plain old Rosalind, and the Miss Pythia thing was an act she was working on to scam the assholes for a few bucks."

If they had been acquainted with each other in the past, then maybe Miss Pythia knew enough about Barb's life to figure out why she hadn't crossed over. And if she could figure that out, they could help Barb finally do it.

"Nish, where are those instructions Miss Pythia gave us?"

Kara called the number printed at the bottom of the sheet, but Miss Pythia didn't answer. She might have been in the middle of doing a reading for a client, or maybe she'd gone home for the day.

"What time is it?"

Nisha pulled her phone from a hidden pocket in her dress. "One." She put her phone away. "I've got to leave soon if I'm going to get to the matinee on time."

"You're a makeup artist, aren't you?" Barb asked. "You used to live here."

"I do makeup at the Wolfman Theater. How did you remember?"

"You were here a long time. Longer than that dip who was here before her."

"Do you think Miss Pythia works all afternoon?" Kara asked. "Maybe we should go see her in person? I don't know why she's not answering her phone."

"I don't think I have time," Nisha said. "I have to go home before I get to the theater. I'm sorry about all this."

Kara didn't want to leave Barb sitting in her living room while she was out, but Barb reminded them, "I've been here alone every time somebody had to go to work. Just because you can see me doesn't mean anything new. Well, except it means you can see me."

"All right, listen," Kara said. "I'll be back in half an hour. Can you just sit here and not get into any trouble while I'm gone?"

"Okay, Mom."

Nisha walked out with Kara until they got to the intersection where they had to go in opposite directions. "I'd say thank you for brunch, but I wasn't expecting a tomato soup cocktail or a surprise guest star."

"Nisha, there's a freaking ghost in my apartment."

"Please!" Nisha said, mimicking Miss Pythia spitting. "*Spirit.*"

"This isn't funny!"

"So, just to check, you *do* believe in ghosts?"

"Nisha!"

"Okay, okay." She put a hand to Kara's bicep and gave it a squeeze. "I'm not trying to make light of this. This is some seriously weird shit, I agree."

"All I want is to find Miss Pythia and make her tell me how to fix this."

"I'd better get the bus. Keep me posted?"

"Have a good show."

Nisha gave a wave as she turned in the direction of an approaching bus. Once she was on it, Kara started the walk down Damen to find Miss Pythia.

The neon light in the front window was off, and the sandwich board had been taken inside. Kara banged on the door anyway. After a few moments and a few curious glances from passers-by, she gave up. Defeated, she returned home, only to realize she'd left her keys and phone in the apartment.

She circled the block a few times, lost in thought, and ended up on an icy bench at the bus stop where Nisha had left. She'd gotten so swept up in the afternoon that she hadn't taken a moment to really analyze what had happened. Some cynical part of her believed this was punishment for wanting to start a new life. Now the past was sitting on her couch. Literally.

If ghosts were real, and if they stayed because of unfinished business, why hadn't Hilary stuck around? Surely they had plenty of unfinished business together. After Hilary's death, Kara had prayed for months for a sign the whole thing was a mistake and Hilary was alive somewhere or a sign that in death Hilary was no longer in pain, so Kara could have peace in her heart. A sign of anything. But there had been nothing.

She sat for a while, reminding herself that grieving was good and natural and that the pain had already dulled and would continue to do so with time.

This will pass, and I can do this. I will be okay.

When she couldn't tolerate the cold any longer, Kara trudged back to her building on her ice-block feet. She buzzed her own apartment in hopes Barb would be able to let her in. A moment later, the lobby door unlatched for her.

Upstairs, Barb was eating pizza out of a delivery box.

"How did you get that?" As Kara said it, she saw her wallet and phone sitting on the coffee table. "You stole from me?"

"Eh, come on, don't call it that." Barb had a thick accent, and it made everything she said sound like a bad comedy sketch about Chicago.

"What would you call it?"

"Making an early dinner for us." She angled the box toward Kara. "It's extra pepperoni."

Kara reluctantly took a slice. It was square-cut and had a thin crust, not the kind of pizza she usually ate, but it tasted good. Even if it had been bought with a stolen credit card.

"I wish Nisha had stayed to supervise you."

"I don't need supervision." Barb ate a slice in two bites and immediately reached for another. "Come on, sit down. Your hovering is making me lose my appetite."

Kara sank onto the sofa beside her. "Can I ask you something?"

"Only yes or no questions."

"Is that a ghost rule?"

"Nah, it just sounds fun." Barb leaned forward and took another slice. Only half the pizza remained.

"Are you the one who hid Nisha's ring in the first place?"

"Yes."

"Did you deliberately wait until Nisha came back in the apartment to give it back to her?"

"Yes."

"How did you know she was going to come over one day?"

"That's not a yes or no question." Barb said it in a singsong voice as she waved a piece of pizza at Kara. "But I'll answer it because I like you. It's not quite knowing. It's more like…feeling. I can sense things that I wasn't able to before, when I was alive. Other people, events, things outside my head. When you moved in, I had this sense that Nisha was supposed to get the ring back when she came here again."

"Where'd you find it?" Remembering the right question format, Kara added, "In the living room?"

"No."

"In the kitchen?"

"No."

This game was annoying. "In the bathroom?"

"Yes."

"I looked there."

"I moved it to the hall closet before you looked. And then I moved it back."

"Why?"

"Not a yes or no question, toots. You're not very good at this."

Kara watched Barb eat two more slices. Admittedly, they were small squares, but surely she had to be getting full now that the pizza was mostly gone. Unless ghosts didn't have stomachs to feel full.

Kara wanted to ask deep questions, the tough stuff that might hurt to ask but that would make her feel better to know. She wasn't sure she had the guts.

"That's all the questions you got?"

"Can you sense Hilary?"

"No." Barb said it with kindness. "I'm sorry."

When Kara's grandmother had died and they'd stood at her grave site, waiting for the casket to be lowered, her mother had leaned over to whisper to her, "It's okay to cry." The comment had confused nine-year-old Kara, who hadn't felt close to crying. Her mother's suggestion had made her feel as if something was wrong with her. She had wished she could summon tears to satisfy her mother, but the whole situation embarrassed her.

She'd been struggling to cry ever since. Sad movies made her sad, but they didn't make her cry. When they lost their family dog a few years after Grandma's funeral, Kara had moped around for a month, but she didn't cry.

When Hilary died, Kara hadn't cried right away. They had known her cancer was winning and that it would take her life, and when she finally passed, Kara was numb. Later, she understood that she had been in shock, and once the shock was gone, she'd burst into full-body sobs. She had shaken and snotted all over the shoulder of Hilary's mom as she wailed about the injustice of how fast it seemed to happen despite the warnings. It hadn't felt fair, and her sorrow and rage had come straight out of her tear ducts and nose. Hilary's mom had held her and sobbed with her until the tears finally abated.

Since that day, she'd been depressed and angry, sometimes despondent, sometimes guilty, over Hilary's death, but she hadn't really cried again.

Now, though, she understood why Nisha had cried when she'd first stepped into the apartment.

Unexpectedly, Barb put her arms around Kara. "It's okay, honey, it's okay."

Barb's body was neither warm nor cool, and Kara couldn't feel a heartbeat through Barb's chest as she rested her head on Barb's shoulder. The hug was supposed to be comforting, and while Kara appreciated the gesture, it was spooky. She abruptly pulled away.

"Sorry. You looked upset."

"I appreciate it. I'm just not much of a crier."

"Neither was I. I think laughing is better anyway. You know how therapeutic laughter is? Tell me a situation when it's wrong to laugh. Never. It's always the right thing to do."

"At a funeral?"

"Well, okay, I see your point, but I hope somebody laughed at my funeral. Because if you're not laughing, then you're probably going to go insane."

"I feel like I'm going insane right now."

"You want to ask me any more questions, or are we done with that game? Cuz the playoffs are on soon, and I kind of want to watch if you don't mind."

"To be honest, I do mind. I wanted peace and quiet. Privacy."

"I got news for you, kiddo. You never had privacy. You just thought you did." Barb finally closed the pizza box and slouched back on the couch. She patted her belly. "Boy, that was good. I missed pizza. Face it, you've had a roommate since the day you moved in. Not my fault you couldn't see me before."

Or talk to her. Or watch her order delivery. This wasn't what Kara had signed up for at all.

"Can you at least tell me why you're still here? That's the reason we were trying to talk to you. We just wanted to figure out how to…. finish your business, so you'd go back to where you're supposed to be."

"You want me to tell you what to do to get rid of me."

"Well, yes."

"Not happening. And let me tell you, there's a lot more going on than you realize. You don't know how naive you are, okay? You have no idea."

There had to be a way around Barb's reticence. It was all a matter of asking the right question. In this case, a roundabout method might work better than direct interrogation.

"You said you lived here in the 1980s? My neighbor has lived here a long time. Maybe you know her? Nan Galt?"

Barb's eyes drifted away for a moment, only to return, steely. "What about her?"

"So you know her?"

"No."

Barb was lying, Kara could tell, but it was going to take finesse to figure out why exactly. Between taciturn Barb and senile Nan, no meaningful details were going to fall into her lap. But Kara enjoyed puzzles.

She decided to try a different approach. "Nisha's really happy to have the ring back. That's why she contacted me in the first place, you know."

"I do know. I heard your conversations." Barb opened the pizza box up and searched for another slice. It had to be cold now, but she crammed a piece in her mouth anyway. "You got any Pepsi to go with this?"

"I think you're being kind of blasé about Nisha. That ring was really important to her, and you hid it for a year. She's been losing her mind trying to find it."

Barb chewed her mouthful quickly. "You don't really know as much as you think you do about Nisha. I was here when she lived here, remember? There are things I could tell you that you wouldn't believe." She gave a long whistle.

"Like what?"

"Things about her and Angie."

Nisha's relationship with Angie wasn't any of Kara's business, though part of her was curious to know what truths lay hidden underneath the perfect exterior Nisha had painted. There had to be a reason she was still pining for Angie a year after their breakup.

"I don't think I should listen to gossip about their relationship."

She took the bowl of herbs into the kitchen and contemplated throwing it away. Apart from keeping a tidy house, though, what was the good in that? Barb couldn't stay in physical form. If they wanted to correct their mistake, they'd probably need the same herbs. She glanced over her shoulder into the living room. Barb was watching television with a happy smile. Kara dumped the bowl into a baggie, sealed it, and hid it under the sink.

She got a bottle of Spotted Cow from the refrigerator and took a long swig. She wanted Miss Pythia's phone to work, so she could get some help figuring out why they could see Barb and how to make her invisible again. She wanted Nisha to be here, so she wouldn't be the only one dealing with the situation. And she wanted to understand how Barb could be so content with her new existence, watching TV and eating junk food. If it had been Hilary who turned up, there was no way Kara would tell her she had to go back to the land of the dead. Kara would smother her with the affection Hilary had so craved. She'd agree to get married and have kids, whatever Hilary wanted to make her happy. If pizza and TV made Barb happy, maybe Kara owed it to her.

As an afterthought, she opened a second bottle of beer and brought it to her new house guest. Barb thanked her but didn't unglue her eyes from the television screen until the commercial break.

"I like how you arranged the sofa. It's better this way."

"You had it set up differently?"

"Sofa there." Barb pointed to a perpendicular wall. "Television in the same place. It was harder to watch, but…"

"But what?"

"But my…roommate wanted a more open flow from the front door."

Kara studied Barb. She'd hesitated on the word "roommate." And, not to rely too heavily on stereotypes, but she was kind of butch.

"Did it bother you that Nisha and Angie were a queer couple?"

"Oh, okay, I see what you're doing. That's a yes or no question, so I'll answer. No. Okay? You happy? No, it didn't bother me. I know what you're getting at, so you might as well just ask."

"Were you gay?"

"Yeah." Barb shrugged and ran a hand through her hair. "Yeah, okay? Yeah, I was. We were."

"But everyone thought you were roommates."

"Things were different back then, you know? Our friends knew. We had a lot of gay friends. You know I volunteered with AIDS patients? It was right before I died. But the stuff I saw. People weren't as accepting back then. They'd kick men out of their houses if they got HIV. Never talk to them again. Didn't matter if they were dying. So we took care of them."

"That's amazing."

"You guys are so lucky now, I'm telling you. Your parents know about you?" Kara nodded. "What do they think?"

"It was a little hard at first, but they're okay with it now. They loved Hilary."

"Of course, not everybody's lucky today. I guess I shouldn't say I had it hard and you guys have it easy. Some people still have it hard."

"Yeah, trans people especially. Is that why you're still here? Some unfinished business about being out?"

"Ah!" Barb pointed a finger at her. "That's a yes or no question, and you're trying to trick me. I can't tell you that, Kara. Come on. I'm not just going to tell you everything direct."

"Of course not."

"Where's the fun in that?"

"I didn't know this was supposed to be fun." Kara sighed. Time to try another tactic. "Why did you write 'love' on the bathroom mirror when I was taking a shower? I hope you know how much it scared me."

"It wasn't meant to scare you."

"Then what was it meant for? Are you trying to tell me how you feel about me or something?"

"Don't flatter yourself, Kara. You're not my type." Barb turned the TV volume back up. "Game's back on."

CHAPTER NINE

Once the actors were made up and the tables and brushes cleaned, Nisha found herself eager to leave the theater. Nobody had a makeup change at the act break, so she didn't have to stay past curtain. It was Nisha's fault they'd manifested Barb, since she was the one reading the instructions, and she felt badly Kara was now in this crazy situation. The least she could do was hurry back to help out. She texted Kara to ask if she should come back over, and Kara immediately sent back *YES!!!!* She dashed off a text to Suni and Maddie, so they wouldn't wonder where she was and jumped on the train a second before the doors closed.

Back at Kara's, Barb was engrossed in the TV, and it looked like the entire contents of Kara's pantry had been emptied around the living room.

"Boy, I don't feel too good," Barb moaned from the couch, where she was sprawled with her feet up. "I feel like Babe Ruth without the home runs."

"Get in here," Kara hissed, gesturing for Nisha to join her in the kitchen. "I'm so glad you're back. It has been a nightmare."

"What happened?"

"First she ordered a pizza, and then she said she was still hungry. She drank all my Spotted Cows—which, by the way, I have to go back to Wisconsin to get more of—and she's been completely obsessed with TV all day. She said we're lucky to live in an age with so many channels."

As annoyed as Kara obviously was, it sounded pretty innocuous for a ghost.

"She had me playing this yes or no question game," Kara continued. "She wanted me to figure out why she was here, but she wouldn't tell me directly. I think she was getting some kind of sick enjoyment out of the whole thing."

"What did you find out?"

"She lived here with a girlfriend."

"Barb's a lesbian?" Nisha peeked around the kitchen door opening to look at Barb on the sofa. She'd unzipped her pants and was rubbing her belly. She belched loudly. "Not to be stereotypical about it, but…"

"She told me she used to play on a softball team."

"Wait, did you? Because if anyone was going to be a softball lesbian, I can totally see it being you."

"I'll have you know our team was co-ed."

Nisha laughed. "So you think that's her unfinished business? Something having to do with her girlfriend?"

"Maybe. She acted weird when I mentioned Nan's name. I'm pretty sure she was lying when she said she didn't know her."

"That's easy enough to figure out. We can just ask Nan."

Kara looked at her skeptically. "You say that like it's so easy to get a cogent answer out of her."

"You have to understand how to talk to her. I'll ask her tomorrow what she knows about Barb."

"Another thing I think we should figure out is how serious our mistake was. See if she'll let us see how solid and permanent her new appearance is."

"Why?"

"Because, frankly, if she can go away where I can't see her and don't have to talk to her, I'd be really glad. I never wanted a roommate, definitely not one so—"

Barb belched again, then moaned. Kara gestured in the direction of the living room, her point clearly made.

"Be nice. It's not as if she chose this."

"For all we know, she did."

When Barb's show was over, they asked her if they could experiment with her manifestation. At first, she protested, saying she wanted to watch something else, but she eventually gave in. They discovered she could pass through furniture and objects, and she could make herself invisible if she tried hard enough, but the effect was temporary. She also couldn't leave the apartment. When she stretched her arm across the threshold to the front door, it vanished, and she cried out in pain.

Kara had acquired a permanent house guest.

They left Barb to go back to the TV and huddled in the bedroom to talk. Kara didn't have any furniture there either, just a sad little air mattress on the floor and a plastic storage tub that was serving as a nightstand.

"This is so much worse than I realized."

"Maybe not," Kara said. "What if we just pushed her out the front door? Maybe she'd be gone for good."

"Okay, one, we are not pushing her out the door to vanish into oblivion. That's cruel. Besides, for all we know, she might just reappear in the apartment, especially if her business here isn't finished. And, two, I didn't mean Barb. I meant this bedroom. This whole apartment. It's so sad."

Kara folded her arms over her chest. "I told you, I ordered furniture. It's on backorder."

"Can we go to a thrift store and get you something in the meantime? A dresser at least?" Nisha pointed to the stack of folded underwear that were leaning against the wall.

"If I had a nicer apartment, Barb would probably want to stay longer. We need to concentrate on how to get rid of her as fast as possible."

"No, we need to concentrate on helping her settle her unfinished business, so she can find peace in the afterlife."

"Frankly, after today, I don't care. I just want her gone."

"She has a right to do this at her own pace."

"No, she doesn't." Kara pulled a folded-up paper out of her back pocket and opened it. It was the instructions they'd received from Miss Pythia. "I called this number all afternoon and nobody answered. And when I walked out with you, I went over there, and her shop was closed."

"Maybe it's a sign this should wait until tomorrow. Today's been pretty traumatic for all of us, Barb more than anyone. Maybe we should take tonight to process what's happened."

But Kara was already dialing Miss Pythia's number. She put the phone on speaker, and in less than a full ring Miss Pythia answered. Kara looked annoyed that she'd picked up so quickly this time.

Fifteen minutes later, they were back in Miss Pythia's shop. She'd left them in the eclectic front room this time, seated at a round table covered in a paisley tablecloth with fringe. The room was infused with sandalwood incense, and the lamps all had pink light bulbs.

"Oh, this is really bad," Miss Pythia said after Kara explained how they'd confused mugworts—and paid twenty-five dollars for a consultation. "The instructions were very clear for this reason. You've made a terrible mistake."

Nisha already felt awful about it. She didn't need recriminations from the woman whose instructions weren't clear at all. If anything, Miss Pythia should be apologizing to them.

"Well, it's already happened, so now what do we do? I think Kara wants her to be invisible again, but I think Barb deserves a chance to stay like this until her unfinished business is resolved."

"We were testing how visible she is," Kara said, "and she could disappear for a little bit before she came back. Is there a way to make her permanently invisible again?"

"Kara, how is she supposed to settle her unfinished business if she can't talk to you?" Nisha asked. "The whole point of what we did was to communicate with her."

"Communicate with her, not listen to her burp all night. Can I ask you something else?" Kara said to Miss Pythia. "She mentioned that your first name is Rosalind, and—"

Miss Pythia held up a hand and said, "Personal conversation is an extra ten dollars. I can't prostitute my private life for free."

Kara made a face but reached for her wallet. She pulled out a twenty, which Miss Pythia swiped and pocketed. She didn't offer any change.

"She said she knew you as Rosalind," Kara said again. "Did you know someone named Barb who lived on Hoyne?"

"Yes." Miss Pythia drummed her red fingernails on the table and looked off into the distance. "When you came before, I didn't realize you lived there, that the spirit you were talking about was her. I feel foolish for not realizing it."

"Is there anything you can tell us about her that might help us figure out what her unfinished business is?" Nisha asked.

"Barb was the life of the party." She got up from the table and disappeared through the beaded curtain.

Nisha looked over at Kara, who said, "Is that it? That's what twenty bucks gets me?"

When Miss Pythia didn't return after a minute, they stood from the table and started to put their coats on. As they were about to walk out, Miss Pythia came back, and they scrambled to sit down. She hefted a photo album onto the table in front of them.

The photos were faded and fuzzy with low resolution and poor lighting, the kind of old photographs that were charming reminders of a time when not every second of every day was captured in perfect clarity. They were stuck behind a plastic film, which Miss Pythia tapped with her nail.

"There's Barb," she said, pointing to the person in the middle of a group shot. Even though the photograph was decades old, Barb looked identical to the person sitting in Kara's living room. "That's me, and that's Nan Galt." Miss Pythia and Nan had both greatly aged. In the photo, Miss Pythia was thinner, her hair a more natural shade of brown than the jet-black it was now, and her makeup was much more subtle. The women were standing, arms around each other, with a fourth person, all wearing matching red tank tops, shorts, and roller skates. "We had just performed in a talent show. It was a fundraiser for the AIDS charity Barb volunteered for. We did a roller-skating routine."

The image of a young Nan roller-skating delighted Nisha, and it was both jarring and comforting to think of the eccentric Miss Pythia doing something as banal as performing in a talent show.

"Who's the fourth?" Kara asked.

"She's the reason I brought this out here. If anyone knows why Barb is still here, it'll be her."

"What's her name?"

Miss Pythia opened her mouth to speak, but Kara jumped in. "Let me guess. Ten bucks to tell us, twenty to call her for us. You didn't give me change before, so how about you give us her name and contact information, and we call it even?"

Nisha feared Miss Pythia would be angry at Kara's directness, but instead the woman cackled.

"I knew I liked you!"

She disappeared once again and came back this time with a Post-It. "Her name is Sonia. I don't have her phone number," she said. "It's been too many years since we've spoken, but this is where she used to live, and I'll bet you she hasn't moved."

Kara took the Post-It and thanked her. "One question before we go. How long can Barb stay like this? Is there any consequence to her being around? Will the effects fade at some point?"

"Oh no, honey, she can stay forever." Miss Pythia frowned. "But, be assured, it will not be pleasant. She will never age. She will never die again. She will be trapped in that apartment day after day, watching everyone around her get older and move on with their lives." She shook her head. "No, it is not a good life, being the dead among the living."

After leaving Miss Pythia's, they walked north on Damen together in the light snowfall and glow of the streetlamp. They decided it was too late to drop in on Sonia without warning, so they were headed back to Kara's.

"I'm really glad you came back tonight," Kara said. "I don't know how I would have handled all this madness without you."

"I don't think you'd be in this madness if it weren't for me in the first place. I feel like this is all my fault."

"I should have double-checked the instructions. I could have been the one reading them and made the same mistake."

"What are you going to do with her tonight?"

"I guess I'll give her a pillow and a blanket and let her sleep on the couch. Do ghosts even sleep?"

"Are you going to be okay?"

Kara arched an eyebrow. "Honestly? If I stop and think about it, no. Not at all. This is absurd, and it's probably more than a little triggering. But if I just keep moving, I'll be fine. For now. Do you want to talk to Sonia with me tomorrow?"

"You're not sick of me yet?"

"Actually," Kara said with a smile, "I feel like we're just starting to get to know each other."

Their eyes locked for a moment, until Nisha forced herself to look away. "I really better get home. I hope you have a fun slumber party."

On the walk to the bus stop, the whirlwind of the day started to catch up to Nisha. As she waited for the bus, she realized how tired she was but how good that felt. For the first time in a long time, she had a goal to work toward. Kara and Barb both needed her, and she'd stand by them and help them however she could.

❖

The address Miss Pythia had given them was for a rundown house on a side street off Damen in the Ukrainian Village, a neighborhood immediately south of Kara's. It was a street that had been recently renovated and gentrified, and the old single-family houses had been replaced by tall brick three-flats with black iron balconies. Each flat probably cost three times what the original house had, even though they were smaller and the lot was now shared. Every building was square and austere, except Sonia's house. Its paint was peeling, and several bolts holding up the metal awning over the front door were missing. Although the front yard was only about five feet deep, there were shrubs, but they were overgrown and ugly. The sidewalk leading up to the door was cracked and pitched upright in various angles. The whole place looked depressing, but Nisha had to give Sonia props for holding on to her house in a neighborhood that had been overrun by real estate developers and yuppies.

"Are you sure this is the right address?" Kara asked.

"That's what it says." Nisha had stuck the Post-It Miss Pythia had given them to her forefinger. "Number 918."

She pressed the doorbell. The street was quiet enough that they could hear the bell ringing inside the house, a sure sign that no one was home. Maybe the house had been abandoned.

But a chain rattled, and there was the sound of the lock being flipped. The front door opened, and a tiny woman about Nan's age stood shielded by the glass storm door. Her face was rugged and wrinkled, and she stood bent over at an angle. Even standing straight, she was probably only five feet tall.

"Que?"

Miss Pythia hadn't warned them Sonia spoke Spanish. Nisha only knew a few words.

"Um, *hola*, um, *me llamo*, um, *esta* Nisha. *Yo soy una amigo* of Miss Pythia." Nisha looked at Kara. "How do you say 'miss'?"

"For crying out loud, just speak English," Sonia said.

"Oh, um, hi."

Kara elbowed in front of her. "Are you Sonia Rivera? We were sent here to ask you about a woman named Barb."

"I don't know any Barb."

"Not now, but you used to. She died in 1986."

The woman scratched her butt. "Talk to Rosie."

"Who's Rosie?" Nisha asked.

"We already did!" Kara called as Sonia started to close the door on them. "She's the one who gave us your address. She said you're the only one who can help us."

The door opened again. Sonia didn't look happy, but she flipped the small lock on the storm door and gestured for them to come inside.

"Who's Rosie?" Nisha asked quietly as they stepped inside.

"I was just guessing it was Miss Pythia. Barb said her name was Rosalind."

Based on the exterior of the house, Nisha didn't have high hopes for the inside, but it smelled like vanilla. They stepped into a living room decorated with immaculately kept Victorian furniture.

"This is incredible," Kara said.

That softened Sonia somewhat. "I dunno why she left. It's nice here."

"Who left?" Nisha asked.

Sonia glared at her. "Rosie."

"Oh, right, of course." Nisha said the words, but in truth she was having a hard time keeping up. Sonia's unpleasant demeanor certainly didn't help explain anything.

Sonia led them into the kitchen, where there was a flan sitting on the immaculate white marble countertop. It was no doubt the origin of the vanilla scent that filled the air and made the place seem so homey. Sonia looked at the flan and then at them, and Nisha could see the resignation pass over her face. She felt obligated to offer them a piece.

The caramel on top of the flan was still warm and gooey, and the custard underneath was creamy and rich. Kara ate hers down fast, and Sonia dished out a second serving without asking if she wanted it.

As they ate, Sonia told them she and Rosie—Miss Pythia— had been involved when they were younger. The way she talked made Miss Pythia seem far less exotic, and her affected speech and eccentric behavior seemed like an act to fulfill the expectations of paying customers. Like Miss Pythia, Sonia showed them an old photo album, and in her pictures they were two ordinary women in T-shirts and shaggy haircuts. In one image, they had their arms around each other like lovers, or at least very close friends, and in another, they were wearing Halloween costumes with two other people. Sonia pointed herself out. She was dressed as a witch in a black cape and black pointed hat with her face painted green.

"No one understood the irony. That was the fun of it."

"What do you mean?" Nisha asked.

Sonia pointed to the photo. "There's me as a witch, Rosie as a fortune teller, and our other friend Nan as a psychic. And nobody knew we were all exactly what we dressed up as. Except Barb." She pointed to the fourth person in the photo, who was unidentifiable underneath a white sheet with two holes cut for the eyes. She closed the photo album and looked at them. "But Barb died a long time ago, so how do you know her?"

Nisha had no idea how to break it to someone that their long departed friend had returned. She looked at Kara as if to say, *You take this one*, but Kara appeared equally uncertain how to proceed.

Sonia pinched the bridge of her nose. "She's a spirit, isn't she?"

"Apparently, she's been haunting the apartment I live in since her death, but now she's visible," Kara said. "You can touch her, talk to her, see her. We did a ritual to try to communicate with her, and it backfired. Massively."

Sonia took their empty plates and spoons into the kitchen and set them in the sink. She ran the water for a moment. When she turned back to them, she said, "I knew something like this would happen."

"You predicted she'd become a ghost and haunt my apartment?"

"Spirit, not ghost, and it's interactive energy, not haunting."

Kara mumbled her apologies.

Sonia put her hands on her hips. "If this is what it's come to, I don't know why Rosie sent you here."

"She said you were the only one with enough information to help us figure out what Barb's unfinished business is."

"Did she?" Sonia said something in Spanish that didn't sound very nice, probably in frustration at Miss Pythia for pawning them off on her. "Listen, girls, if you want to see pictures of Barb from back then, I can show you, but I can't help you with whatever you're trying to find out."

"Who can?" Nisha asked.

Sonia looked at them like they were idiots. "You two—you're a thing?"

"A thing?" Kara repeated.

"We're not in a relationship, no," Nisha said.

"But you're in the family. Otherwise, Rosie wouldn't have sent you here."

"I'm queer, if that's what you mean," Kara said.

"Me, too, but what does that have to do with the spirit?"

Sonia picked the photo album up and moved toward the living room. Out of curiosity, Nisha rose from the table to follow. As Sonia set the album on the bottom shelf of her bookcase, Nisha peeked at the rest of the books. They ranged from leather-bound and dusty to newer paperbacks, but there was one commonality: they were all books about the occult.

"You really are a witch!"

"Nish, witches aren't real," Kara said from the doorway.

"Bruja," Sonia said.

Nisha had no idea what that meant. "If you're really a witch, does that mean Miss Pythia can really tell fortunes?"

Sonia snorted. "If you mean, can she feel the vibrations and does she understand auras and karma, yes. If you're asking if that hooey she charges money for is real, then no. She majored in theater in college. That's probably why your ritual got screwed up."

"I think I messed it up," Nisha said, feeling a strange need to defend Miss Pythia in her absence. "I didn't realize we had Chinese mugwort, not Korean mugwort, and we accidentally put the thyme in after instead of before."

Sonia looked at her like she was speaking gibberish. "Mugwort?"

"I'd never heard of it before either," Kara said, "but somehow instead of being able to communicate with the ghost—the spirit—now she's at my house in the flesh. Sitting on my couch and ordering pizza."

"This is very serious." Sonia sat on a perfectly upholstered settee. "It's probably going to take all of us to get this settled. Assuming the others will even talk to me anymore."

"You mean Nan and Rosalind?"

"Why wouldn't they talk to you anymore?" Nisha asked.

"They blame me for what happened to Barb."

"Why on earth would they do that?"

Sonia was facing in their direction, but her eyes were glazed over, like Nan's when she was in touch with "the gift."

"I killed Barb," she said at last. "That's why I can't be the one to help you."

"You couldn't have killed Barb," Kara argued. "She said she died of a heart attack."

Sonia waved a hand. "This is too much for one afternoon. I want you to go now."

To be on the verge of learning something and dismissed so suddenly was frustrating. It had felt like they were finally getting somewhere, but Sonia was slumped over, head in hands. Learning about Barb was a huge shock, and the only decent thing for them to do was to respect her wishes and leave.

They thanked her for her time and the flan and let themselves out.

❖

After they left Sonia's, Kara suggested they take a walk around the park, so they could talk about what they'd learned without Barb overhearing. She asked Nisha everything she knew about Nan, so they could piece together why Barb had pretended they didn't know each other.

The truth was, as much as Nisha adored Nan, and as much time as they spent together, she didn't know much about her. By the time she and Angie had moved into the building, Nan was already somewhat senile. They'd met in the laundry room one day when Nan couldn't lift her basket, and Nisha had offered to carry it for her. After that, Nisha had made a point to check in on her from time to time.

Nan had lived alone, except for her cat Bernie, whose litterbox Angie had sometimes cleaned. Bernie had died in the year between Nisha's and Kara's residence, and Nan had decided she was too old to get another cat.

"Do you know anything about her family?" Kara asked.

"She doesn't seem to have any family. Nobody ever comes to check on her. It's really sad. She keeps in touch with friends, mostly through email, but sometimes they talk on the phone. She won't get a smartphone, and she doesn't text."

"What about her past?"

"She tells stories about her glory days. Mostly scandals about people cheating on their partners and selling drugs before the neighborhood was this affluent, when it was a lot of Puerto Rican families and artists. I know she used to be fluent in Spanish, and one time she told me she'd had an affair with a lesbian head of a Puerto Rican gang."

"Nan's a lesbian?"

"Yeah, you didn't know that?"

"No, and that has to be connected. What are the odds two lesbians lived next door to each other in the 1980s and didn't know each other?"

Nisha shrugged. "I don't know. Maybe slim, but maybe also very good? I think the neighborhood was a magnet for queer people back then. Think about the photos Sonia showed us."

"I'm wondering if she and Barb ever had a relationship."

"Nan and Barb?" Nisha couldn't picture it, but maybe that was because of the decades between them now. Would Nan of the 1980s had gone for someone as crass and butch as Barb? "Maybe."

"I'm also wondering if the Puerto Rican gang leader Nan told you about was Sonia."

Nisha's jaw dropped. "Of course! But, wait, Sonia said she used to live with Miss Pythia, so if she and Nan were also involved—"

"And we still don't know which of them was the girlfriend who lived with Barb."

It sounded like a real-life soap opera, with couplings and re-couplings. To Nisha's mind, it was a total mess. But maybe none of them had ever committed to monogamy, in which case changing partners was a different story. Maybe it wasn't drama, just the thrill of different sexual and romantic encounters.

"Don't you think it's weird they're all pretending they don't know the full story?" Kara asked.

"They're eighty years old. Maybe they just can't remember."

"We need to get Nan to talk if Barb won't. She has to remember something useful."

Nisha's protective instincts came roaring out. "Okay, I need you to understand something about Nan. You can't push her. She's tough, but she won't open up because you demand it. When she tells stories, it's on her schedule, when she's having a good day. Asking doesn't always work the best, and if you push her too hard, you'll drive her into more confusion."

"I promise not to push Nan too hard. But if she really is in such bad shape, why doesn't anyone take care of her? Isn't it dangerous for her to live by herself?"

"She's okay most of the time. She doesn't use the oven anymore, and she only uses the stove to make tea. Oleg put handles in her shower, so she won't slip. Mostly she just forgets to eat, like she did the other day."

They found a bench and sat down. The sun was hiding behind a dull gray sky, and a cold wind whipped through the park. Nisha was wearing a cape instead of a proper coat, and she regretted how exposed her front was to the cold air. She pulled the excess material across her chest and let it cover her like a blanket.

"I agree with you it's sad," she continued. "I wish she had a better support system, and I feel terrible I don't check on her as much since I moved out. Oleg makes sure she's okay when he can. But maybe you could from time to time?"

"Of course. But maybe—I know you live on the other side of town now—but maybe you should come over more to see her?"

"Are you inviting me to hang out in your building?"

"I guess so."

Another gust of wind blew a discarded plastic bag and a few crinkly brown leaves in their direction.

"Are you cold?" Kara asked. "Do you want to get some coffee?"

"I'm okay. My new philosophy is to try to find beauty and enjoyment in all weather." She adjusted the cape so her arms were covered. "I just need to remember to dress right to do that."

"Maybe we should make a list of what steps to take next." Kara pulled out her phone and opened the notes app. "I can do some research tomorrow at work. I'll try to find out Barb's full name based on the year of her death. She told me she used to be an AIDS volunteer. Maybe one of the obituaries from 1986 will mention AIDS work, and from there we can get her last name. That would also help us pinpoint the exact date, which may help us figure out the unfinished business." As she spoke, her thumbs hastily typed out a summary of what she was saying. Then she added a K after the note. "You should talk to Nan. See what you can find out about her relationship with Barb, and if she won't tell you directly about their relationship, find out whatever you can about what was going on in the building in the 1980s, and see what else she'll tell you about Sonia and Rosalind. Are we calling her that now? Or should we still say Miss Pythia?" She added N next to the new note. "One of my neighbors said Oleg is supposed to be back tomorrow, and I think it would be better for you to talk to him, since he still doesn't like me."

"What do you want me to ask him? He wasn't in the US in 1986."

"Anything about the building's history or anything he might know that happened before you moved in." Another N next to the line item in her notes. "I'm texting you a copy of this list so you have it."

As she said it, Nisha heard her phone beeping with a new message. "Is this what you're like at work?"

Kara locked her phone and looked up. "What do you mean?"

"Never mind."

Kara slid her phone into the front pocket of her hoodie. "The piece that doesn't make sense yet is your ring. What does it have to do with these three women?"

Nisha touched the fingers on her left hand protectively. Her own ring was on the ring finger with Angie's next to it on the middle.

She'd kept the rings in her pocket until she'd left the house, so Suni wouldn't judge her for wearing them.

"I've been thinking about that, too."

"Barb told me she can't say directly, or maybe she *won't* say it directly. I've been trying to brainstorm how to ask her more indirectly, but it's not going well." Kara reached for her hair and tightened her ponytail, a gesture Nisha recognized from their first meeting at the wine bar. It was a sign Kara was anxious about something, she realized. "Obfuscation and passivity only cause problems, so I'm going to be candid. Barb tried to tell me things that happened when you and Angie lived in the apartment."

Nisha clenched her hands into fists and steeled herself to hear what Kara had learned.

"I told her I didn't want to gossip," Kara continued. "I have no intention of invading your privacy. As far as I'm concerned, it's none of my business what went on between you and Angie."

Nisha's hands relaxed. "I appreciate that."

"The only reason I'm bringing it up now is because Barb says she can't tell me anything, but she keeps making hints. I think there's a reason why she hid the ring, and I don't think it was just to be a jerk."

Nisha hated thinking about how much Barb must have witnessed when she and Angie lived in the apartment, and she definitely hadn't expected to hear that Barb was trying to tell Kara about it. That would be awful.

She'd probably tell Kara the whole story of her breakup with Angie at some point if their friendship continued to evolve. But once she did, Kara would likely drop her the way her other friends had. Until then, she'd prefer Kara to remain in the dark and their friendship to remain unspoiled. It was a blessing Kara had arrived in Chicago on her own without friends, in need of Nisha, and Nisha wasn't ready to lose that.

She looked at Kara's face in the cool, diffuse light. Kara wore makeup but kept it natural-looking. A swipe of mascara to darken her pale eyelashes, no eyeshadow, and just a little concealer under her eyes that was a shade too yellow for her skin tone. Her cheeks and lips were naturally pink in the cold air, a contrast to her creamy complexion.

On a whim, Nisha tucked a loose strand of hair behind Kara's ear. Kara's mouth fell open, and she reached out to touch Nisha's jawline, letting her hand slide to rest on the back of Nisha's neck. They gazed at each other, Nisha's pulse quickening, and the moment felt suspended in time.

Then Nisha shut her mouth and looked away. "I have another matinee. I should probably get going."

Kara offered to walk her to the train, but things were quiet and awkward between them.

"I'll call you," Kara said.

After Nisha climbed the stairs to the platform and watched Kara walk in the direction of her building, she felt relieved.

On the train, she let her head rest against the window as she reflected on the dizzying moment in the park. She had felt something as they looked at each other, the air around them swirling with tension and possibilities. What was that about?

CHAPTER TEN

The next few weeks passed for Kara in a blur of work and baby-sitting her ghost. Barb made increasingly ridiculous demands every time Kara left for the office in the morning. "Bring home some Tab," she said once, as if Kara had any idea if they still even made it. Another time she asked if she could get a cat to keep her company during the day. Absolutely not.

When she wasn't working, Kara's social life was pretty pathetic. She'd met people. Sure, she could say that. She'd met a building manager who didn't like her, a pretend medium, a neighbor who sometimes didn't remember if they'd met before, an elderly witch, and the former resident of her apartment who was possibly the only remotely normal person on that list but who was obviously not over her ex.

Kara had dutifully checked off the K items on the ghost to-do list, most of which were a resounding failure. With the help of Ruthie, the front office assistant, she'd hired the firm's private investigator to look into Nan's background, but she still didn't know Barb's last name or date of birth, and Barb refused to tell. Every night when she got off the train, she headed away from her building to check Miss Pythia's shop, and every night it was closed. One day, the curtains were gone, and she was able to peek in the windows. Inside was an empty space. The next day, a "for rent" sign was posted to the door. When Kara saw Nan in the mail room a few days later, she asked if Miss Pythia had relocated, but Nan insisted she'd never heard of anyone by that name.

The one person who was easy to get a hold of was Nisha. Actually, Kara didn't have to get a hold of her. Nisha texted night and day to check on Barb. She'd called Kara's office the day after their walk in the park to ask if she should come over to help, but Kara had told Ruthie to say she was in a meeting and unavailable.

She kept seeing Nisha's earrings brush against the delicate brown skin of her neck as the wind blew, Nisha's plush lips smiling as they talked. She kept thinking about how close she had come to kissing those lips and how terrible an idea that was.

Nisha was fixated on Angie. She had been wearing Angie's engagement ring that very day. She was still living in the past.

And Kara's ideal plan for moving forward into the future didn't involve starting a new long-term relationship. It involved hot, casual sex, something she was getting absolutely none of.

So there they were. Kara was avoiding Nisha, and Nisha was relentlessly trying to contact her.

On a Tuesday afternoon in late November, the first heavy snowfall of the season came, and by evening the streets of the Loop were full of plows. As Kara watched the maintenance crew from the building across the street shovel the sidewalk and scatter salt, she felt reluctant to leave the warmth of her office. She'd called her mom and sister to catch up, and she'd sent text messages to some friends in Wisconsin who asked if Chicago was amazing.

With no one left to talk to, Kara was scrolling through Instagram on her phone, wasting time, not ready to face another evening with Barb, when she saw Nisha's latest post. It was a picture of her on the train, looking out the window while holding a cup of coffee. Her thick black hair was loose around her shoulders, and she was wearing a red scarf with a gray coat. The caption said Sunita had made her pose, and Kara wondered where they had gone together that had sparked the impromptu photo session. It was funny how most of Nisha's photos were her alone. To someone who didn't know Nisha, it seemed as if she led a solitary life, but she had Sunita and Madeline—and Nan and Oleg—a whole host of people who loved her and wanted to be around her.

Meanwhile, Kara was ignoring her texts.

She pulled up Nisha's contact info and hit the call button.

On the third ring, Nisha answered. "I really think you should come over, so we can talk."

"Tonight?"

"Yes."

At six forty, Kara ran down the stairs to the train station and through the tunnel. It was her first time riding the Red Line, which she took north to the Bryn Mawr stop. From there, she hiked a few blocks in the cold to a nondescript red brick low-rise that looked almost identical to the other buildings on the street.

Her hand was shaky as she buzzed unit 215, a mixture of anxiety over whatever was bothering Nisha and eagerness to see her.

When the front door hummed to signal it was unlocked, she let herself inside. The building had no lobby, just a small vestibule with mailboxes. She found the stairs and began climbing, uncertain which direction 215 would be, when a door to her left opened, and someone waved at her.

It was Madeline. Her blond hair was in a messy bun with pieces falling around her face. She was wearing a T-shirt, pajama pants, and gray slippers, and Kara realized Nisha hadn't said if they were eating with her roommates or just the two of them. Kara wasn't sure which would be more awkward.

"Welcome!" Madeline called as Kara made her way down the hall. "Do you remember me? We met that night at Perimeter."

She sounded friendly, as if all the anger Sunita had leveled at Kara that horrible night at the club had been long forgotten.

"Of course, you're Madeline, right?"

"Maddie, please. Come on in."

She escorted Kara through a dark stained door and into a living room separated from a dining room by a half-wall with built-in china cabinets. It was obviously an older building but recently refurbished. The space was bright and warm and modern, even with its beautifully preserved original features. So this was Sunita and Maddie's condo, where Nisha had been crashing since she moved out of Kara's sticky, smelly apartment. Not a bad place to recover from heartbreak.

"Nisha's changing her clothes. Can I get you something to drink while you wait?"

"A glass of water, please."

Maddie left Kara alone on the gray corduroy sectional. When she came back, she was carrying a tall glass of chilled water with a lemon wedge. Kara hadn't expected such formality and wasn't sure what to make of it. She gave her thanks, and Maddie left her alone again.

Eventually Nisha emerged from a door farther down the hall. "Sorry it took me so long. I slipped and fell on my way home, and I was soaking wet."

"Are you okay?"

"Maybe a bruise on my butt, no big deal." She shuffled across the pristine wooden floors in a pair of fuzzy green socks and sat cross-legged next to Kara on the couch. "So what's going on?"

"What do you mean?"

"You sounded so upset when you called me earlier."

Kara frowned. "When I called you earlier, you said to come over tonight, I said okay, and you asked me what time I'd be here, and then you hung up. How did you get that I was upset from a twenty-second phone call?"

"Before that. When you left me the voice mail saying you were having a tough day and needed someone to talk to."

"Nish, I never did that." But Nisha had been on her mind. Had she called and forgotten? She reached for her bag on the floor and took her phone from the inside pocket. She pulled up the call history.

"It wasn't from that number. It was a 312 number I didn't recognize. I assumed it was one of your office lines."

"I think someone is pulling a prank on you. I was thinking about you all day, but didn't call."

"You were thinking about me?"

Kara couldn't tell if Nisha sounded hopeful that she occupied Kara's attention or annoyed that thinking about her was all Kara had done. She decided to put her guts on the line.

"I know I said I'd call the last time we saw each other, and I didn't. I'm sorry about that."

"I don't understand. If you were avoiding me, why'd you agree to come over?"

"You made it sound like we had something important to talk about." She'd thought Nisha might have an update from her half of the to-do list. But, in her heart, Kara knew that wasn't why she'd rushed over. She'd come because she was glad Nisha wasn't angry at her lack of communication. She was grateful Nisha had made the first overture. Or the tenth.

"Do we have something important to talk about?"

Nisha's big brown eyes did that soul-searching thing, and Kara took a sip of water to avoid falling into them and never coming out again. Nisha wasn't talking about Barb, that was clear. As much as Kara wanted to get lost in her, it was too much.

"I don't need to bust in on your evening. Sorry for the misunderstanding."

She rose to her feet and slung her bag over her shoulder. She moved to the front door, but as she reached for the knob, Nisha said, "Please don't go."

Kara turned to look at her and felt the same swelling in her chest she'd experienced at the park.

"I didn't call because I didn't know what to say," she admitted.

"Because I've been texting so much, right? It was probably overkill. It's just that when you helped me search for the ring and made me brunch—"

"I made you toast."

"You invited me over for brunch, and you were good to me and Nan. And now that you're stuck with Barb, I wanted to return the favor."

Kara leaned her back against the door. "You were good to me when you took me out to that club. I was the one repaying the favor. Anyway, I shouldn't have avoided you. I…I missed you."

Her throat felt dry, and her heart was racing now. She hated the words she was saying and how vulnerable they made her feel, but she liked how they made Nisha's eyes soften.

"When you said you wanted a hookup, I thought maybe you were the kind of person who can't be trusted with anything more serious." Nisha quickly added, "I mean friendship. How some people aren't reliable. Not that everyone who has casual sex is unreliable. I'm not trying to make a moral judgment about monogamy. Man, I'm floundering here."

"You were scared."

"Yeah."

"Why?"

"Because I haven't been with anyone since Angie."

There it was. The reminder that while for Kara there was a bubble of feelings growing between them, getting bigger each time they talked, Nisha wasn't ready for it.

"You have to let her go."

"It's not that easy. I'm not saying she was so perfect I can never imagine anyone living up to her. But when we broke up, it wasn't just us breaking up. It was splitting up furniture and bank accounts and friends. I lost nearly everybody but them." She tipped her head toward the hallway, meaning Sunita and Maddie. "My life completely fell apart. I couldn't face getting hurt like that again." Nisha turned to lean against the wall beside Kara. "When I met you, and you were here in Chicago all alone, it was like the universe was giving me a sign that I should get to know you. Then Barb happened, and I was the only other person who knew about it, and I thought, well, you need me."

So Nisha's attentiveness had only been out of pity for Kara's loneliness, nothing more. "I don't need you. It was nice having you around, but I'm fine on my own. That was my whole goal in moving here, right? Now if I can get Barb to go away, I can finally have what I want."

Nisha frowned at her. "Is that really what you want?"

There was the sound of a key fumbling in the lock a split second before the door pushed into Kara, and she fell a step forward. Nisha caught her. Then the door opened all the way, knocking into Kara's back.

"Sorry." Sunita stepped inside and twirled her key ring on her forefinger. She didn't sound very sorry. "Are you all right?"

An ache where the doorknob had pounded into Kara's back was growing stronger and hotter. She'd probably have a bruise.

Once again, Sunita looked at her with cold eyes. "I didn't realize Nisha had invited you over."

Did they require Nisha to get permission before having guests? Kara just returned the stare and waited for Sunita to say something else.

They were saved by Maddie, who came out of a bedroom door in the narrow hall. "Suni! I need your help in here!"

Sunita studied Kara one last time before hanging her coat on a hook and heading toward Maddie. Kara suspected the demand for help was a clumsy attempt on Maddie's part to give Nisha and Kara time alone, and she appreciated it. Whatever social skills Sunita lacked, Maddie seemed to have in spades. Unless Sunita reserved her coldness especially for Kara.

"Does she hate me?"

Nisha shrugged noncommittally. "Do you want some ice for your back?"

"I'm fine."

"Humor me."

She trailed Nisha to the rear of the unit, where the galley kitchen looked onto a small eating area, far from the dining room by the front door. "Weird setup but nice place."

"It's typical of these kinds of buildings. Maddie and Suni own, so the finishes are a little nicer. They were the first to buy after the place was converted into condos. They got a really good deal, and now it's worth twenty grand more than they paid for it."

Nisha's voice was tinged with uncharacteristic bitterness. She reached into the freezer drawer of the stainless steel refrigerator and pulled out a handful of ice cubes. She put them in a sandwich bag and wrapped the bag in a dish towel. Instead of handing the bundle to Kara, she pressed it gently to Kara's back. Kara wasn't really in that much pain, but she appreciated Nisha's tenderness.

"I'm really sorry," Nisha said after a moment. "I don't think Suni meant to open the door into you like that."

She had definitely meant to open the door like that.

"I was in the way." Kara took the ice pack from her and sat gingerly in one of the barstools at the counter between the eating area and kitchen.

Nisha leaned on the opposite side of the counter facing her. "She's actually an incredible person. She saved me when I was at my lowest."

When she had broken up with Angie, she meant, but Kara couldn't imagine someone as self-actualized as Nisha being such a mess that she needed rescuing. What had Angie seen in Nisha that had made her leave? Or maybe the better question was: What had Angie stopped seeing?

"I think I'm a little jealous of you," Kara said.

"Of me?"

"You have such a handle on life. You talk about your feelings, you're insightful. You're…How do I say this nicely? You're stuck in the past in a way that seems kind of unhealthy, but at the same time you're also incredibly healthy, mentally."

"I'm a walking contradiction." Nisha came around the counter to sit on the stool beside her. "Actually, every day feels different, and I never know which kind of day it's going to be until it's halfway over. You caught me on a good day today. Suni and Maddie could tell you about my bad days. The truth is, I think I've been a little angry at you."

"Why?"

"You're ready to go out and meet people, and part of me is jealous of you. I think it makes me a little angry because…"

"Because what?"

"Because you being ready to move on makes it seem like you didn't know what a good thing you had."

Kara supposed she could understand that. All Nisha wanted was for Angie to love her again. Kara had had Hilary's love, and she was looking for something from someone else instead of just appreciating it.

"I still love Hilary. I will always love Hilary, even if I end up in another relationship. Nothing could ever change that. I think that's why I keep saying I don't want another relationship right now." Kara placed one hand atop the other against her chest. It was something she'd started doing after Hilary died. She liked to think that's where Hilary was now, in Kara's heart. "It took me a really long time to figure out how to keep going, not despite Hilary's death but in honor of it. But you—you're missing out on everything that's in front of you. Angie walked out on you. You don't owe her your loyalty anymore."

"I know it's stupid to still want her back," Nisha said. "I would give anything for the chance to see her again, to talk to her, because I feel like if we had talked one more time or maybe gone to counseling, we could have worked through our problems, and she would have changed her mind about getting married and getting the house. Or, if she didn't change her mind, maybe we could have at least ended on a decent note."

Nisha wanted closure. That was a reasonable enough request, one Angie should have granted. In a long-term committed relationship, people owed it to each other to end it graciously. Kara was lucky that she and Hilary had gotten time to find closure with Hilary's diagnosis.

"Hilary wanted to get married." It wasn't something Kara talked much about. Her sister Becca and a few friends knew, but her parents didn't. She wasn't sure why she was telling Nisha.

"Did you?"

"No." Nisha looked at her in surprise, and Kara felt a little defensiveness kick in. "I know, as a lawyer, why it makes sense, but it seemed dumb to me, since so many marriages end in divorce. I didn't see the point in putting that kind of pressure on us when we already had a great life together. Hilary always said she understood how I felt, but I could tell it was a disappointment to her. After she died, all I could think was how stupid I'd been. Why couldn't I have worn a ring and signed a piece of paper if it would have made her happy? I could see the fallacy in my argument, you know?"

"How do you mean?"

"Well, my point was that we already had a marriage, functionally, just not legally, so what was the point of actually filing the papers? But the inverse is also true. If what we had was basically a marriage anyway, then signing papers and wearing rings wouldn't have changed anything, so I had nothing to be afraid of. When she died, I regretted it so much. I think I'll probably regret it for the rest of my life." Kara didn't want to go too far down this road for fear she might open a door she'd have a hard time closing again. She looked at Nisha. "And then you showed up—"

"And I had the ring you'd said no to."

"Yeah."

"But you and Hilary had real love for each other. I just have an empty symbol."

"If it's so empty, take it off."

"I don't know…"

Kara reached for Nisha's left hand, so they could look at the two matching rings. "If you want closure and you can't get it from Angie, give it to yourself. Take these off, put them away, sell them, give them to someone else, whatever, but don't wear them anymore."

Nisha's face scrunched in distress, and Kara thought she'd pushed too far. If she pressured Nisha into doing something she wasn't ready to do, she'd only end up resenting Kara for it.

She was about to dial it back when, to her surprise, Nisha said, "You're right," and pulled the two rings off. "I don't need these anymore."

"Wooo!" Kara applauded and whistled, savoring how it made Nisha blush. Her hands came up to her cheeks, but she was smiling.

Sunita popped out of the bedroom. "What's going on?"

Nisha held up her empty left hand. "I took off the rings!"

Sunita pursed her lips and was about to say something when Maddie yanked her back into the bedroom, and the door slammed shut.

"Will you take these?" Nisha pushed the rings toward Kara. "I don't care what you do with them, just as long as I don't have to see them again."

"Are you sure?"

Nisha nodded, and Kara put the rings in her pants pocket. Not the safest place to transport them, but her work bag was in the living room. She'd put them in the inside pouch before taking the train home. After that, who knew? She'd probably hide them in a dresser drawer in case Nisha called the next day and said she'd made a mistake.

"I'm proud of you," she told Nisha.

"I don't think I'd have gotten here if we hadn't met."

Maddie came out of the bedroom then, apologetic. "I was trying so hard not to interrupt, but if I don't start pressing the tofu now, we won't be eating until bedtime. Can I come in for one second?"

"It's fine, Maddie." Nisha sounded long-suffering. "You're not interrupting anything private."

"I'm gonna go put these in my bag," Kara said, tapping the pocket with the rings.

Her bag was in the living room. She put the rings in the inside zipper pouch, where there was no chance of them falling out or getting lost on her way home. Her phone buzzed, and she felt a little dread mixed with annoyance. It was probably Horowitz calling with another one of his after-hours ideas that could wait until morning. But when she looked at the phone screen, Kara saw she had already missed six calls from a 773 number she didn't recognize. She accepted the incoming call.

"Finally! Do you know how many times I had to call you?"

"Who is this?"

"It's Barb."

"How did you get a phone?"

"From Nan."

"Nan's in my apartment?"

"She was. Now she's on her way to the hospital."

"What? What happened?"

"She collapsed, so I took her phone and called 911. You'd better get to the hospital. And bring Nisha."

CHAPTER ELEVEN

In the emergency room, they couldn't get any information. "I'm sorry, you're not her next of kin," the person at the reception desk said three times. Nisha was about to yell, since asking nicely wasn't getting her anywhere, but Kara tugged her by the sleeve toward the waiting area.

"Who's her next of kin?" Kara asked. "If you have their number, we can call them directly to find out what's going on."

"I didn't know she had kin! She never talks about family, only other queer people she used to know." Nisha slumped into the chair beside Kara. She felt guilty she hadn't been to see Nan in a while and frustrated she didn't know more about Nan's family. She'd thought they were close. It was embarrassing to be confronted with what she didn't know. In all the time they'd spent together, why hadn't they talked about Nan's plans for an emergency like this?

"What if it's something serious?" she said. "Why does someone who never even sees her get to know what's going on and I don't?"

Before Kara could answer, Nisha sprang to her feet and went back to the reception desk. "Can you at least get us in touch with whoever *is* her next of kin? Can we talk to them? I just want to know what's going on. She's like a grandmother to me."

She knew on some level she was pissing off the staff, but she couldn't help it.

"I'm sorry, I can't do that. I can tell them you're here, and they can decide if they want to update you."

"That's the best you can do?"

"That's the best I can do. Now, I've got a lobby full of people, so I need you to take a seat."

Nisha returned to Kara, ready to hear her suggest going home, but instead Kara reached for her hand. She gave it a squeeze and didn't let go.

Thirty minutes later, Oleg came through the door and nodded when he saw them. "What has happened?"

"I don't know." Nisha stood and gave him a quick hug. "Nobody will tell me anything."

"How did you know to come here?" Kara asked.

"Strange thing." Oleg took a seat beside Nisha. "I get a call from emergency service to come to your apartment to fix overflowing toilet. I go. Is not you there. The toilet is fine. Woman there tells me to come here. I say why can't you tell me that on phone. She say she no have number, just emergency service number."

Diabolical Barb.

"Who is this woman?" Oleg asked Kara. "Only you are on the lease."

Kara opened and closed her mouth and looked to Nisha for help. As fond of Oleg as Nisha was, she wasn't going to try to explain Barb. She opted for a white lie instead.

"She's Kara's cousin from Wisconsin. She's just visiting for a few days. I'm glad she figured out how to get in touch with you. We don't know what's going on with Nan. They won't tell us anything."

Oleg went with her back to the reception desk, to the clerk who looked ready to snap. She said the same thing again, much less gently this time. Oleg thanked her, and once again Nisha sat on the stupid hard chair.

"I can see if Eric has a number," Oleg said, scrolling through his phone.

Eric was his direct supervisor. He lived in a nearby building run by the same management company. When Nisha had lived in the building, she'd sometimes seen them hanging out together. Oleg made a phone call and explained what was going on, chatted for a minute, and then said, "Da," and hung up.

"Well?"

"He's going down to his office to look through the files. You know every year we ask for updating information? He thinks maybe he have something in there."

Nisha let out a sigh of relief. Finally someone was doing something. "You're the best."

A few minutes later, Eric called back, and after a minute Oleg relayed the conversation to Nisha and Kara. Nan hadn't responded to the annual request for updated information in a few years, but the last time she'd done it, she'd included the name and number of a friend as her emergency contact.

"Well, who is it?" Kara asked.

"Is Sonia Rivera," Oleg said. "I call now."

"Sonia?" Nisha said to Kara. "Sonia is listed as her next of kin?"

"No answer," Oleg said. "Maybe she is here now."

Kara went back to the reception desk. Nisha watched as the staff person opened her mouth, ready to yell at them, but Kara swiftly and smoothly said, "I know we've been a nuisance to you, and I'm sorry about that. I get that you're really busy and just doing your job. The thing is, we know who our friend's emergency contact is, and she's not answering our calls. Could you at least tell us if she's here in the hospital right now? Because if she's not, we know where she lives and we can go get her, so she can make the decisions she needs to and so we can all get updated on our friend's condition. Her name is Sonia Rivera. I can give you her phone number as proof I'm not lying."

"Just a minute." The receptionist picked up the phone.

Kara turned to them and gave a thumbs up.

Ten minutes later, Nisha was in a cab with Kara headed toward Sonia's house to bring her to the hospital.

❖

By the time they got to Sonia's house, it was around nine, and all the lights were off. Nisha had misgivings about waking her, but for all they knew Nan's life was in danger, and Sonia was the only one the doctors would talk to. For Nan's sake, she thought, some impoliteness was allowed.

Sonia answered the door in flannel polka dot pajamas. She was holding a baseball bat, ready to take a swing. When she saw who her visitors were, she set it down by the door.

"You never know at this hour," she explained. "What the hell are you doing here in the middle of the night?"

"It's nine," Kara said.

Nisha pushed in front of her. "Nan's in the hospital, and they told us you're the only one they'll talk to."

"Me? Why me?"

"I guess she listed you as her next of kin."

Sonia laughed. "That's a bunch of hooey." She squinted at them. "Why are you the ones telling me this? Shouldn't somebody official call me?"

"Do you turn your phone on silent when you go to bed?" Kara asked.

"Oh, well, yeah. But listen, I'm not paying for anybody's hospital bill. If she thinks I'm rich, she's crazy."

"I don't think you're expected to pay just because you're her emergency contact," Kara said. "I think they just want someone to give updates on her condition and to make decisions on her behalf. But we don't know anything that's going on, so we have no idea what they need you for. The hospital won't say anything until you're there."

Sonia left them in the living room while she went upstairs to change. Nisha took the opportunity to look more closely at her bookshelves. In addition to the books on the occult, there were small figurines of animals and a few photographs. None of Barb, Nan, or Rosalind. In one, a much younger Sonia was standing with two children of about ten or twelve. The three had a very strong resemblance.

"Kara!" She waved for Kara to come look. "Do you think Sonia has kids?"

"Maybe. Do you think that's important?"

"What if Sonia dumped Barb to marry a man? Maybe that's what she meant about killing her. She broke her heart."

"That's a lot of speculation."

"We should ask her."

"Ask what?" Sonia came down the stairs in jeans and a hoodie, a fashion twin to Kara on her off-hours. "How are we getting to the hospital?"

"I'll get us a ride," Kara said, pulling out her phone.

Sonia rolled her eyes. "I have a car. Gonna lose my parking space, though."

Sonia's car looked as frozen in time as Barb. It was the size of a small boat, its hood and trunk extending a yard away from the cab. Its lines were angular, and there were patches of rust on the maroon paint. The interior smelled like stale cigarettes, the leather seats were torn, and the carpet was stained. Worse was Sonia's driving. She didn't seem to care that she lived on a residential street with stop signs at every intersection. She took them as loose suggestions, slamming on the brake, threatening to launch them all through the windshield with the force of it, and a split-second later she'd jam her foot on the gas pedal, hurtling them back against the seats like a roller coaster making its ascent. By the time they turned onto Augusta, Nisha was ready to throw up.

"We were wondering if you have any children," Kara said.

"Yes."

"May I ask how old?"

"Carlos is fifty, and Luis is forty-seven."

Nisha did the mental math. If Sonia's kids were around fifty, they would have been born before Barb died. Her hypothesis that Sonia had broken Barb's heart to go live as a heterosexual married mother was wrong.

Kara must have been thinking the same thing because she said, "So you had kids when you lived with Rosalind? Did that pose any problem back then with you being queer?"

"You have to understand, mija, things were different. Almost all of us had relationships with men at some point. Some of us did it to cover up who we really were, and some of us were just looser about who we loved. If you were attracted to women at all, you were called lesbian, but what you'd call 'lesbian' today isn't really what we were."

"It sounds as if you're saying most people were bi or pan," Nisha said.

"I'm not saying that either. Anyway, what does this have to do with Nan being in the hospital?"

"We were hoping it had something to do with why Barb's spirit is still around," Nisha explained. "Maybe that's how you broke Barb's heart."

"My kids don't got nothing to do with that."

"Do you have any grandchildren?"

Sonia looked at her from the rearview mirror with cold eyes. "What's that gotta do with this?"

"Nothing, I was just asking to be polite."

Kara turned to look at Nisha, shaking her head as if to say, *Let me handle this.* She was, after all, the one Sonia had kept feeding flan.

Kara steered the conversation back to Nan as they arrived at the hospital and looked for a parking space. When they got inside the emergency department, Sonia introduced herself to the staff person at the desk. This time, the staffer smiled and said, "All right!" as if congratulating them on finally being able to circumvent the draconian next-of-kin policy.

Eventually, Sonia was allowed to see Nan, and she let Nisha come with her.

Nan wasn't conscious. An IV was sticking out of her hand, and she was on a heart monitor. In bed, surrounded by so many machines, she looked old and frail, and it hit Nisha how precious Nan's life was and how she'd taken for granted that Nan would always be around.

A doctor came to update them, and Nisha held one of Nan's limp hands as he explained that Nan had suffered a stroke and would need to remain in the hospital for a few days for tests and observation. They'd look for signs of paralysis or speech impairment and begin any necessary rehabilitation before they discharged her.

"We won't know her home care needs for a few more days," he said, adjusting his glasses, "but it's pretty common in cases like this that the patient will need someone to take care of them for a while."

"She lives by herself," Nisha said.

"Then, depending on her home life and her health circumstances, we might be talking about assisted living."

"A nursing home?" Sonia clarified. "She'd rather fucking die."

If the doctor was scandalized by her swearing, he didn't show it.

"Well, as I said, it'll be a few days before we know anything definitive. I just want you to be prepared. She could lose mobility, speech, even memory."

He said a few more things to Sonia about transferring Nan to a regular room, but Nisha was too busy thinking about Nan losing her special memories of a world that didn't exist anymore. Her stories from when she was younger were invaluable, and if Nan wasn't able to tell them, it would be a loss to the community.

And she was worried about Nan losing her ability to take care of herself. On a good day, Nan's independence was already somewhat questionable, and if she couldn't walk or feed herself anymore, who was going to help her?

A nurse told them it was time to leave Nan alone to rest. Nisha didn't want to comply, but knowing that Nan was at least stable was some comfort.

Back in the waiting room, they told Kara and Oleg everything they had learned. Since Nan was sleeping and there was nothing to be done until she was awake, they decided to go home. Oleg volunteered to take Kara and Nisha with him, but before Sonia left, Nisha had to ask again.

"Why are you her emergency contact?"

"Are your feelings hurt that it's not you?"

"No." Nisha adored Nan, but she wouldn't have expected to play that significant a role in Nan's life. What she had expected, once the idea of an emergency contact had been presented, was that it would be someone she knew, someone who was regularly around. Until recently, she'd never heard of Sonia. Nan had never mentioned her by name, and Sonia certainly hadn't given the impression they were still in touch.

"I didn't know I was her emergency contact, okay? I don't know why she would have done that. But I'll try to do right by her because we have a long history. Maybe she did it because she and Rosie had a falling out. You'd have to ask them about it."

"I can't ask Nan anything. She's unconscious."

"Then ask Rosie."

"She vanished."

"What do you mean, she vanished?"

"I don't know. Her store is for rent, and she's just gone."

"Damn Rosie," Sonia said with an affectionate smile. She shrugged, said good night to Oleg and Kara, and left.

"Everything okay?" Kara put a comforting arm around Nisha's shoulder.

"Have you noticed how incredibly blasé they all are about whatever happened in the past? It's so frustrating."

"Aren't you the one who said we have to let them tell us in their own time?" Kara said. "Not much we can do now but wait."

CHAPTER TWELVE

Despite what she'd told Nisha, Kara couldn't wait. If the key to Barb's mystery rested with Miss Pythia, who was gone without a trace, and Nan, who was unconscious, then Kara was going to pick the lock. She didn't want to upset Nisha, so she maintained the facade of patience. Nisha was stressed about Nan's health and well-being, and Kara didn't want her to have to worry about anything else. It also helped to have her conveniently absent, since she probably wouldn't have approved of what Kara was up to, anyway.

And so Kara's quest to figure out Barb's unfinished business continued alone, without satisfactory progress. The stupid amount of money she'd spent on the private investigator didn't yield much. In fact, she'd learned more about Nan's private life in one night at the hospital. The investigator's findings would have been more useful if he had looked into Barb's past, but without Barb's last name, birthday, or any real details other than that she was a dead lesbian from the 1980s, it was hardly worth spending money on.

While she was working out the unfinished business, Kara thought she could at least try to make Barb invisible and quiet again. If Barb weren't sleeping on her couch and eating all her food, Kara would have a lot more patience about the whole situation. She'd saved the herbs and candles they'd used the night they accidentally manifested Barb, so one evening when Barb was taking a shower, she decided to reverse the ritual.

Maybe it was reckless to assume that doing everything in the opposite order might make Barb invisible again, but these were desperate times.

First, Kara did the embarrassing throat-singing. Then she said the incantation backward, word by word, and put the ground herbs into a bowl in reverse order, making sure not to mess up the mugwort and the thyme. She placed the candles around the room in the same pattern Nisha had and lit them one by one. Then she waited.

After a minute or two, Barb came storming out of the bathroom, her hair still wet, and hollered, "What the hell did you do to me? I'm strobing like a disco!"

She was, indeed, blinking in and out of visibility.

Assuming she hadn't done the incantation to its full effect, Kara recited it again, quickly, with Barb scrambling for the paper. When Kara finished, Barb had permanent stripes of invisibility.

"Are you happy now?" Barb yelled.

"Maybe if I read it one more time?"

"Give it up, kiddo. You don't know what you're doing." Barb tried to blow out the smoking bowl of herbs, but she was missing the lower half of her jaw and couldn't. She reached for the bowl, but she was missing half her fingers. She still had eyes, though, and they glowered at Kara. "I can't believe you did this to me."

She looked like some kind of ghost zebra.

"I thought we had a better relationship than this by now."

"You won't tell me your unfinished business," Kara said. "You won't tell me anything about you, so I can figure out your business on my own. What do you expect? I'm getting desperate."

Barb waved a hand through where her stomach should have been. "Do me a favor? Just read the stupid thing in the right order, and then we can talk."

Or she could read it backwards one more time to see if the rest of Barb disappeared. She started to, but Barb figured out what she was doing and grabbed the paper from her hands.

"Read it in order, or so help me, I will go full-on horror movie ghost on you."

"What does that even mean?"

"Chains rattling in the middle of the night, objects flying across the room. I'll dump your beer in the toilet."

"You wouldn't!"

"Try me, Kara." She waved the paper. "Read the damn thing. Go on."

"I'm not going to be threatened by a ghost."

"What would Nisha say if she knew you did this to me?" Barb reached for Kara's cell phone on the coffee table and missed. She tried again, but her invisible hand kept waving right through it. "Hey, Siri, call Nisha Rajchandra!"

"Okay, calling Nisha Rajchandra."

The screen of Kara's phone lit up. How did Barb know about Siri?

"It's ringing," Barb warned her.

The phone rang again.

"How long do you think it'll take her to pick up?"

If Nisha answered and Barb told her what Kara was doing, Nisha would be furious.

The line rang a third time. Then the call connected, and they could hear Nisha's voice saying, "Hel—"

"Hey, Siri, hang up!" Kara shouted in panic. The phone screen went dark again. Then to Barb, she said, "Fine. Give me the stupid paper, and I'll put you back."

She read the incantation again, and slowly the missing parts of Barb's body came back into view.

Barb sighed with relief. Then she lunged at Kara, grabbed the paper, and set it on fire. Before Kara could think, Barb took the bowl of herbs to the bathroom and flushed the contents down the toilet.

"Don't mess with me, Susie Q," Barb said, sauntering into the living room. "If you don't like living here with me, maybe you're the one who should move out." She plopped onto the couch and leaned back with her hands behind her head. "I'm not going anywhere."

❖

After the failed attempt to un-manifest Barb, Kara concentrated her energies on learning more about the AIDS charity. In 1986, could there have been that many? If she could find out which one Barb had volunteered for, she could perhaps find records of their activities, and maybe that would lead to more information about Barb.

The problem was that while Kara thought of herself as someone incredibly well-trained at reading the finer points of legal documents,

JANE KOLVEN

she was not a trained archivist. Other than typing "Barb," "AIDS," and "1986" in an internet search bar, she had no idea how to go about looking for records from a charity that might not even exist anymore. She needed help from a professional.

She also needed a break from Barb. Her ghostly roommate had gotten tired of wearing the same clothes and had asked Kara if they could order something from the JCPenney's catalogue. In a fit of foolishness, Kara had shown Barb the Amazon website, and now her apartment housed, in addition to Barb's new wardrobe, a PlayStation and gaming chair. Barb liked first-person shooters, which she said allowed to her vent her aggressions in a socially acceptable way, and she played them, night and day, until Kara felt crippled with headaches from all the noise.

One Saturday, she told Barb she was going to see the new modernist exhibit at the Art Institute. Barb looked disappointed that she couldn't come, but that was out of their control. She'd vanish if she crossed the door to the apartment.

"You can get a pizza for lunch if you want," Kara said. "I'll leave a credit card."

That mollified her somewhat.

Outside, Kara headed north toward Uptown instead of toward the Loop and the tourist area where the Art Institute was located. She'd done some research while at work and had discovered another possible medium, this one located off Wilson Avenue.

The medium, Pauline, had actually answered the phone, which had been a pleasant change of pace from Miss Pythia. And she'd agreed to an appointment to discuss the situation with Barb. Kara met her at a small store selling imported art objects from West Africa alongside mass produced goods from China. Once they introduced themselves, Pauline took her into the break room to talk.

"The problem now," Kara said, after explaining how they'd accidentally manifested Barb, "is that she's always around. She's loud. She's rude. She knows how to use my Amazon Prime account. Living with her is intolerable."

"She cannot go away until she feels at peace with what has happened in her life."

It was more or less what Miss Pythia, Nan, and Sonia had said, though Pauline made it sound like a choice on Barb's end, rather than something that would automatically happen to her once her business was finished.

"I'm trying to find out what might be causing her to stay around. After this, I'm meeting someone who studies LGBTQ history in the area. I guess I just wanted to know if there's a way she can be un-manifested while her business is still unfinished. So I was wondering, do you know what incantation the other medium might have given me? Maybe you have a copy of it, and I could recite it again?"

"You'd prefer to interact with her as a spirit rather than a person."

"Yes."

Pauline made a slight face of disapproval.

"It's not that she's a bad person," Kara explained. "I just don't want a roommate. I moved here to get a fresh start, on my own, and her presence is impeding my ability to do that."

Pauline nodded now. "I think I understand."

"You do? So you can help me make her vanish?"

"If you're hoping I know exactly what the other person gave you, I'm sorry to disappoint you. I have no idea. If you want me to sell you a crystal and tell you it's magic and can make your ghost go away, I'm sure there's something up front we can pick out. But that's not your problem. Your problem is that the spirit represents the past, and you are focused on the future. You're unwilling to look the past in the eye."

"I am?"

"Until you do, you will never be comfortable with Barb's presence."

Pauline's interpretation of the situation wasn't one Kara had considered before, and it was in some ways a reversal of what Kara had said to get Nisha to take off the ring. She'd encouraged Nisha to stop looking backward, but now it sounded as if Pauline thought she needed to do the opposite.

"I don't understand. You're asking about me, but I thought it was *Barb's* unfinished business that was keeping her around. Are you saying her business is connected to me?"

"It must be, if she appeared first to you. What happened in your past that brought you to Chicago?"

Kara gave a taut smile. She did not want to talk about Hilary. That had nothing to do with Barb.

"Are you sure you can't just sell me that crystal?"

Pauline laughed lightly. "Like I said, I can if you want, but it won't help your situation. Let me ask you something. Are you a Christian?"

Kara nodded. Her family was Lutheran, but she didn't really attend church or think much about her own belief system.

"There is great historical conflict between the practices of witchcraft and Christianity and Islam. Many say these religions stand in opposition to witchcraft, but of course what some call witchcraft others say is ancient spirituality, the religion of people before crusades, not dark magic or something to be feared. It has different names in different cultures: Wicca, hoodoo, voodoo. The common thread is that the practice is always seen in opposition to the three major monotheistic religions."

"I wasn't trying to practice witchcraft," Kara said. "If you'd have asked me before if I even believed in witches and ghosts, I'd have told you no."

"I was not finished. There is also a long tradition of these practices being associated with women."

"Like the Salem witch trials?"

Pauline smiled. "This is not unique to America. In Ghana, where my family is from, and around the world. Accusing a woman of being a witch is often a way to suppress her education and empowerment."

Pauline continued to explain, giving a history and culture lesson as she went. Spiritual practices, she said, were sometimes derided as "witchcraft"—as if witchcraft was something bad, something dealing with dark and scary forces. It was a way of suppressing indigenous and marginalized religions. Anything a woman did that was powerful or enlightened could be chalked up to her being a witch, and therefore her accomplishments could be negated as evil.

The obvious correlation, Kara thought, was with the queer community. How often were people accused of being gay as a way of dismissing them from mainstream society? And if those people were also accused of witchcraft, then homosexuality itself would be seen as evil.

"Barb told us she lived in the apartment with a girlfriend, and as far as we can tell, the other women who are somehow involved were a circle of lesbian friends."

"Is there any connection between that and whatever brought you to Chicago that you refuse to talk about?"

"Am I that transparent?"

Perhaps it was more than a coincidence that the queer ghost had appeared when she, another queer woman, moved in. But maybe not, since Nisha and Angie had lived there before.

"I'm not sure. I'm gay, if that's what you're asking, but I'm not the only gay person to live in that apartment since Barb died."

"What do you know about the others who lived there?"

She told Pauline what she knew about Nisha and Angie's relationship, which wasn't much, and about the missing ring.

"There must be a connection between these events now and what happened to your spirit in the past."

"The problem is that I just don't know that much about Barb. She won't tell me much about herself, and every time I ask about her unfinished business she says she can't tell me directly. She says I have to wait."

"What's wrong with waiting?"

"She's going to bankrupt me in the meantime."

"Do you know anyone who does know more about her?"

Kara explained that Nan was in the hospital, essentially unable to tell them anything, and that Sonia was reticent and Miss Pythia had disappeared.

"You don't know her by any chance?" she asked hopefully. "Her real name is Rosalind. I don't know her last name. She used to have a shop on Damen."

"We don't have a Facebook group if that's what you're asking," Pauline said. "I'll ask around, but it's not likely we move in the same circles. I do have a recommendation for what you can do in the meantime."

She led Kara to the main part of the store, where she picked out two books, one on the history of witchcraft and the occult in West

Africa and another about how the Atlantic slave trade had globalized indigenous religious and spiritual practices. Kara dutifully bought the books, certain they'd be zero help with Barb—who'd said she was from a Chicago suburb called Cicero, not West Africa. She thanked Pauline for her time, especially since it had been free, unlike Miss Pythia's expensive consultations, and Pauline directed her to a nearby café to try egusi soup.

After lunch, Kara took the bus north on Clark to the LGBTQ library, where she met Harold, a sixtyish, soft-spoken staff person who had responded to her email request for help using the library's archives.

"Most of our special collections begin in the early 1990s," he explained as he took Kara into a room with a few file boxes on a table. "Your aunt was really at the forefront of things to be volunteering as early as 1986. The HIV test only began to be used in 1985." Harold patted one of the boxes. "Fortunately, we do have the personal papers from one of the founders of an early organization, and some of the records date as far back as 1984. You didn't give me much to go on, but this is our best start."

Kara felt a little chastised. "I'm sorry I don't know the name of the organization. All I really know is that they had a talent show in 1986."

"And you don't know your aunt's maiden name?" Harold seemed to find that a little suspicious, and rightly so.

"Just Barbara. She and my uncle died before I could get much other information. I guess everyone else in my family who might have known her is dead, too. That's why I wanted to learn more about her. My family history, you know."

She hoped her hasty lies sounded more believable than the truth would have.

Looking at old records turned out to be very dull and painstaking work, and not that much different from the discovery process. For a solid hour, Kara sat in silence with Harold as they skimmed page after page from the boxes, looking for any sign of a talent show or any mention of someone named Barb or Barbara. Kara's appointment was only for an hour, and as the clock ticked down, she started to worry they wouldn't find anything useful before her time was up.

With only ten minutes remaining, Harold gave a small "hmm" that caught her attention.

"Did you find something?"

"This monthly newsletter mentions the unexpected passing of a devoted volunteer, Barbara Kowalski, but of course that couldn't be your aunt, since she obviously lived to marry your uncle."

"What's the date on that newsletter?" Kara asked.

"February 20, 1986." Harold showed her the paper he'd been reading. "Didn't you say your last name was Eckhardt? It must have been another volunteer."

"Must have been," Kara agreed, faking a disappointed face. She put the minutes from a board meeting she'd been reading back in the box. "I don't think we're going to find anything here. I guess I just don't have enough information. But I really thank you for your time."

"This is what we do," Harold said with pride. "Preserving our queer history."

"It's wonderful." And she meant it. Reading the files had been a dreary task, but it was comforting to know a history the world often erased or forgot was being meticulously kept at places like this. She shook Harold's hand and departed, eager to find out more about Barbara Kowalski who died around February 20, 1986.

❖

A week later, Kara told Barb she was going to the Museum of Science and Industry to see the submarine and suggested Barb order Thai food to see if she liked it. But instead of heading to Hyde Park, where the museum was located, Kara took the Blue Line downtown to the Harold Washington Library to look up old newspapers in search of Barb's obituary. The library was a beautiful red brick building with a glass and steel roof and giant owl sculptures looking down on pedestrians. It served as the main branch of the Chicago Public Library system, and the librarian Kara had talked to at the Wicker Park branch had explained that old newspapers were kept there on microfilm.

A kind staff person helped Kara locate the *Sun-Times* and *Tribune* film cartridges for January and February of 1986. She showed Kara how to work the machine, warning her not to advance or rewind too fast in case the film came off the spool, and left Kara to work.

If looking through an old file box had been boring, this was excruciating. The newspaper was hard to read on screen, and obituaries were buried under all the news stories. There was no way to find them except to slowly advance through each week's entire paper, and if Kara went too fast, she missed them and had to go back.

After two hours, she'd been through the *Sun-Times* with no luck. She turned her attention to the *Tribune*, wondering how long she was going to sit at the library and where she could get some coffee when this project was done. She tried to do what the librarian had shown her and what the instructions on the machine said as she replaced the *Sun-Times* spool with the January *Tribune* one, but the spool flew off the machine as soon as she tried to advance it.

When her phone rang, Kara scrambled to silence it. Her nephew Levi was calling, and she took it as a welcome sign of a break.

"Hey, Aunt Kara. I just wanted to tell you I miss you."

At twelve, Levi was at the awkward age when one day he was still an open-hearted child and another he was a hard-shelled teenager. Kara preferred the days when he was still unashamed of his emotions.

"I miss you, too, bud. What's new?"

"I need your advice."

Levi had grown up knowing Kara was gay, and it had never been a problem because he got two really good aunts out of the deal. Kara was the cool one who took him to sporting events and went snowboarding with him while Hilary had been the nice one who made cookies and gave the best birthday presents. As an only child, Levi had often turned to Kara for advice about how to handle problems at school and with his parents, and she had treasured that bond because she expected it would fade as he got older and pulled away from the family. Now, hearing him ask for her help, Kara felt heartened that he still needed her.

"Desi's mom said he could have a boy-girl party for his birthday."

"And you don't know how to tell your mom."

"Well, do I have to tell her, or can I just say it's his birthday party?"

Kara remembered "boy-girl parties," those awkward affairs that had started in junior high when parents decided it was okay for their kids to socialize across gender lines. Most of the time, they had been terrible parties in carpeted basements with parents lurking upstairs. It was a significant turning point in one's life to be old enough to attend, but for Kara those parties had been a source of anxiety and dread. Her friends acted unnatural and nervous, more interested in getting the boys to notice them than in having fun together. Kara had preferred sleepovers and camping—times when she and her friends could hang out without boys around. Once she'd come out, she'd understood why.

Now, as an adult, the whole idea of a "boy-girl party" as some marker of moving into adolescence seemed dumb. It was a surefire way to pressure kids into thinking they had to feel some excitement about spending time with the opposite sex. And what if they didn't? Why couldn't they spend time together without it being flirty and awkward? Couldn't boys and girls just be friends? And, these days, weren't half of the kids nonbinary, anyway?

As fine as Becca was with Kara's homosexuality, she was still fairly conservative about these sorts of things. Kara knew instinctively Becca would consider the party a big deal and would not be okay with Levi going without her knowledge.

"You have to tell your mom," she said.

"What if she says I can't go?"

"Then I'm sure there are other things you can do that night. Maybe you and Desi can do something special on a different night."

"But *everyone* will be there!"

Kara remembered that feeling from school. If everyone but Levi went, he'd look completely uncool, even if it wasn't his choice not to attend. The politics of junior high were rough.

"You want me to talk to your mom?"

"I just want to know what to say to her. If I get good at asking her stuff now, then when I'm sixteen, I'll know how to get her to let me drive her car."

Kara thought about what made Becca tick. She was a pretty strict parent, so appealing to her sense of cool wouldn't work. She wouldn't care if the kids made fun of Levi for being the only one not allowed to go. Trying to convince her that her objections to the party were heterosexist and outdated wouldn't work. Becca did, however, care that she was coaching her son through life appropriately.

"How about if you tell her this is an important milestone in your adolescent development?"

"I don't even know what that means!"

"All right, here's what you do. You just tell her directly. 'Mom, Desi's birthday party is a boy-girl party, and I really want to go. I think I'm ready for it.'"

"But I don't know if I am ready for it."

Kara definitely hadn't been. Still wasn't. "Do you even want to go to this party, or do you just feel pressured because everyone else is going?"

Levi breathed into the phone a few times, not responding, and that was all the answer Kara needed. "Did you know you were gay when you were my age?"

The question threw Kara for a loop. She wondered if Levi was trying to tell her he wasn't ready for the party because he wasn't interested in girls.

"I didn't think about kissing girls or anything when I was your age," she told him. "I just didn't like it when boys were around. And I didn't understand why my friends were so obsessed with them."

"Would you like me better if I was a girl?"

"No, I like you the way you are."

"Would you like me better if I was gay?"

Did he think they would have a closer relationship if that was something they shared, or was he again trying tease his own sexuality? Was Levi about to come out to her? But if he wasn't gay, and she said yes, would he think she didn't connect with him as well?

"I would like you the same," she said carefully.

"But you like gay people better than straight people."

Where did he get this stuff?

"I like people to be who they are. Would it be cool if being gay was something we had in common? Maybe. But I wouldn't wish for you to be anything other than who you are, the same way that parents of a gay kid love their kid because that's how their kid is. It's not really about gay or straight. It's about being true to yourself." Kara took a moment to figure out how to ask what was motivating these questions. "You don't think I moved to get away from you, do you? That maybe if we had more in common I'd have stayed? You know I miss you a lot, right?"

"Not enough to stay here."

"Moving here had nothing to do with you, bud. I wish we still lived close to each other. Being far away from you was one of the reasons I didn't want to leave."

"Then why did you?"

"I don't know if you can understand right now, but maybe when you're a little older and ready to go to college, you will. I had to leave because I needed to figure out who I am, and I couldn't do that if I stayed. Sometimes the people around you expect you to be a certain way, and it's hard to separate their image of you from who you really are without a little space from them."

"I guess that makes sense."

"So what's this phone call really about? I mean, other than how to ask your mom about the party? Why is this party such a big deal for you?"

"Sometimes I have thoughts about girls. I think I might be straight."

Kara grinned. So he was teasing his sexuality, but a different identity than she'd expected. She loved that he felt the need to come out straight.

"That's awesome," she said. "If that's who you are, then that's all that matters."

"I wish you would come home for a visit. It's not the same without you. Do you like Chicago?"

Tough question. Did she like her new job and the pace of the city? Yes. She appreciated the opportunities living here presented, like exploring different neighborhoods and eating food she'd never even heard of.

Did she like her apartment and the fact that most of her life in Chicago was tangled up with some ghost story? No. Did she wish it was all over? Yes.

"You're gonna come home for Christmas, aren't you?" Levi said. "Or maybe I can come visit. Can I? I could stay at your apartment one weekend. Please? Can I come visit?"

There was no way in hell Levi was coming to visit until Barb was gone. Kara said yes to Christmas, remained noncommittal about the possibility of him visiting her, and eventually they hung up.

She turned her attention back to the old newspapers and finally found it: an obituary for Barbara Kowalski, deceased on February 14, 1986. Valentine's Day.

CHAPTER THIRTEEN

It had been three weeks since Nan had gone into the hospital. Three weeks since the doctor had said she'd be released "in a few days," and three weeks since Sonia had given Nisha any meaningful update on Nan's condition. Something had to have gone wrong for Nan's release to be delayed so severely, but Sonia rarely returned Nisha's calls. And when she did, she explained what she understood from the doctor in confusing terms. At the hospital, Nan wasn't much help either. Although she was receiving speech therapy for the paralysis on the left side of her face, she didn't talk much because of how difficult it was, and when she did, her words were too slurred for Nisha to really understand.

On days without snow, the hospital staff let Nisha push Nan outside in a wheelchair. They'd make a loop around the building in the fresh air, and they'd come back inside before Nan got too cold.

As the days passed, the ward became decorated for Hanukkah and Christmas. On Christmas Eve, Nisha and Oleg came with gifts of non-slip socks and contraband sweets. It was one of the most pathetic Christmas parties Nisha had been to, but the spark in Nan's eye said it meant a lot to her.

The holidays were Nisha's busiest weeks at the theater because they put on an annual performance of *A Christmas Carol* that played every single night. When she wasn't working or visiting Nan, Nisha still managed to squeeze in visits to the apartment during the daytime, so Barb wouldn't be lonely while Kara was with her family in Wisconsin. Most of the time, Barb pretended not to care that Nisha was there. She kept her attention on her video games and the new sixty-four-inch TV set that occupied most of the living room. Once, she decided she needed a change and asked Nisha to give her a makeover.

"Nothing fancy like you do," Barb said.

"Of course not. Good makeup isn't necessarily heavy makeup. It's not about turning the person into someone they're not. It's about finding the beauty in the person and bringing it out." She studied Barb's face. "In your case, I think we should darken the eyebrows a little. It'll provide a nice contrast between your eyes and your forehead to give your face a little definition. Then I want just a little more color on your lips, nothing too dark or shiny because they're thin and that would make the thinness stand out."

Barb closed her eyes and sat patiently while Nisha worked on her. After she applied a very light coat of makeup, she brushed Barb's hair and thought about what contemporary style would be the equivalent of the 1980s feathering. Barb might look good with a medium-length pixie, something textured but short enough that she didn't need to style it.

"When I come over next time, I'll bring my hair supplies." She handed Barb a hand mirror she'd found in Kara's bedroom. "For now, what do you think?"

Barb looked in the mirror and frowned.

"What's wrong? Do you hate it?"

Barb handed the mirror back. "I can't see myself."

Nisha angled the mirror, so she could see. Sure enough, the mirror showed an empty chair. Barb didn't have a reflection.

"Thanks anyway." Barb slouched her way back to the couch and turned on the TV.

For the first time, Nisha considered that Barb's couch potato act might have been motivated by depression. It was negligent of her not to have seen it before.

The next time she came over, she brought three vintage home workout videotapes from the thrift store. She told Barb how her morning runs had helped improve her mental outlook, and if Barb couldn't leave the apartment to exercise, then they were going to do it in the apartment together.

They laughed their way through *Jane Fonda's Workout* and decided to order lunch as a reward.

"Do you like noodles?" Nisha asked.

"Yeah, like pasta?"

"No, noodles, like…Asian noodles."

"Oh, you mean Chinese food. Moo goo gai pan and all that."

"Didn't people eat noodles when you were alive?"

"We had a Chinese takeout. There were some Polish restaurants. Some good Mexican places."

"No Thai? Ramen? Sushi?"

"I've never had sushi, but I've seen people who live here eating it. It looks so fancy."

"Okay," Nisha decided, "you're going to try sushi for the first time today."

She showed the menu of a restaurant off her phone screen, but it was all too unfamiliar to Barb. As a vegetarian, Nisha didn't have that much more knowledge. She ordered a small assortment of hand rolls and sushi pieces for Barb to try and made sure to get several vegetarian options for herself.

When the food came, they sat on the couch together with a reality show about house hunting on TV.

"Well," Barb said, opening a plastic container, "let's try this."

"I think that's the crab."

Barb used her fingers instead of chopsticks to pick up a piece. "It's cold!"

"Well, yeah, it's sushi. What did you expect?"

"What's this junk?" Before Nisha could warn her, Barb swiped a finger through the wasabi and tasted it. Her eyes squeezed shut, but tears were already dripping out. "My mouth! My mouth!"

After a glass of water and some crackers, Barb settled down. She came back to the sofa and pushed the containers toward Nisha. "I guess it's not for me."

"You should have seen your face when you ate that wasabi." Nisha took a bite of the asparagus tempura roll, which was an amazing combination of soft and crunchy. "You were actually crying! Seriously, you're missing out. This is so good."

"You know, when I was young, being adventurous about food wasn't as big of a deal as it is now. You people today, you eat all kinds of things from all over the world. Except—well, some women I've seen in this apartment, they don't really eat. In my day, women weren't scared of eating meat and cream."

"It always freaks me out to be around women who pick at their food. I love eating."

"My mom, she used to make the best lasagna. With ground beef and cheese and tomato sauce she made herself. It would simmer on the stove for three hours before she'd use it. This lasagna was loaded with calories, but it was delicious. One time, I brought my friend Elaine over to the house for dinner, and she asked if she could have salad instead. My mom had cooked all afternoon. I thought she'd die."

"No! She didn't even pretend to eat?"

"That's worse, isn't it? Because then you waste a portion someone else could eat the next day."

"I'd never be able to save a piece of lasagna for the next day," Nisha said. "I love carbs."

"Work hard, play hard, I always say." Barb settled into the couch. "You know, this has been a really nice day."

"I'm so glad to hear that!" Nisha put the lid on the empty sushi container and carried it to the kitchen garbage can. "I've been a little worried about you, to be honest. You must be sick of being stuck in this apartment after all this time."

"I've had better vacations." After a moment, she added, "I'm not the only one stuck somewhere, though."

"You mean Nan?" Nisha said as she came back into the living room. She handed Barb the bottle of beer she knew Barb would want and got comfortable on the sofa again. "I'm hoping she's going to be released soon, but I'm worried about how we're going to take care of her when she is."

"I wasn't talking about Nan."

"Me? Where am I stuck? I can go wherever I want."

"I'm glad you realize that," Barb said. "Just make sure you don't forget it."

Barb's cryptic warning stayed with Nisha through the uneventful blur of New Year's. Although she had a show that night, she made it home in time to watch *Mean Girls* and drink champagne with Suni and Maddie. At midnight she accepted a pity kiss on the cheek from each of them before going to bed.

Ringing in a new year made Nisha take stock of her life. When she'd first moved in with Suni and Maddie, she'd planned to stay a few weeks until she got her grounding. It had now been over a year. When Angie dumped her, she'd committed herself to paying off debt and trying to improve her income stream. The job at the Wolfman was a massive step up from the off-Loop theater work she had been doing before, which barely paid at all, but it wasn't enough to keep her afloat if she wanted to get her own apartment.

She wondered if this was what Barb had meant about being stuck. Had she overstayed her welcome with Suni and Maddie? Was she actually getting herself together, or was she wallowing at this point? She didn't have an answer to that question, but as a resolution, she decided she was going to prioritize thinking about it.

❖

When Kara returned from Wisconsin, Nisha was itching to see her. She'd waited to give Kara and Barb their Christmas presents until they could do a little group party. They even told Oleg that Kara's cousin was in town again and invited him to come up. He said he was busy, but given how strange Barb could sometimes be, Nisha thought maybe his absence was a good thing.

She brought several bags of groceries to make dinner, as well as the presents, and there was a spring in her step as she made her way up the five flights of stairs to the top floor of the building.

"Hey, Miss Makeup," Barb greeted her as she opened the door. "Don't you look nice today."

Nisha was wearing gray leggings, a long-sleeved T-shirt, and knee-length cardigan. Hardly anything nice.

"She's not home yet. She called me and said Horowitz was keeping her late to talk about something."

"How did she call you?"

Barb beamed and held a cheap black plastic flip phone to her ear. "I'm in the twenty-first century now, baby. Look at me. It's like I work for NASA."

"Kara bought you a cell phone?"

Barb flipped the phone shut and crammed it in her jeans pocket. "Technically yes, but let's just say I'm better at picking out Christmas gifts for myself than she is."

"Oh, Barb, she's probably furious at you." Nisha set down the bags of groceries on the kitchen counter and noticed the new wine rack with six bottles lying sideways in it. More of Barb's work, she guessed. "I brought stuff to make dinner. You know, we've never talked about whether you like Indian food?"

"I love it! What is it?"

"I have a bunch of different stuff to make, some lentils and okra and samosas—they're like fried potato dumplings. It's really good."

"What's the main dish?"

"It's a bunch of little dishes."

"Chicken? Beef?"

"Vegetarian."

Barb didn't even try to hide her disappointment.

"Just promise me you'll try it. You might like it. You can fill up on rice."

"Fun! I'm always saying how much I like filling up on rice when there's nothing of substance to eat."

Nisha tried not to take Barb's cynicism personally. She loved cooking, but Maddie prided herself on being the family cook. That was her contribution to the household, since Suni earned more money and worked longer hours. Even if Maddie refused to buy her spices at the Indian stores on Devon Avenue, having said on many occasions how intimidated she felt there, and made bland food as a result, Nisha had to respect that it wasn't her kitchen.

That was part of the reason why she'd been looking forward to making dinner tonight. She'd finally get a chance to prepare some of the dishes her nani had taught her. Plus, she thought it would be fun to introduce Barb to new food.

"I'm doing this as a gesture for you," Nisha said, though her voice was gentle. "It's a lot of work."

Barb put her hands up. "Okay, okay, you're right. I can be gracious." She went into the living room and put soft jazz on the stereo at a low volume, then came back into the kitchen. "Anything I can help you with?"

Nisha shook her head as she began unpacking. "I saw Nan yesterday. She looked a little stronger."

"That's good. I don't like picturing her sick."

Careful not to look at Barb and to keep her tone neutral, Nisha asked, "What happened that night? Why do you think she came over?"

"Boy, you and Kara, you're both determined to get stuff out of me."

"I'm not asking because of your unfinished business. I'm asking because I care about Nan."

"You really do, don't you?"

"She's like this fun old queer grandmother who tells me stories about how things used to be. I love her."

"You want stories, babe, I got stories." Barb waved a finger. "Not about what's keeping me here. That's off limits. But I can tell you stuff." She whistled. "Back in my day, I did a lot more than Nan ever did. I don't know what she's told you, but she was the innocent one of the group."

"She was?"

"Oh, yeah, she was the one who always said, 'We're gonna get in trouble,' every time the rest of us had an idea."

"What kind of ideas did you have?"

Barb thought for a second. "Okay, here's a good one. See, there was this bar Monique's on Irving Park, and on Tuesdays they had a special night called Titillating Tuesdays. It was for the lesbians, and everybody knew it, but Monique wasn't going to come out and say it. So they called it Titillating Tuesdays. You get the pun? Because of tits."

"Yeah, I get it."

"So this one time, Sonia and I cook up an idea. What if we really make it about tits? So we decide not to wear bras, and we get these shirts and cut out the holes right here." Barb gestured a circle around her breast. "Then we put on coats, so it looks like we're wearing regular shirts. Rosie does it, too, because she always liked to fit in, and Nan's going, 'I don't know. I think we're gonna get in trouble.' But we finally convince her to do it with us. So we get to the bar and we all take off our coats, and there we are, titillating them."

"What happened?"

"Monique threw us out because she didn't want to lose her liquor license for having nudity in the bar. But the next day, she called up Sonia and said she thought it was hilarious and asked if we'd be willing to come back every week and do it and get thrown out, kind of as a stunt to get customers."

"Did you?"

"Nah, once was enough."

Nisha tried to picture a younger Nan flashing everyone, and though Barb said she was the innocent one of the group, in Nisha's eyes Nan had always had a wild streak.

"I'd love to hear more stories," she said. "Maybe you should write this stuff down."

Barb gave Nisha a warm nod of approval at this idea. "I'm gonna think of some stuff." She reached into the refrigerator and pulled out a bottle of beer. It was Spotted Cow. In fact, the whole bottom shelf was stocked with Spotted Cows. Kara must have brought them back after visiting her family. "You cook, I'll think."

"Deal."

When Kara finally came home, Nisha realized she had let herself in and started making dinner, as if she lived there, though neither she nor Barb were on the lease. Kara didn't seem to mind. She was mostly apologetic at how late she'd gotten home, and she griped about how her boss had summoned them to a six o'clock meeting that could have waited until the next day.

"Smells amazing in here." Kara came behind Nisha to look at the pots on the stove, and Nisha held her breath in anticipation of Kara's touch.

But instead, Kara murmured into her ear, "I didn't have a meeting. I have news about Barb. After dinner, let's get coffee and talk? Don't say anything, just nod if you're in."

Nisha nodded. "Here, taste this," she said to continue the subterfuge.

She lifted a spoonful of the potato and eggplant. As Kara's lips closed around the spoon, so did her eyes, and she gave a low, sensual moan of pleasure. The sound and proximity of Kara's face to hers sent sparks of electricity through Nisha. Kara opened her eyes, and Nisha held her breath for the brief moment they gazed at each other.

All Nisha could see were Kara's pink lips, which she wanted to feel against her own. Then Kara's expression closed off, self-conscious, and Nisha hastily turned away to put the spoon in the sink.

While dinner was simmering, Nisha gave Barb and Kara their Christmas presents. She'd seen a beautiful aqua pashmina that would complement Kara's skin tones and provide a nice pop of color against the gray wool coat she wore to work. For Barb, Nisha had a special surprise: a gift certificate for an at-home massage.

"Since you can't leave the apartment, I thought spa day could come to you."

"Nish, that had to be really expensive," Kara said quietly.

The massage had cost more than Nisha usually spent on her friends, but it was a perfect gift for Barb, who was cooped up all day. Barb gave Nisha a hug—the first time she'd ever done that—so Nisha figured it had been worth the expense.

They ate dinner while watching Barb's newest obsession, a true crime series that Kara said sensationalized the facts of the case and that Nisha found to be the stuff of nightmares. And afterward, Kara suggested they go out for coffee.

"You have coffee here," Barb said. "You put that little plastic cup in the machine, and badda-bing, you have coffee."

"But I don't have an espresso maker," Kara explained. "Sometimes it's nice to have espresso. It's a stronger flavor."

"I can order one on Amazon. I bet there's same-day delivery." Barb opened Kara's laptop.

"No!" Kara slammed the laptop shut. "We aren't buying an espresso maker, and we aren't getting same-day delivery. Sometimes I wish you still thought everything had to be ordered by mail from a catalogue and took a month to arrive."

Barb looked at Kara and seemed to understand something from Kara's eyes. "Oh, I see. Yeah, espresso has stronger flavor. Yeah, you have to go out to get that. It's not the same as regular coffee."

"Do you want us to bring you something back?" Nisha asked.

"I like Sanka," Barb said. "They have that?"

"I don't even know what Sanka is."

"Well, I guess no coffee for me. I'll stay here, you know, since I can't leave the apartment. But, yeah, that espresso—it's definitely worth leaving the house for."

"Okay, weirdo," Kara said, putting on her coat, "we'll be back soon."

Once they were out of the apartment, Nisha asked if Kara knew why Barb had acted so strangely.

"No clue. But that's how she is. Maybe it has something to do with her unfinished business?"

"How could espresso have anything to do with that?" Nisha wondered.

The café around the corner was open until nine. Nisha ordered a decaffeinated ginger tea since it was so late, but Kara went for a triple shot without hesitation. They took their drinks to a table in the window.

"How was home?"

Kara had texted and called a few times, but mostly she'd seemed busy, as Nisha had expected. She didn't take it personally. Although she didn't have a close relationship with her parents, she understood how important time with her family was for Kara, especially now that they didn't live in the same city.

"You know how worried I was that visiting would put me right back where I was before I moved? It wasn't like that at all. I felt like the person I am here, but also like the person I used to be. This probably doesn't even make sense."

Actually, it did, and Nisha told her as much. Kara had grown and changed in the months she'd been in Chicago, but she also valued reconnecting with her roots. It was a balance Nisha had craved for years with her own family until, after a lot of time and emotional work, she had accepted it wasn't going to happen. That was why she invested so much in her friendship with Suni, to connect to her culture, and with Nan, to give her a sense of generational legacy. Nisha wasn't jealous that Kara's situation was different. She was incredibly happy for her.

"You seem lighter," Nisha said.

Kara's face lit up at that. "It was really nice to see some of my old friends. And my nephew, Levi. I think he's grown a foot since I moved here. I probably annoyed the shit out of him trying to be with him every second I could. He came out straight to me. Isn't that adorable?" Kara took the lid off her coffee to help it cool faster. "But

I knew when it was time to come home. How were things here? Did you have an okay time?"

The significance of Kara calling Chicago home didn't escape Nisha, and she dared to hope she played some part in that feeling.

"I missed you." She took a sip of her tea, so she wouldn't see Kara's reaction.

"I missed you, too," Kara said to Nisha's relief. "One of the things I realized while I was gone was how much I like having you as part of my day. Not just because of Barb and all the stuff I can't tell other people about. That's a huge part of it, but…I guess it's easy to be around you."

"That means a lot to me."

They shared a smile.

"So, listen, I found Barb's obituary." Kara took a folded piece of paper from her coat pocket. "I printed it out." She opened the paper and rotated it for Nisha to read.

Barbara Kowalski, age 50, originally from Cicero, passed away February 14, in her home from natural causes.

Nisha skimmed the rest of the obituary as Kara told her, "She had several siblings, so I had the private investigator we work with look for them. Two are dead, but she has a brother, Abe, who's still alive. He's in a nursing home, but I called his daughter and talked to her. She said they were estranged from Barb when she died, but she definitely remembered a group of lesbian friends coming to the funeral. She said they stood away from the family and only interacted with each other, and they were all anyone could talk about."

"You called Barb's niece to ask about Barb's funeral thirty-five years ago? Don't you think that's a little invasive?"

"She didn't seem to mind."

"How on earth did you explain why you were calling?"

Kara shrugged. "I told her my aunt Nan was in the hospital with a stroke, and she always told us stories about her old friend Barb, and I wanted to try to track Barb down in case my aunt didn't make it."

"Wow. That's actually a pretty good cover story. I didn't think you were that good at lying."

"I couldn't exactly tell her the truth, could I?"

"Did you learn anything useful?"

"Not a thing. I thought maybe if you looked at the obituary, something might stand out for you. I'm going to keep trying Sonia. Since Nan's in the hospital and Miss Pythia vanished, Sonia's the one we need to be pursuing."

"Kara, we're not 'pursuing' anyone." Nisha pushed the obituary across the table. "She's old. If she doesn't want to talk, don't make her talk."

"Sonia doesn't act old. Besides, I think she likes me."

"You need to leave it alone. Whatever Barb's here for will happen on its own time. You pushing isn't going to help."

"You don't know that. Maybe her unfinished business is something that can't happen without us. Pauline said—" Kara cut herself off mid-sentence and looked down at her coffee.

"Who's Pauline?"

"I don't know, who is that?" Kara's cheeks were pink, and she couldn't make eye contact.

Nisha supposed it was reassuring that, although Kara could tell plenty of white lies to others, she didn't seem capable of lying to her. "Kara, who's Pauline, and what did she say?"

"A medium in Uptown." Kara's voice was barely audible.

"You went to another medium? Without me?"

"Since Miss Pythia is gone, I thought we needed to find someone else, so I found this person, Pauline, and I went to talk to her."

"And what did you find out?"

"She suggested that maybe Hilary's death and your breakup with Angie are all connected to the fact that Barb lived in the apartment with a girlfriend. She said maybe Barb's unfinished business is *our* unfinished business."

"What unfinished business do we have? I took the rings off."

"And I'm proud that you haven't even asked for them back yet."

Nisha appreciated the praise, but she wasn't going to be distracted from what she was learning. "You're so frustrating. You told me we should wait and be patient, and the whole time you've been chasing down mediums and hiring private investigators."

"Are you mad?"

Nisha took a moment to process her feelings as she took another sip of tea. She was impressed with how much work Kara had done, but she felt a little left out. She'd thought they were a team. It had been nice to be on a team again.

This was Kara, though. She was relentless, but at least she was charming about it. She had made it clear she didn't want a roommate, so Nisha should have known she wasn't going to leave it alone.

"I'm not mad," she said finally. "I'm disappointed at myself for not expecting this. I'm going to do everything I can to give Barb the time and space she needs for this. I need you to accept that."

"And I need you to accept that I'm going to keep doing everything I can to figure out what it is that she won't tell me to get this over with."

"I wish you wouldn't, but at the very least, can you tell me what you're up to?"

Kara fiddled with the discarded lid of her coffee. "There are so many things I want to tell you, but I always worry that I shouldn't."

"You shouldn't keep things from me. That was a huge part of what happened between Angie and me. Secrets are bad news."

"What happened between you and Angie was that she dumped you because she's a fucking idiot."

"Hey, don't talk about her like that. You didn't know her. She was a good person."

"I'm not saying she was a bad person. I'm only saying she was an idiot. Ultimately, no matter how great and perfect you think she was, she clearly had one major flaw, which is that she was too blind to realize what a good thing she had with you." Kara licked her lips. "Right now, I don't see how anyone could make that mistake."

The words sounded good, but Nisha couldn't let herself melt over them because she knew Angie hadn't been blind and Kara was still in the dark. "You don't know the things I've done."

"Try me."

Nisha shook her head. "I can't."

Because Angie wasn't stupid. She'd learned what Nisha had done to her—to them and their future—and she'd walked away. That was smart.

And here was Kara, acting as if Nisha cooking dinner in her kitchen was an ordinary weeknight and whisking her away to a secret coffee date. And right now what Nisha saw was someone who'd been gone for a week, someone she'd missed to the core, someone who had become one of her closest confidants. Kara whose lips looked plump and pink in the overhead light, whose blond hair always looked happy, no matter what the weather was.

From the first night together, Kara had made Nisha feel off-kilter. She'd squirmed and giggled, and she kept coming back for more.

"What can you tell me?" Kara asked, and Nisha had no idea what they'd been talking about. "What are you thinking about?"

"I'm thinking about how much I want to kiss you."

To her surprise, Kara said, "Me too," and slowly, sensually, slid out of her seat and came to sit beside Nisha. Kara waited a breath before tilting her head to the right and leaning in.

The kiss was tentative at first, a question on both ends rather than a declaration of interest. It was a rolling moment, forward, then retreat, and when they came forward again, their lips parted. Kara's tongue performed an elaborate tango with her own. Nisha felt the blood rushing from her head, and she was glad she was sitting down. She wondered when they might stop and why it had taken them so long to reach this point in the first place.

And finally Kara broke it off, gently, with small, lingering kisses and one final touch of their lips together. She was smiling. "You're an incredible kisser."

"I wish I could take credit, but it wasn't me. I thought that was you."

Kara crumpled a few strands of Nisha's hair in between her fingers. "You're so beautiful."

"Oh, stop." Nisha could feel herself blushing, but she liked the attention and praise. "What do we do now?"

Kara shook her head. "Whatever we want. We can still be friends. We can pretend this never happened if you want."

A cold gust of wind blew away the fog of love that had been circling Nisha. Of course Kara just wanted to be friends. Kara had made it clear on many occasions that she wasn't looking for a relationship. Kissing certainly didn't mean they were in a relationship.

Feeling stupid, Nisha finished her drink and made her excuses to get home.

The next day, she told Maddie she was ready to start dating again.

CHAPTER FOURTEEN

The phone logs Ruthie was required to keep of every incoming call at Horowitz and Stein probably made it seem as if Nisha and Kara were deeply involved in a relationship. Although Kara had never looked at the logs, she imagined the number of times Nisha called during the work day had to rival the number of calls her married colleagues got from their spouses. Most of the time, Nisha spent a solid minute apologizing for bothering Kara at the office, followed by a meandering discussion about something Barb had done and the same fears and concerns about Nan she'd already expressed a hundred times. Eventually she'd get to the point, which was usually something that could have been expressed in a single text.

Kara didn't mind. Since their kiss that night at the coffee shop, Kara couldn't stop thinking about how beautiful Nisha was. She liked makeup and fashion, and the photos she staged for Instagram were the kind that professionals took, but there was nothing boastful or superficial about her. Kara was pretty sure Nisha didn't even realize how gorgeous she was.

And not just on the outside. Nisha was a compassionate person, always worried that everyone else's needs were being met. Like the massage she'd gotten Barb.

And, of course, there was the kiss itself. Maybe it was adolescent to fantasize about something as innocent as a kiss, but Kara found herself doing it all day. In the shower, she'd be washing her hair, and suddenly she'd think about how Nisha had tasted. During meetings, someone would be talking, and her mind would remember the tingling that had spread throughout her body when they'd finally connected.

Kara didn't have Ruthie send Nisha to voice mail anymore, and some days she did as much talking as Nisha.

That particular day, the point of Nisha's phone call was nothing Kara could have ever anticipated.

"So Maddie and Suni made me a profile on this new dating app, and they exchanged messages with someone, and now I have a date."

"They what?"

"Maddie said it's time for me to go out. And Suni said it'll be like riding a bike."

Kara wasn't really sure where this conversation was going, but in principle she agreed with Maddie and Suni, even if their methods were controlling and she hated them for steering Nisha toward someone else.

It had only been a kiss, after all. She could hardly expect fidelity from one kiss.

"Sounds like something somebody else said a few months ago," she teased, hoping her disappointment couldn't be heard. "So are you going?"

"I told them I'd go," Nisha said with hesitation, "if…"

"If what?"

"If my good friend Kara goes with me."

"A threesome?"

"A double date."

"But a double date means I'd have a date, too, and I don't know anyone, and I'm not on any dating apps."

Nisha had suggested a dating app the first night they met, Kara remembered, and if she had taken Nisha up on that suggestion, maybe she wouldn't feel like a starstruck teenager getting crushed by her idol right now.

"Apparently, Maddie and Suni told my match that you're new to Chicago, and the person said she would bring a single friend for you. I guess she thought it was a smart move if we each brought someone for safety or something. Anyway, she has a friend who's free and interested in meeting an attorney. Suni found a photo I took of us and sent it, and I guess the friend thinks you're attractive."

"So I'm going out with someone who's already seen a picture of me but I've never heard of until now?"

"Yeah."

"What if she's ugly? Do I get to see a picture of her?"

Nisha groaned. "What do you even care if it's not a real date for you?"

Nisha had a point, but Kara didn't like that Maddie, Suni, and random people off an app all colluding to decide who she'd get to date.

"Who says it's not a real date for me?"

"Oh, right, of course. I mean, this is a good opportunity for you to get to know more people. So tell me what your type is, and I'll make sure she's a real looker."

"'A real looker'?" Kara laughed. "Who talks like that?"

"What's your type?" Nisha asked again. "Skinny? Curvy? Covered in tattoos? Sophisticated older lady? Sad artsy type? Polyamorous with a zest for life?"

Creative types who are somehow both outgoing and introspective? Come to think of it, that described Hilary, too. They were also both deeply devoted to the people they loved and thoughtful in ways Kara didn't know how to be. Caregivers. Although Kara had never seen it until now, Hilary and Nisha had a lot in common.

She turned her attention back to the conversation. "If there's already a specific friend interested, I guess it doesn't matter what my type is. What does your date look like? Is she your type?"

"I don't think I have a type," Nisha admitted. "Everyone I've dated has been totally different. I've dated tall and short, thin and overweight, white, not white. I don't know."

"You're making a collection. What's left?"

"Actually, I've never been with anyone blond, if you can believe that."

At the moment she said it, Kara happened to catch her own reflection in window. She saw her light hair and wondered if Nisha had made the same connection.

"Well," she said, clearing her throat, "I need to get back to work, so I hope your date is the blonde of your dreams."

"So you're in?"

"Do I have a choice?"

"Not really. Meet me tomorrow night at Maddie and Suni's after work, and we'll go from there."

"How will I know what to wear?"

Nisha sighed. "Because I'll come over tonight and pick out outfits with you, duh."

"If you're coming over tonight, why did you bother calling now?"

"I think this could be a chance for me." Nisha was serious now. "But I'm scared. I need you there to help me get back on my feet in the dating world, okay? I think…I think I might be ready to try to move on, but I don't think I can do it without you."

"I'll be there. You know I'll be there."

❖

When Kara got home from work, she started laying out clothes for Nisha to consider. Barb watched, eating neon orange cheese balls directly out of the can.

"Awfully nice clothes for a pizza and TV night."

"Did we have plans to watch something specific?"

"Not really. So you don't have to feel bad about blowing me off."

"I'm not blowing you off," Kara began, but Barb forestalled her with a wave of her hand.

"It's fine. I'll ask Nisha if she's in the mood for veggie lovers or vegan cheese. It's hardly the same as sausage or pepperoni, but I guess it'll have to do."

Kara's face went hot.

"Oh," Barb realized. "I see."

"It's not even tonight. She's coming over to help me pick clothes. We can all have pizza tonight if you want. The clothes are for when we go out tomorrow."

"And leave me by myself. I guess it doesn't matter too much, you know, what with me being dead and all."

"Her friends set it up, and she didn't know how to back out, so I said I'd go along, too. We won't even be out late. How about if I bring dessert home?"

"And ruin this figure?" Barb patted her bulging gut. "You and Nisha have fun, and don't do anything I would."

Kara put a hand on Barb's shoulder. As it was every time she touched Barb, it took a second to adjust to skin that was neither hot nor cold, neither clammy nor dry. "Are you sure? I can cancel. Nisha's capable of going on a date without me." She dropped the striped shirt she was holding. "Maybe this was a bad idea."

"It's not a bad idea." Barb tipped the empty cheese ball container up to her mouth and gulped down the remaining crumbs. Then she wiped her mouth with the back of her hand. "These taste different than they used to. They change the recipe or something?" She put the plastic lid on the canister and tossed it in the direction of the trash can. It didn't make it, and she made no move to pick it up.

Kara suppressed a growl and put the can properly in the trash. "Why don't you think it's a bad idea?" she asked. "You think the idea of four queer women going out together is a good idea? Is that something you used to do? Maybe with Nan and Rosalind and Sonia?"

"Oh, boy, you really suck at asking questions, you know that? On TV the attorneys go right in for the kill. They ask a question, and the guy on the witness stand cracks, and he confesses to everything, and they yell, 'No further questions, Your Honor!' And the credits roll."

"Barb, I work in contract law."

Kara knew Barb's tangent was intended to distract from the main issue, which was Kara's admittedly clumsy attempt to find out more about what had gone on in Barb's life before she died. Barb smiled at herself, proud of her distraction.

"I think something real good is gonna come out of this," Barb said. "Something really big indeed."

❖

Nisha said the booties didn't work with the skirt and tights because they made her legs look stumpy. She liked the heels, but they were impractical with all the snow outside. The flat knee-high boots were practical, but apparently they were all wrong for the outfit. And now she was looking at a pair of nondescript black flats.

"These make me look like I've given up on life. Maybe it's not the shoes that are the problem. Maybe I should change my outfit."

Kara let out a long, slow breath, looking to the ceiling for salvation. "You already texted me your outfit. You had it planned yesterday."

Nisha unzipped her skirt and kicked it off. "This is a pants situation, clearly."

"I thought the whole point was that we dressed—what was the expression you used? Not coordinating but—"

"Stylistically compatible." Nisha held up a pair of pants and considered them in the mirror. "I can't wear these. What was I thinking? These are just plain dumpy."

"Okay, that's it." Kara got to her feet. "You picked out my outfit. I'm picking out yours."

She really had no clue what she was doing, but somebody had to take charge of the situation.

Nisha's closet was jammed tight with clothes, too many to look through quickly. Kara reached for a random hanger and pulled out a navy blue dress with white dots and ruffles around the neck. She couldn't imagine Nisha wearing it, and anyway it looked like it was for summer. Nisha looked good in rich colors, like those burgundy pants she'd been wearing the first night they met.

Kara grabbed another dress at random. It was mustard yellow with a split neck and a drawstring waist. Nisha would look good in the color. As for the style, who cared? Kara was hungry, and she knew Nisha wouldn't be upset if she made them late because she didn't like being impolite.

"This is the one. Take your shirt off, put this on, let's go."

Nisha made a face as she took the hanger.

Kara turned her back to give her a sense of privacy while she changed.

Shoes. Even if Nisha accepted the dress, they'd spend twenty more minutes picking out shoes to go with it. Kara reached down to the shoe rack. Heels? No, heels in the snow seemed wrong. She grabbed the brown booties Nisha had rejected earlier.

"And these."

Nisha made another face of displeasure but dutifully put them on. She looked good in the dress and shoes, but something was missing. Kara remembered the day in the park when the wind had ruffled Nisha's earrings.

She moved behind Nisha and gathered her hair into a low side ponytail. "Like this, with your jade earrings. What do you think?"

As they looked at their reflections in the mirror, Kara was eager to hear whether Nisha approved. If she didn't, Kara was going to hustle her out the door anyway, so they could make their reservation on time. But she'd be disappointed she wasn't better able to pick something out, considering how well Nisha had chosen Kara's outfit.

But Nisha smiled. "I never would have put this together, but it looks really good."

"You always look good," Kara said, returning the smile.

"Okay, let me fuss with it, and I'll be out in a second. Will you wait in the living room?"

"You won't change again? Because it's time to go."

"I promise. I just need to fix my hair and makeup."

As Kara went back to the living room to wait, she could feel herself smiling. As frustrating as it was that Nisha took forever to get ready, Kara enjoyed being able to participate. If someone was able to pick out an outfit for you, it was a sign they knew you well, wasn't it? When Nisha picked Kara's clothes, she brought the best version of Kara out, a version Kara wanted to be but didn't know how to find on her own. She hoped she had reciprocated.

When Nisha came out, her side ponytail was smoothed and coiffed, and her dress was accessorized with a brown belt. She was wearing heavier makeup, her eyelashes thick and long and her lips plumped with a nearly nude shade of lip gloss.

Maddie praised what Nisha called her "final look," but Kara was too awestruck to talk. She looked like a model. She looked like a movie star. She looked like someone was about to become a very lucky person to have such a kind, amazing person as their date.

Kara didn't feel as excited about dinner anymore.

"It's about time," Sunita said drily.

Nisha gave a coy smile that put Kara's stomach in a knot. "Don't wait up!"

❖

The restaurant in Roscoe Village was bustling, and they had to cluster in the entryway while servers moved around them and more diners kept pushing their way in the door. It wasn't the best environment for meeting new people, and when their dates, Sarah and Jill, arrived, they could only manage half-waves in the crowd. To make room for them, Nisha leaned back against Kara, who was pressed tight against a window. She put a hand on Nisha's hip to warn her not to step on her toes.

"Which one's mine?" she murmured into Nisha's hair. It smelled like oranges and coconut.

"Jill." Nisha craned her head to the side to be heard, her breath tickling Kara's nose.

Jill heard her name and raised her eyebrows in expectation. Kara gave her a polite smile. Jill was what Kara would call a high maintenance super-femme. Although it was winter in Illinois, she was tan, and not from having recently been in the tropics, if the slight orange cast was any indication. She had thick fake eyelashes that feathered out from her brown eyes and accentuated her high cheekbones. Her lips were filled with collagen, the kind of lips that always looked like they'd been stung by a bee and made Kara feel squeamish to look at. Her skin was flawless, but that was because it was paved in foundation and concealer. Nisha wore a lot of makeup, but Kara could never actually see the layers of it caked into her skin like Jill's. She looked like she was trying too hard. She looked too artificial. She didn't do anything for Kara.

When the hostess called Nisha's name, the four of them moved like a less than enthusiastic conga line through the crowded restaurant and to their table. Kara and Nisha accidentally sat opposite each other, but Jill and Sarah took the two empty chairs before Kara could move. Realizing their mistake, Nisha raised her eyebrows across the table at Kara, who shrugged back at her. This way, she could still get to look at Nisha. She was way less fake-and-bake, less injected lips, less hair product. Much nicer to look at over dinner.

Sarah suggested ordering a bottle of wine because it would be cheaper than each of them ordering two glasses individually. A bottle might be more practical, but Kara didn't like Nisha's date going for something just because it was cheaper. Or assuming everyone was going to drink two glasses. Something about her immediately put Kara on alert.

Jill, by contrast, readily agreed to the wine suggestion. She seemed like one of those self-proclaimed "social drinkers," who swore they never drank, except when they were out, which was all the damn time. And when they were out, all the damn time, they drank too much. She'd rarely met people like that in Wisconsin. Most people born and raised in Wisconsin freely acknowledged how much they drank because beer was such a part of the culture that there wasn't a stigma against it, and that meant they were experienced enough to be able to hold themselves together. Kara voted Jill most likely to get wasted.

Nisha hesitated at the bottle suggestion before agreeing.

Kara supposed if they ordered a bottle, she didn't have to pick out her own wine or face the embarrassment of asking Nisha to do it for her.

"Whatever you decide is fine with me," she said to Sarah. Next to her, Jill beamed at her agreeability.

The appetizer also caused a group discussion that ended in Kara saying, "Whatever you decide is fine." The pretend date was quickly turning into a battleground, and she was losing turf inch by inch. She didn't join in the eating of the caramelized onion and wild mushroom crostini, and she internally groused the whole time about how she'd no doubt be expected to cough up for it anyway. Nisha ate. Delicately. Like she was worried about cramming the whole thing in her mouth, the way Sarah did, or getting crumbs everywhere, which Jill did. There really wasn't a way to eat flaky toast without looking a little like an ass. Unless you were Nisha, apparently.

Sarah suggested splitting two entrees, and that was a line too far.

"It might be easiest if we each order our own," Kara said, hoping she sounded disarming. "That way, we don't have to waste a lot of time trying to agree on something."

That was what she said aloud. The internal dialogue was something like, *Order your own damn meal, you cheapskate. Are you afraid of eating?*

Over their entrees, the conversation covered mundane topics: work (Jill managed a specialty pet boutique on Armitage), the weather (Sarah had heard more snow was coming), and then the news (they all agreed the latest military intervention in the Middle East was cause for concern, but to Kara's annoyance no one seemed capable of saying anything more specific). When Sarah asked Jill to talk more about all-natural dog birthday cakes, Kara excused herself to the restroom.

Nisha came in while she was washing her hands. "Jill's pretty."

"She's all right."

Nisha leaned against the countertop near Kara. "Sarah's not bad. She's kind of taking the lead and making everything easy."

If you find overbearing freaks attractive. "Uh-huh."

"What do you think we should do after we get the check? Should we go for coffee or something?"

This night was important to Nisha. If Kara's sour mood spoiled it, that wouldn't be fair to her. She gave Nisha a little hip-check. "Depends on what you want. You want to split up, so you can have time alone with Sarah?"

Nisha's eyes grew in size. "Kara!"

"You said she wasn't bad."

Nisha's cheeks were turning pink. "I think my standard is a little higher than 'not bad.' Unless you wanted time with Jill?"

Kara was too stupefied by the suggestion to respond. Jill was awful. In no universe did she want time alone with Jill.

Nisha's jewelry reflected the light in the bathroom. Her eyes were wide, her eyebrows raised. Everything about how stunning she looked, how expectant, made Kara want to kiss her again. To feel the touch of Nisha's silken lips against her own.

As she looked at her, Kara knew the problem wasn't Jill. It was that Jill wasn't Nisha.

But Nisha was trying to grow in new directions. She'd agreed to this date to try to branch out in her social life. She wanted to meet new people and get back into the world. Kara cared too much for her to hold her back.

"We should probably get back to the table."

❖

After the server took their plates away, Sarah suggested they go for coffee at a place around the corner, and Jill agreed enthusiastically. She looked to Kara for confirmation.

"I'm pretty beat. I think I'm going home." Jill gave a little pout, and Kara added, "I have a client meeting at eight tomorrow morning."

She pretended not to notice the disappointment etched on Jill's face, which wasn't hard to do when Jill beamed at Sarah as they gathered their coats.

"I'm going home, too," Nisha said.

Sarah and Jill seemed to have forgotten Nisha was there. They were already talking to each other and heading for the door.

"It was very nice meeting you!" she called after them. "Thank you for a lovely evening."

Only Nisha could be utterly blown off and still finish the night with a touch of class.

She turned to Kara. "Can you believe that?"

She reached for her coat, but Kara suggested they wait a minute in case Sarah and Jill were loitering on the sidewalk.

When they finally went outside, they ran past the coffee shop, squatting down below the window in case Sarah and Jill saw them together. At the corner, they crashed into each other and exploded with laughter.

"That was the worst date ever!" Nisha said. "Is that what dating's like?"

"I sincerely hope not. That was so bad!"

"Do you think—I mean, am I crazy, or did they seem more interested in each other than us?"

"You weren't imagining it."

"But that's weird, right? They were friends who agreed to go out with other people. Why would they do that if they were really interested in each other?"

Kara shrugged. Why had she agreed to go on this dumb date? To make Nisha happy because she couldn't tell Nisha what she really felt, since they wanted different things. Maybe it was the same for Sarah and Jill.

"I'm going to spy on them," Nisha announced.

Kara whispered her name several times to come back, but Nisha marched, head up this time, toward the bright windows of the coffee shop and looked inside. She gasped.

"What?" Kara called. "What do you see?"

"Oh, shit!" Nisha ducked and came running back. She grabbed Kara's hand and pulled her around the corner, flattening them against the brick exterior of a building. She laughed again.

"What? Tell me!"

"Sarah was wiping whipped cream off Jill's lip, but then she saw me and starting coming toward the door."

Something bubbled up inside Kara and came rushing out in a fit of uncontrollable laughter. She doubled over, holding her side, struggling for breath.

"Breathe," Nisha said through her own laughter. She rubbed a gloved hand on Kara's back.

"Worst. Date. Ever."

"Worse than the time we tried to have brunch and ended up manifesting a ghost?"

Kara nearly collapsed onto her knees then. Her face was hot, and her laughter was coming out in loud guffaws.

Nisha was laughing, too, but not nearly as hard. She held out a hand to steady Kara, and in another fit of laughs, Kara slipped on some ice. She tumbled to the sidewalk, pulling Nisha with her.

They lay there stunned for a few seconds.

"You know what?" Kara said as she got up and dusted the salt off her pants. "I take it back. This wasn't the worst date ever." She reached out a hand to help Nisha up, but once Nisha was on her feet, she didn't let go. "It's probably one of the most memorable in my life."

Kara's words were serious now, directed at Nisha. Whatever had happened with Sarah and Jill, however dreadful their dinner together had been, the thing that mattered the most was that Kara had gone through the experience with Nisha.

And the terrible brunch that ended up causing the mayhem that was Barb? Another experience she'd gone through with Nisha.

"Kara," Nisha murmured, closing the distance between them. "I—"

"I know," Kara said, and their lips found each other.

They kissed a few gentle, sensuous times before their lips parted and their tongues entwined. Despite all the ways Nisha could be tentative in conversation, she kissed with precision and intent. It was soft and meaningful, and it built a fire in Kara's belly log by log until it was roaring hot. She and Nisha pressed against each other, trading little moans.

It went on and on, until Kara couldn't take it anymore. She pulled away and cupped Nisha's face, staring deep into those endless eyes of hers.

"Would you like to come home with me?"

And Nisha nodded.

CHAPTER FIFTEEN

On the ride back to Kara's apartment, they held hands, but Nisha wondered how they were going to do this with Barb around. Then other doubts started creeping in. This would be the first time she'd had sex with anyone since Angie, and after so long with one person, what if she didn't know the moves anymore? What if she didn't know how to do the things that made Kara's body respond? Since she hadn't anticipated tonight being anything more than a dinner date, she hadn't fully waxed and groomed, and she felt self-conscious about the idea of taking off her clothes in front of someone, especially someone she knew as well as Kara. In some ways, casual sex might have been easier because if it was terrible and she was embarrassed, she never had to face the person again. If sex with Kara was terrible, what would happen to their friendship?

She was starting to change her mind when the car dropped them in front of the building. Kara got out first and offered a hand to help Nisha. She closed the car door, and the driver pulled away to pick up his next passengers. Kara didn't move toward the building but stayed there on the sidewalk, holding Nisha's hand.

"I want to make sure you're still up for this," she said. "No pressure. It has to feel right to us both."

Nisha wanted to ask if it felt right to Kara for them to start a relationship, whether Kara had changed her mind about commitment, but what she'd settle for was knowing if this step they were about to take together felt right.

Maybe Nisha needed to do more living in the moment. Maybe "setting yourself up for success" was sometimes just overthinking.

Kara was waiting patiently, not rushing her, not pressuring her. She knew Nisha. She wasn't going to hurt Nisha.

The light from the building framed Kara's silhouette, giving her a heavenly glow around the edges, and Nisha was overcome with the urge to see Kara glow from the inside out. She stepped forward and kissed her, hard and intense this time, and Kara met her intensity.

She wanted this. She needed it. She was going to move on from Angie, and she was going to do it with someone she had come to trust and…

She wouldn't use that word until she knew how Kara felt.

For now, she'd settle for the fact that Kara wanted her, badly.

They stumbled inside and up to the fifth floor, hands searching each other between kisses, until Kara managed to unlock her door while Nisha nibbled her neck. Inside, the lights were off.

"Barb?" Kara called. "Where are you?"

Nisha flipped on the light to the kitchen, but Barb wasn't there or in the living room.

Kara shrugged. "A problem for another time," she said, pulling Nisha down the hall.

The only light in the bedroom was the glow from the streetlights outside, and in the dimness Nisha didn't feel as self-conscious about her body as she'd anticipated. She peeled off Kara's sweater and took a moment to trace the contours of Kara's breasts, letting her mouth capture one of the sharp pink nipples, before she worked on Kara's pants. Then Kara coaxed Nisha to sit up enough for her to unclasp Nisha's bra, which she slid down Nisha's arms inch by inch until Nisha felt goose bumps.

"Is this okay?" Kara whispered, and Nisha nodded. Anything Kara wanted to do was okay right now.

Kara concentrated her attention on Nisha's left nipple, kissing it with care and then nipping at it when Nisha least expected. She heard herself whimper, but it wasn't a protest. Her body arched closer to Kara's mouth, and Kara turned to focus on the right side.

When Nisha's nipples were hard and taut, Kara made her way downward. She kissed each inch of skin left bare as she slid

Nisha's underwear down and off. She put her hands on Nisha's inner thighs, not yet nudging, and asked Nisha if she'd feel safer with a dental dam.

"I was tested after Angie broke up with me. I haven't been with anyone since then."

"I was tested before I moved here."

Nisha nodded her consent, and Kara pressed her thighs apart. She slid down the bed, settling herself between Nisha's legs, and she paused for a moment to look up. Their eyes met, Kara smirking at what she was about to do and knowing she was in control of when it was going to happen.

"Please," Nisha begged.

Kara started with careful, delicate licks and kisses, one hand tracing lines on the sensitive skin of Nisha's inner thigh and two fingers of the other hand inching slowly toward Nisha's opening. When at last she was inside, Nisha's body began moving in time with Kara's strokes and the circles of Kara's tongue. She grabbed a fistful of Kara's hair, which inspired Kara to go faster and harder, and everything behind Nisha's eyelids turned white. As they moved together, she felt herself teetering over the edge, the white becoming an explosion of colors. She bucked against Kara's face and moaned, and the moan rose in pitch until she heard herself letting out a sound she'd never made before. Kara continued as Nisha came completely apart at the seams. Shudders rippled through her body until she was floating above it and thought she had died. She put a hand on Kara's shoulder to signify it was more than she could take, and as Kara slowly withdrew, the shudders turned into warm waves rolling across her body as every muscle relaxed deeply into the mattress.

She reached for Kara, who held her until the ripples subsided, giving her sweaty forehead gentle, loving kisses.

When at last her breath and heartbeat had come down, Nisha opened her eyes. She expected that everything would look different now, but it was the same dim room with its spartan decor. And there was Kara, looking at her with a satisfied smile but with something expectant in her eyes, and she wasn't the same Kara anymore at all. She was someone different now, someone who had seen the most intimate side of Nisha, and the way she looked at Nisha was different, too, and maybe, Nisha thought, recklessly, maybe that look had something to do with love.

She tipped her head for a kiss, slow this time and deep. Their legs entwined, and Nisha tried to channel everything she was thinking and feeling into the kiss.

Eventually, she found her way on top of Kara. She leaned down, her breasts grazing Kara's, and they savored the touch of each other's bodies as the kiss grew in intensity. Nisha pushed away Kara's navy boy shorts as fast as she could, wanting to get to the prize that waited inside. But once she was there, she took her time.

Later, after Kara had moaned her own long, slow release, they lay together naked. Kara traced meaningless patterns on Nisha's back with the forefinger of one hand while the other arm reached around Nisha's torso. It felt protective. Possessive. They stayed that way for a long time, not saying anything—definitely not "I love you"—and eventually they drifted off to sleep.

❖

At 6 a.m., the alarm on Kara's phone went off. It was still dark outside and entirely too early for Nisha. Kara had a meeting first thing, though, so she sat up without hesitation and rolled out of bed.

The steady sound of the shower running lulled Nisha back to sleep. When she awoke again, it was from the mattress dipping as Kara sat beside her legs. Kara was fully dressed, putting on her shoes.

"You have to get to work, don't you?" Nisha stretched against the cool cotton sheets. She sat up, holding the sheet in front of her naked breasts, self-conscious once again in the light of day and in the face of Kara's fully clothed state. She reached for her bra on the floor.

"You don't have to rush out just because I am. You still have a key, right?" Nisha nodded. "Go back to sleep, and you can lock the door when you leave."

"Where's Barb?"

"She's still not here. I'll have to worry about that when I get back from work tonight, but for now I'm going to be late." She leaned down and gave Nisha a quick kiss on the lips. It was a closed-mouth kiss—no tongue, no lingering—the kind of kiss a straight man would give his wife before he rushed off to work and his younger, more attractive secretary.

And that was it. There was no talking about what had happened, no plans for what was going to come next, just "I'm going to be late." Then Kara was gone.

Nisha felt as if a rock had settled in her stomach. Although it was way too early in the morning to be awake, there was no way she could go back to sleep now. She couldn't lie in their sex sheets, smelling reminders of how freely they'd given themselves to each other, without knowing what Kara was feeling now.

The truth was, she already knew what Kara was feeling. Kara regretted it. Or maybe she didn't regret it, but she didn't think it was a big deal. It was just sex, not some spiritual union or the start of anything bigger. "I'm going to be late" was her way of brushing off what had been, for Nisha, a pretty major milestone in their relationship.

Nisha padded to the bathroom and looked for toiletries she could use. The tub of cream in the medicine cabinet made her smile because she knew it belonged to Barb. Cream-based facial cleansers were making a comeback, but this was old-fashioned cold cream, straight out of another era. There was also a five-pack of plastic toothbrushes, one of which had been taken out and used. Nisha helped herself to another one.

She thought about visiting Nan before going home, but she didn't want to go to the hospital looking and smelling like the morning after sex. Would Kara mind if she took a quick shower?

The hot water felt good in the chill of the morning, and it relaxed the muscles that had been stretched the night before, muscles that weren't used to work because of how long it had been since she'd had sex with anyone. She spent longer in the shower than was necessary, but she was too tired and too deep in thought to rush.

Sex with Kara had been unexpected but incredible. Nisha had gone out the night before with the intention of changing her life, and she had—in a very different way than she'd meant. The repercussions their night together had on their friendship remained to be seen, but the sex itself wasn't just hot. It was compatible and tender. It was so much more than Nisha had expected from her first time post-Angie, and it was exactly why she didn't like the idea of casual sex with someone she didn't know very well. They'd responded to each other as if they knew intuitively how each other's bodies worked. How could a stranger do that? That took trust and intimacy, didn't it?

She stepped out of the shower and reached for the nearest towel. If Kara hated that she'd used it, she could offer to do a load of laundry. Or maybe she could do one before she left anyway. Maybe she could clean a little, too.

That would probably be a little much.

She toweled her face off by patting it gently, the way her mother had taught her, instead of rubbing it. As she lowered the towel, she noticed a word in the mirror fog.

LOVE

Nisha gasped. She wrapped the towel around her body and tucked the corner in.

"I know you're here, Barb. You might as well show yourself."

She looked at the word again. *LOVE*. Angie used to write messages to her while she was showering in this very room. Sometimes Angie would write *I love you*, and sometimes she'd draw a heart. Barb had to have known because she was haunting back then, but why was she imitating it now?

"I love you, too, Barb!" Nisha called. "You want to come out now?"

Barb appeared in the bathtub behind her, making Nisha jump in surprise.

"God, don't do that!"

"You told me to come out." Barb was wearing a Bears sweatshirt today.

"Where have you been?"

"I can't leave the apartment, Einstein. Remember?"

"So you've been...here...the whole time?"

"I didn't listen last night. That would be inappropriate."

"And it's not inappropriate that you're standing in the wet shower while I try to get dressed?"

"Oh, gosh, I'm sorry, I forget sometimes how modest you guys are cuz I can see you all the time, even if you can't see me."

Nisha couldn't bring herself to ask if that meant Barb had seen her nude in the shower.

"What's up with this?" She pointed to the mirror. "You did it before when Kara was showering."

"Should be pretty obvious by now." Barb stepped out of the tub and slid past Nisha, sending chills across Nisha's bare arms.

"Your unfinished business has to do with someone you loved?"

Barb opened the bathroom door, letting in a rush of cold air. "I gotta eat. I haven't had anything since lunch yesterday. Being invisible is hard work."

"Okay," Nisha called after Barb as she walked away, "I'm going to get dressed, and then we can talk about who you love!"

She felt a little silly wearing her going-out clothes so early in the morning. Without product, her hair was a frizzy mess that she could only salvage by putting into a bun. She always carried makeup in her purse, but the minimum needed for touch-ups. She supposed it would have to do until she got home and put on her full face. Nan wouldn't be particular about how well made-up a visitor was, but without being able to fully primp, Nisha felt self-conscious that her look screamed "morning after" or, worse, "walk of shame."

Barb was sitting at Kara's new kitchen table, where she was having a bowl of cereal and cup of coffee. "Hey, you want something? I can make you coffee." She laughed at this, slapping the table at her own joke. "You get it? Because it's just a little plastic cup and you push a button. You can have guests over any time, and you can pretend you always have a pot on. Just push a button, and there's coffee."

The Keurig must have been thrilling to someone who had last made coffee in the age of percolators that took forever to drip a whole pot, but Nisha didn't really see why it was funny.

"I'll get my own coffee."

She opted for dark roast this time, since it was so early in the morning and she needed to wake up. When she was seated next to Barb with her cup, she broached the subject of love. "When we talked to Sonia, she sounded like she really regretted what happened."

"Do you think Kara's going to regret what happened?"

Whoa, change of topic. Nisha definitely didn't want to talk about that with Barb. Even if Barb had seen and heard everything that had happened the night before. Especially then.

She took a sip of coffee, regretting it as the tastebuds on the front of her tongue were scalded. "I thought we were talking about you right now."

"I never agreed to that. That's what you decided." Barb picked up her empty cereal bowl and tipped the leftover milk into her mouth. "You guys decide a lot for me, you know. It's not very nice."

"I'm not trying to decide anything for you. Kara's the one who wanted you gone months ago. I keep telling her you should get to take all the time you need to figure out your unfinished business. It's too important to rush."

"Well, thanks, Nisha," Barb said in a show of uncharacteristic sincerity. "I always liked you better." She set her bowl down and wiped her mouth with the cuff of her sweatshirt. "It's going to be okay, you know? It probably doesn't feel like it right now, but it is."

Nisha didn't want to cry, and she wasn't ready to share all her fears about what Kara must be thinking and feeling and how those thoughts contrasted so sharply with what Nisha experienced. Instead, she gave Barb a wan smile and thanked her.

❖

One of the advantages of working at odd hours was that Nisha had the condo to herself for the rest of the day. She did yoga, cleaned the bathroom, and watched several video tutorials on a new contouring technique. It was a pretty chill day, exactly what she needed after the unexpected surprise of sleeping with Kara the night before.

She was scrolling through Instagram over a bowl of noodle soup when she saw a photo of Sarah and Jill together. They were clearly in bed, pillows behind them, their cheeks pressed together as they smiled for the camera.

#girlfriend #LGBTQ #bedtime

Everyone on their double date had gotten laid. By all measures, that was the mark of a really good date. Except the pairings weren't what Maddie and Suni had planned.

Nisha took a screenshot of the post and sent it to Kara in a text message. *Sarah and Jill went home together last night. Sarah posted it on Instagram.*

She didn't expect Kara to text back right away, since she was often in meetings or on the phone when she was at work. But after two hours passed without response, Nisha could only assume that Kara didn't care.

The more the afternoon wore on, the worse Nisha began to feel about what they'd done. Sex complicated friendships. In the past few months, Kara had become important to her, and if she lost that, she'd be back to where she was before Kara moved to Chicago, when Nisha was lonely and still trying to figure out her path.

Kara had been clear about what she wanted. She had never misled Nisha in any way. From the first night they'd met, she'd said she wanted casual sex without a relationship. She wasn't looking to replace Hilary, who must have been perfect to have left Kara pushing everyone else so far away.

While their sexual chemistry had been great, Nisha couldn't agree to casual sex, not with someone she knew as well as Kara. Not ever, really. That wasn't her style. She could respect that it was what Kara wanted, and in that case there seemed to be only one thing they could do.

They'd have to stop spending time together to give Nisha some emotional distance.

If they tried to keep their friendship going at the same pace, it would be a constant reminder to Nisha of the sparks between them that she had to let die. Or she'd give in and agree to some casual fling she didn't want at all, making herself miserable and sacrificing their friendship on the altar of a quick and easy fuck. Remaining friends with Kara would not be setting herself up for success.

And sleeping with her did?

Even if she let herself fantasize about Kara somehow changing her mind, there was still the problem that Nisha was fundamentally unworthy.

You're worthy of love. You did a bad thing. That doesn't make you a bad person.

Once Kara knew everything that had transpired with Angie, there was no way she'd want to be in a relationship with Nisha. Nisha didn't think she could stomach telling her the whole story, and if she didn't tell her, she'd always be lying by omission.

What Nisha needed was something else to focus on because the Kara situation was, frankly, done. There was nothing to brood about. By choosing to sleep together, they'd effectively chosen to end their friendship, and now Nisha was going to have to find something else to occupy her overactive mind.

She needed fresh air. Exercise and a break from being inside would give her some perspective. She bundled up, went down to the front door, and took a steadying breath before pushing it open to the cold winter air.

The walk to the corner was less meditative than she'd hoped, really more of a study in staring at the pavement to make sure she didn't lose her footing among the salt and ice. She headed westward, away from the lake and toward Broadway, a main thoroughfare where she could feel like part of the crowd. Back in the swing of things. One of a million moving parts to the city.

As she walked under the L, a pigeon came flapping out of the steel girders, and Nisha felt something warm and wet land in her hair. Thinking it was snow, she reached up to brush it off, and her fingers sank into bird poo.

She stood on the sidewalk, looking at the white mess in her hand. This had to be a sign. She decided to give up on the day. She turned around and went home.

By the time Maddie got home from work, Nisha was lying on the couch in her pajamas with some stupid fake court show blaring on the TV and a half-eaten bag of chips resting on her stomach. Maddie could tell right away something was up. Nisha had never stayed out all night before, and she never sprawled on the couch like a lifeless sack of vegetables.

"Do you want to talk about it?"

"Might as well wait for your wife to get home. No reason to tell the same story twice."

"You don't have to tell us anything if you don't want to."

Nisha made a face. "Like Suni would ever allow that."

Maddie looked uncertain about what to do or say. She finally said she was going to change out of her work clothes and left Nisha alone in her misery.

When Suni came home, she didn't even remove her coat. She stomped into the living room and turned off the TV. She crossed her arms over her chest and stared down at Nisha.

Maddie came out of the bedroom, and the two of them sat in the armchairs that faced the sofa. Nisha sat up, feeling a little like a kid facing Mom and Dad after doing something bad. But looking at Suni's face, which was a mix of sternness and excitement, Nisha realized they thought she'd hooked up with the date they'd picked out from the stupid app. They were expecting a good story.

They had no idea what had really happened.

"Rhymes with Sarah," she said, "but wasn't her."

Suni's face morphed from excitement to confusion and then, once she recognized whose name rhymed, disapproval.

"Oh, Nish," Maddie said, her eyes widening. "You didn't?"

"I know you don't like her—"

"I never said I don't like her," Suni argued. "I don't even know her."

"I love you," Nisha said, "but you're…really mean whenever you see her. Like that one night, when you shoved the door into her."

"I thought Maddie had piled up junk for Goodwill again. And I said I was sorry!"

Maddie looked at Suni as if to gauge whether she was telling the truth.

"I might be a little tough, but that's because I saw how hurt you were after Angie left. I don't want you to get into that kind of situation again."

Nisha gave a cynical laugh. She'd managed to get into "that kind of situation" again, even with Suni acting like her emotional bodyguard.

"Maybe you're a little overprotective," Maddie suggested. "She's an adult who can make her own choices." She turned to Nisha. "How did it happen? Are you okay?"

She told them about how terrible their dates were, and Maddie made the appropriate noises of regret. Nisha wanted to tease her that it was her fault she'd slept with Kara, since Maddie had picked out Sarah in the first place. But the situation wasn't funny.

She told them how they'd gone back to Kara's place and had sex.

"And this morning she said, 'I'm going to be late,' and left. I haven't heard from her since."

Suni shook her head. "She left you alone in her apartment?"

Close enough to alone, Nisha supposed. Suni and Maddie didn't know anything about Barb, which was probably another reason they were so confused by the amount of time Nisha spent with Kara.

"Well, that means she trusts Nish, right?" said Maddie, ever the optimist. "If she regretted what happened, she'd want you gone right away. She was trying to do the decent thing by letting you sleep in even if she had to leave."

"It was lazy of her," Suni argued. "That way, she didn't have to face anything. She probably didn't even have an early meeting. She was probably avoiding the situation."

"You think the worst of everyone."

"No, she's right," Nisha said. "She had bad vibes about Kara from the first time you guys met her at Perimeter, and now we can't be friends anymore because Kara is only interested in hooking up, and that's not what I want."

Suni prompted, "Because you want...?"

"Does it matter what I want? I can't have it, so I have to move on."

Nisha appreciated that they weren't pushing her.

"At least tell us the juicy details," Suni said.

"It was good." She couldn't tell them how Kara had made her feel safe and exposed at the same time, how worried Nisha had been about her body and her abilities and how needless all that worrying had been because everything they had done together was smoking hot but also sacred and loving. "Really good. That's all I'm saying."

"Damn."

"Well," Maddie said after a pause, "this is good, right? I mean, you had sex with someone who wasn't Angie. That's good."

"True," Suni said. "You used to be 'all I want is Angie back' and 'I'll never love anyone else for the rest of my life,' and now you've been with someone else. That's progress, right?"

It didn't feel much like progress when it had left Nisha wallowing in misery on the couch all afternoon. It felt like a massive backslide.

She flopped down on her side and curled into the fetal position. She wasn't going to cry over her mistakes. She wasn't going to punish herself for being too impulsive to think through the consequences of her actions.

But she really wanted to.

Maddie gave a little noise of sad empathy. "Maybe if you just told her how you feel...."

"I can't, Maddie." The tears started to flow. "I don't want to make her feel bad that she doesn't feel the same way back."

Suddenly there were two other people sitting on the couch with her, offering hugs and reassuring pats. More than Suni's admittedly terrifying judgment, the comfort was how Nisha knew she really had fucked up her life.

CHAPTER SIXTEEN

Dear Kara,

There's a special event tomorrow night at the Gene Siskel Film Center I thought you might enjoy. There will be a screening of a new documentary about AIDS activism in Chicago in the 1990s, followed by a Q&A with Prof. Jen Rankin from U of C, an expert on early AIDS cultural history. Tickets are $15 and benefit the Howard Brown Center. Given your interest in your aunt's work in the 1980s, I thought of you when I saw the flyer. I hope you don't mind me contacting you.

    Best,
    Harold

The email came when Kara was swamped at work. When she saw the return address was from the LGBTQ library and not a client or colleague, she had to triage, and it wasn't until the day of the event that she actually read the message. What the hell, she thought. What else was she going to do that night, other than go home and watch Barb play video games? She probably wouldn't learn anything useful to Barb's situation, since Barb had died before the 1990s, but it might be an interesting way to pass the evening.

The film center was only a few blocks from her office, so after she finished work for the day, she figured she'd walk over to get a ticket. Then she'd find a bar or coffee shop where she could hang out until it was time for the screening.

She only made it as far as the corner of Washington and Dearborn, a half block from her office building, when she saw Nisha emerge from a restaurant. Her arm was linked through someone else's, and they were laughing loudly. She looked happy and carefree.

Then she spotted Kara, and time stopped.

Kara hadn't seen her since the night they'd spent together, and it was like seeing her for the first time. Her mind hadn't done a good enough job remembering the shape of Nisha's nose or the little crease that appeared above her left eyebrow when she was thinking. A visual memory couldn't reconstruct Nisha's larger than life presence, the way her big emotions and heart made her seem to take up more space than her small body actually did. There on the street in the middle of rush hour, Nisha might as well have been the only person. Like the world put a spotlight on her.

Their night together had been Kara's first time with someone who wasn't Hilary since college, and it had clarified for her that her plan for casual sex had been a disastrous one. Thankfully, it hadn't come to fruition. She hadn't expected to feel so vulnerable or to be so concerned about how sharing intimacy with someone else might alter what she and Hilary had had. She'd spent time "processing her feelings," as Nisha would say, and she'd realized two things. First, if Nisha regretted what happened between them, Kara didn't. She would forever be grateful that someone she cared for so much had been the one to help her take this huge step. Second, sex had only increased Kara's affection for Nisha. She'd reflected a lot on whether her feelings were just spurred by hormones, and she knew now they weren't.

But Kara could read between the lines. Nisha hadn't called or texted, other than to tell her their dates had also hooked up. If she'd been to the apartment to see Barb, it was always when Kara was out. Nisha obviously regretted what had happened, and Kara wasn't going to push.

"Everything okay?" the other person asked Nisha. A new lover, Kara thought, given how intimately they were holding each other.

Still looking at Kara with an expression Kara couldn't read, Nisha nodded. "Yeah, it's fine. Come on, we don't want to be late."

They crossed in front of Kara, heading north on Dearborn, still arm in arm. About halfway up the block, Nisha turned to look over her shoulder at Kara, who was still rooted in place, too dumbstruck to move.

The Wolfman, where Nisha worked, was only a block away from Kara's office, but their paths had never crossed before. Usually Nisha worked weekends when Kara didn't, and when she had shows on weeknights, she had to be at the theater before Kara left the office. Seeing Nisha tonight was something Kara never imagined happening, and so she'd never thought to emotionally prepare herself for it.

She walked to the film center, aware of how alone she was while Nisha had been on the arm of someone else. Someone who made her look happy.

The film was interesting and educational, but the Q&A dragged on as the audience asked irrelevant questions that frustrated Kara. The professor answering the questions did so with grace and poise when Kara wished she'd tell people to shut up.

As the crowd was making its way out of the theater after the Q&A, Harold from the library called her name and came over to say hello. He introduced her to his partner and a few other people.

Kara's heart wasn't into schmoozing. Her mind replayed the encounter with Nisha on a loop. It was a sore reminder that Nisha had never really needed Kara, not the way Kara needed her.

She rode the train home, melancholy and, for some reason, eager to see Barb.

❖

"Did you know you don't have to watch TV when it's on the air?" Barb said as Kara walked through the front door. "They have this thing where you can watch it whenever you want. You can even fast forward through commercials. You don't need a videotape or anything."

Barb was at least good for a chuckle, Kara thought as she took off her coat and the scarf Nisha had given her for Christmas.

"So you've discovered the joys of on-demand." Kara joined her on the sofa. "What are you watching, anyway?"

"*Barney Miller*. They have the whole series on this TV. I missed a lot of the later episodes because I baby-sat Sonia's kids on Thursday nights while she worked."

A loud retro show was playing, something about police and the criminals they caught. Kara was glad Barb had found something from her era to watch, and she was too broken down to care what was on the screen.

"You don't usually say much about Sonia or the old days."

"All I'm saying is that I baby-sat."

"She must have trusted you a lot to let you watch her kids." Kara couldn't restrain herself from adding, "Must be nice to have a friendship that deep."

Barb paused the TV. "Another thing you can do. You just push this button, and it pauses. You can restart it whenever you want." She turned to face Kara. "You want to talk about it? You've been moping around here ever since—"

"Don't say it."

"Come on, ever since Nisha spent the night."

"I saw her tonight with someone else."

Barb looked stunned. "You did?"

Kara nodded. "They were walking down the street, and they were laughing and they had their arms around each other. She looked happy. Really happy."

"Are you sure?"

"The funny thing is, I once told her she was stuck in the past, and I was congratulating myself on how well I was moving forward. But, actually, she's the one who keeps moving forward. She doesn't need me at all. So now I just want to sit here and watch TV with you and forget about my life."

"Suit yourself." Barb picked up the remote and pressed play.

Somewhere in the middle of the next episode, Kara realized they were arranged on the couch in a picture of domestic familiarity. Barb's feet were propped on the coffee table, and she had one arm stretched along the back of the sofa in Kara's direction. It wasn't touching Kara, who was sitting cross-legged, but she wasn't shying away from it either. They looked like people who knew each other and had lived together a while.

She supposed they had. It had been nearly four months.

After the third episode, Barb yawned and stretched. "I'm ready for bed. Pretty weird for a dead lady, huh? I have all of eternity to sleep. You'd think I'd stay awake now."

"There's a lot about you that's weird." Instead of being a joke, it came out tenderly.

Barb looked pensive. "I lied to you," she said at last.

"About what?"

"Hilary."

Kara felt a wave of anxiety rolling through her stomach. Tonight had already been difficult enough, and the mindless TV show had only just started to take the edge off. She wasn't sure she was ready for more.

Through a dry mouth, she managed to ask, "What'd you lie about?"

"You asked me if I could communicate with her, and I said no. It wasn't totally true. If I concentrate hard enough, I can feel her. I can't see her or talk to her the way I can talk to you, but I can sense her out there."

"Is she...how is she?"

Barb closed her eyes. "Safe. Content. She isn't in any pain anymore. Everything is okay now." Her voice was gentle, pitched almost like Hilary's, a very different Barb than the loud-mouthed food addict she normally was.

Kara didn't want to ask because it seemed selfish if Hilary was content, wherever she was, but she couldn't not ask, all the same. "Does she miss me?"

Barb's eyes filled with tears. "She loves you so much. She wants so much for you, Kara. But mostly she just wants you to know it's okay."

"What's okay?"

"Everything that's happening, everything that's about to happen. It's all okay. You just have to accept it."

Kara wanted to ask what that meant, but Barb wiped her eyes and took a sip from the bottle of beer on the table. Then she was back to her usual self.

"Don't make me do that again. That was really hard."

"Thank you," Kara said slowly. "I don't know what it all means, but hearing that Hilary's okay, that's more than I ever expected. It's a relief to know."

"We all need closure." Barb took another sip of beer. "Just make sure you're not giving yourself closure on things that aren't actually closed."

"Unfinished business?"

"Exactly."

"You're talking about Nisha," Kara said, but Barb just shrugged. "We just have bad timing." Kara stole Barb's bottle and took a swig. "And speaking of unfinished business, are you ever going to tell me what happened with Sonia? Not so I can banish you, but because we're friends?"

"Are we friends?" Barb teased, grabbing the bottle back. "Is that what'd you call us?"

"I guess, technically, you're an uninvited guest who never left, but, yeah, we're friends, right? You know Nisha once told me she was my best friend in Chicago. I'd only lived here about three days when she said it."

"I guess you're my friend," Barb said, "since you're the only one I talk to anyway."

"If we're friends, tell me what happened with Sonia."

"Why do you keep fixating on Sonia?"

"She said she's responsible for your death."

Barb rolled her eyes. "She's a drama queen."

"Are you saying that of the four of them, she's not the one your unfinished business is connected to? Then what about Miss Pythia— Rosalind? Where did she go? Why did she disappear after you came back?"

Barb grinned and waved a finger at Kara. "I can't tell you that."

"Come on, Barb, the 'I can't tell you that' routine is getting old."

"I really can't tell you," Barb said. "I have no idea where she is. Hand to God."

"Sonia told us that she and Rosalind used to live together at her house," Kara said, "so can we assume that Nan was the one who lived here with you by process of elimination?"

Barb smiled and shook her head.

"I didn't think so. I think we're assuming you and Sonia were talking about the same time, but the four of you were friends for a long time, weren't you? Whichever one of them lived here with you, it wasn't necessarily when Sonia and Rosalind were together, was it?"

"What makes you think it was one of them who lived here with me?"

That was another assumption Kara had made, Barb was right. For all she knew, there was a fifth woman in the mix. Maybe more. She didn't have any evidence that Barb's live-in girlfriend was Nan, Sonia, or Rosalind, but instinct told her it was.

"Everything keeps pointing to the same three other people. I think if there was a fifth one of you, I'd have heard some clue by now. I'm convinced your girlfriend was one of those three."

"You're right." Barb took another sip of beer and didn't bother to stifle the belch that followed. "It was one of them."

"Which one?" Kara nearly shouted with frustration, but that was the end of the conversation.

After she got ready for bed, Kara lay in bed for an hour, thinking over what Barb had said about Hilary. Knowing that Hilary's soul was out there somewhere, still full of love but now free from pain, was a huge relief to Kara. She placed her right hand atop her left and brought them to her heart.

She wants you to know it's okay.

Kara wanted to know what it was that Hilary was okay about. She wished she'd asked Barb what Hilary thought of the chaos Kara had made of her relationship with Nisha. Hilary had had an unending capacity for forgiveness, and she'd probably laugh fondly at Kara's mess and tell her to lighten up about it all.

Kara wished Nisha could laugh about it. But she should have known better. Nisha's mind had been firmly stuck on Angie. Then she'd taken off the ring and been ready to date again, but of course that didn't mean she wanted Kara. She was looking for new adventures with new people, and rightly so. First it was the stupid app, and now she was thriving with whoever she was with tonight. She didn't need Kara interfering in that. If Kara really cared about her, she was going to have to let Nisha go.

CHAPTER SEVENTEEN

It was a bitterly cold Wednesday, the kind of day when winter had lost its appeal, and instead of the magic of a dusty snowfall, they got razor-sharp icy wind whipping off the frozen lake. On days like this, Nisha struggled to see the joy in winter and wanted to hibernate until spring. Instead, she and Sonia were making their way across the crowded hospital parking lot as the wind drove needles into their faces.

Nan had a blood clot and had been taken into surgery. From her hasty googling, Nisha knew it was a serious condition, and Nan's prolonged stay in the hospital was about to be lengthened. If she made it out of surgery.

They caught the clot in time. She will be all right. Have faith in the ability of these people to do their jobs.

For the first time since Nan was taken to the hospital, Sonia looked genuinely worried. In the waiting room, she held Nisha's hand.

"Rosie should be here," she said. "Maybe she thinks it's cute that she's gone, but this is serious. She should be here."

Sonia still didn't speak much about her friends, and the one or two times they'd talked about Rosalind's disappearance, Sonia had only seemed proud of her for going underground.

"Do you think something happened to her?" Nisha asked. "Should we be going to the police?"

"I'd feel it here," Sonia said, tapping her chest. "She's still out there, somewhere, but I'm not happy with her right now."

Neither was Nisha. Vanishing when she and Kara needed help with Barb's manifestation was one thing, but vanishing on a friend in the hospital was another. It didn't seem fair to Nisha that Sonia, who was in her late seventies, was expected to handle Nan's situation by herself.

Sonia's son Carlos had come to the hospital to give his mom support, and Nisha had gotten to meet him. He was fifteen years older than Nisha, and he lived in Arlington Heights, a northwestern suburb far enough that it was inconvenient for him to check on Sonia every day. He'd seemed to think it was strange his mother was hanging out with a thirty-five-year-old he'd never met, but Sonia had said a bunch of things in Spanish. After that, Carlos had been polite to Nisha.

He had three kids of his own, all in high school. When Nisha asked Sonia if she wanted to live closer to them, Sonia had asked why Nisha didn't live closer to her own parents. She'd understood what Sonia meant. Sometimes, even when you loved people, you needed distance.

That afternoon, Carlos said he would come by the hospital after work, so Nisha could go to the theater without leaving Sonia alone.

"When he and Luis were little," Sonia said, "Barb used to baby-sit them at night while I waited tables. My parents hated the idea of a dyke watching them, but Barb was a good baby-sitter."

"Did Nan ever baby-sit?"

Sonia nodded. "We were all in each other's business all the time. Barb's brother dated my sister at one point, but my parents hated it. 'You have to marry a boricua.'" She imitated her parents' thick accents. "Carlos and Luis's dad, he and I were married for a few years. I thought it would make my family happy, but it didn't work out. It's not who I was."

"That must have been difficult for you."

Nisha's parents were disapproving, and they'd spent a long time trying to persuade her to marry a man. She couldn't imagine actually going through with it for the sake of appearances.

"I don't know why I'm telling you all this," Sonia said, rubbing her forehead. "Nan's up there, getting cut into, and I'm facing my own mortality. There are so many stories from the past I never told anyone."

Nisha knew what a gift it was that Sonia was finally opening up to her. "It's funny you say that because I've been thinking about how much I love hearing Nan's old stories and how I wish I'd gotten her to write them down before this happened. These stories need to be shared."

"Our stories need to be shared? Nah, we were just a bunch of dumb kids who became dumb adults, trying to figure things out."

"Oh, no, you're our grandparents," Nisha said. "You're our history. People my age wouldn't be where we are today without your generation fighting so many battles for us."

"You make it sound like it was all protests and arrests," Sonia said.

"And getting kicked out of Titillating Tuesday because you flashed everyone."

"Barb told you that? I'd forgotten about that!" She laughed at the memory, then shook her head. "Sometimes we weren't fighting battles against homophobia. Sometimes we were just battling each other for no reason. Maybe it's time I told you what happened between Nan and Rosie."

Nisha held her breath in anticipation. Finally, a part of their history would be revealed. While it might help Barb process her unfinished business, it would also be nice for Nisha to hear after so many weeks of Barb and Sonia being tight-lipped about their past.

"After Barb died, the three of us stayed pretty close for a long time. It was in 2005 when everything started to fall apart. You know Prince Charles over there in England?"

Nisha nodded that she knew who he was, wondering what on earth he had to do with Nan.

"Well, they announced that he and that woman he'd had an affair with—what was her name? Kamala or something?"

"Camilla?"

"Yeah, they announced the two of them were getting married. Lady Di had only been dead maybe five or ten years. And Nan, she said good for them if they were in love, but Rosie adored Princess Diana. She'd made us all watch their wedding—that was when Barb was still alive—so she thought this new marriage was in bad taste. She and Nan had a big fight about it, and one thing led to another, and finally Rosie said she didn't want to see or talk to Nan again. That put me in the middle, and I couldn't pick sides. They were my best friends. Finally, I couldn't manage going back and forth between them anymore, listening to them hate on each other, and that was it. They weren't talking to each other, and I was done with both of them."

Nisha gave herself a moment to process before she tried to say anything. While she appreciated that Sonia had opened up to her, she couldn't believe the big, secret falling out among three best friends had been over something as dumb and distant as a British royal wedding. But she didn't want to say that and insult Sonia.

Sonia must have sensed what Nisha was feeling because she added, "You have to understand how huge Lady Di was."

"Of course." Nisha nodded as if it was all perfectly reasonable.

She resolved at that moment that if they ever found Miss Pythia, she was going to organize a reunion to make them talk out why their friendships had crumbled over something that had such little bearing on their lives.

People shouldn't throw away relationships because of a difference of opinion about something that didn't directly affect them. Like her relationship with Kara. Or non-relationship, as it were. When one person wanted a relationship and the other wanted casual sex, that was a reason to go separate ways. When one person thought some famous rich guy's remarriage to some rich lady was a bad idea, that was no reason to throw away something special that had lasted for decades in the face of adversity.

"Do you ever think about their falling out?" Nisha said. "And wonder if the reasons for it really outweighed the reasons for you all to stay together?"

"How do you mean?"

"My ex, Angie, the one I used to live with in the apartment Barb's haunting—we were going to get married. We'd put in an offer on a condo we were going to buy together. Everything was perfect, you know? All the plans for the future I'd wanted. But then Angie found out I'd taken out two credit cards she didn't know about, and I had about fifteen thousand dollars in debt. She got really mad and said I'd betrayed her trust because we were trying to build a life together, and that life included shared finances. She took off her engagement ring and threw it at me and called off the wedding."

Confessing to Sonia felt good, especially after Sonia had been willing to share her own story, but it was a reminder of the painful choices Nisha had made that had led her life down this path. Why hadn't she told Angie her income couldn't keep pace with their spending? Why had taking out credit cards seemed like the only solution? And why hadn't she told Angie about those credit cards, especially before the mortgage broker ran their credit reports and everything came out in the open? Nisha had made foolish choices, hurtful choices, but she understood now that regretting those choices was futile. She couldn't change her actions in the past. What she could do was learn from the consequences and accept that the actions in the past had led her down a path to the present.

And at present, she was alone and homeless.

"Your girl threw a ring at you?" Sonia said.

Nisha nodded. "It actually got lost in the apartment, and I spent a year looking for it until Kara moved in. I guess Barb was hiding it. Then, the first time I came over to have brunch with Kara, Barb gave it back."

"That's funny," Sonia said, "because Barb once threw a ring at me, too."

"She did?"

"This was a while before she died. We'd been involved, and I was going to try to make things work with Javi, my boys' father. In those days, women couldn't get married to each other. We could barely act like a couple in public. But Barb and I had matching mood rings. I'd gotten them for Valentine's Day one year. Nobody knew what they stood for but us. But when I told her I was going back to Javi, she took hers off and threw it. I'd broken her heart."

"Oh my gosh, that's so similar to what happened with Angie and me."

Sonia nodded. "That must have been why she kept your ring, because it reminded her of what happened between us. You said you got it back when you came over to the apartment for the first time?"

"Yeah. Kara has both rings now. She's keeping them safe for me until I can figure out what do with them."

"How much are they worth?"

Angie's parents had given them some of the money for the rings, and the rest had come from money she and Nisha had saved together.

In the process of moving out and dividing their stuff, Nisha had offered to give Angie her ring back, in case she wanted to sell it and repay her parents, but Angie, communicating through a mutual friend, had said Nisha was free to keep the ring as long as they never spoke again. Their friend had also made it clear that if Angie's missing ring ever turned up, Angie didn't want any part of it.

"They each cost a little more than three thousand dollars."

For some people, that probably wasn't very much money for a ring that was supposed to last a lifetime, but for Nisha it had been a staggering amount. If she hadn't been so emotionally attached to her ring, she would have sold it long ago and used the money to pay down her debt or put a security deposit on an apartment of her own. But getting rid of the ring had been unthinkable, since it was her last remaining symbol of the life she'd been trying to build with Angie.

Now that she didn't want that life anymore, though, what was preventing her from using that money to build the life she did want?

❖

After yoga class the next day, Nisha and Carter went to the Swedish restaurant for pancakes. Nothing beat rewarding yourself for working out by immediately replacing all the calories you'd burned and then some. It also gave Carter a chance to check in on Nisha's progress with the anatomy portion of her yoga teacher training.

"Have I told you how grateful I am that you're cutting me a discount on this?" Nisha said as a plate of thin, rolled pancakes with a giant dollop of lingonberry jam was set in front of her.

"Yoga is stupidly expensive." Carter wasn't vegetarian and had opted for the salmon and dill quiche. "I hate that it's become this thing only rich people can afford, as if rich people are the only ones deserving of spiritual enlightenment and body-mind connection. My biggest problem, though, is that if you get certified, you'll be my competition."

Nisha smiled. "I'm sure there are enough rich people who want to take classes for the both of us."

"Seriously, I think it's such a great idea that you're doing it." Carter forked the quiche and took a delicate bite. "This is so good!"

"Carter, you know I feel like I've learned a lot from you in the past year? I was wondering if I could run some other ideas by you—things that aren't about yoga."

"If this is about that woman we saw on the street by the Wolfman, I would love to hear the whole story, every juicy detail."

The night they'd run into Kara after Nisha had started teacher training and thanked Carter with tickets to a show, they hadn't pushed Nisha for many details—they'd just accepted it when she'd said the bizarre encounter was the result of a "friendship gone sideways"—but it was obvious there was a lot more to the story.

"Actually, this is about another idea I've been mulling over."

Carter was useful as an advisor because in addition to their in-person yoga classes, they were an influencer whose social media and YouTube channel were dedicated to mind-body wellness advice, especially for trans and nonbinary people. Nisha followed Carter's videos and saw how many people logged in and left comments, and she knew Carter was able to monetize that popularity into an income. She assumed it wasn't much money, but if her goal was to focus less on Kara and Angie and more on putting her life back on track, she figured every bit of extra income would be useful.

"I want to expand my makeup business beyond theater," she said. "I was thinking that maybe you could help me figure out how to build my brand online."

Carter's eyes widened. "Yes, I love this idea! Some makeup tutorials, maybe some lives where you do a makeover in real time, you could be a big hit."

"But nothing gross. Not about teaching people to look like someone they're not," Nisha explained. "What I like about your yoga classes is that when you guide us through meditations, it always feels really personal, like your advice is handpicked for me. I want to do that with beauty. I don't want to teach people how to slather on makeup to feel beautiful. There are plenty of people on the internet doing that already, and I just don't think that's what makeup and hair should be for. I want to help people see the beauty that's inside them already."

Carter put their fork down. "Oh, honey, you're gonna be a star."

CHAPTER EIGHTEEN

In the lobby of the building, Oleg was fighting with a giant red foam heart to get it to stay on top of the mailboxes without falling down. Kara tried to shut her mailbox as carefully as she could, but it shook the whole rack, and the heart came tumbling down again.

"Nice Valentine's Day decorations."

Oleg glared at her. "I put package at door."

"Okay, thanks."

Kara's birthday was in early March, and she wondered if someone in her family had sent an early present. More likely, she thought with dread, Barb had been shopping again. Although she'd canceled her Amazon Prime account, Barb had learned to buy things directly from retailer's websites.

The box sitting in front of the door to her apartment was large, nearly two feet cubed. Kara didn't recognize the return address, which was some business with a bland name in Ohio. She brought the box to the kitchen table.

"Hey, Barb, did you order something online again?"

The TV was off, and Barb wasn't in the living room.

"Barb?"

Kara found a pair of scissors and slit open the tape sealing the box.

Inside was a hot pink vibrator. Kara pulled it out, turning its box over to look at the model. She had definitely not ordered a vibrator. There had to be a mistake with the package.

Underneath some crumpled brown packing paper was a set of fuzzy pink handcuffs and some hideous lace thong that looked like something Becca would have gotten at her bachelorette party. There were two red silicone...teething rings? Oh no, they were cock rings, weren't they?

"What. The. Hell."

There was also a feather tickler, a jumbo box of dental dams in assorted flavors, and at the very bottom of the box was the packing slip. It had Kara's name at the top and listed the last four digits of her credit card as the form of payment tendered for the grand total of $322, which had included expedited shipping. And there was a gift message: *Dear Barb, play safe and play fun! Love, Kara.*

"Barb! Where are you? Show yourself!" Kara took off her coat and scarf while she waited, but there was no answer. "Barb, I want to talk to you right now!"

The prickling on the back of her neck told her Barb was lurking, but she didn't return to visibility. Chicken. They'd talked about Barb using Kara's credit cards without permission, and it was one thing when Barb spent $15 on pizza because she refused to cook, but $322 on sex toys? This crossed the line.

This shall pass, and I can do this. Kara took a few deep breaths.

What did Barb plan to do with this stuff, anyway? Well, her plans for the vibrator were pretty apparent, but why did she need handcuffs and lingerie? And what on earth were the cock rings for?

Kara thought back to when Barb was still invisible, when she'd written *LOVE* on the bathroom mirror. She wasn't planning to seduce Kara, was she?

It occurred to her that if Barb could use her laptop to buy a vibrator, she could use it to join a dating site. Maybe she already had. When Kara was at work, Barb had no supervision. Maybe she had a parade of women coming in and out of the apartment all day.

Kara really, really hoped they didn't use her bed without changing the sheets.

"I don't care about your unfinished business anymore. I want you gone."

The box flew off the kitchen table and crashed into the floor.

"Oh, so now you're pissed, huh? Good. Imagine how I feel."

The table rattled.

"I am not scared of you, Barb." Rattling furniture and flying objects might have seemed scary on their own, but not when she knew the beer-guzzling ghost behind it. "I don't care if you can turn off the lights and go boo. I've put up with a lot from you for way too long. And I am not going to let you interfere with my life anymore."

The lights went out.

Kara was undaunted. She knew it wasn't the work of some horror movie killer. She flipped the switch a few times, and when nothing happened, she found her way to the fuse box. Using her phone as a flashlight, she saw that Barb had switched off the main breaker.

When the lights came back on, the box had been put back on the kitchen table. The cock rings were sitting on top of it with a heart drawn around them in Sharpie.

A voice behind her said, "I'm not interfering in your life."

Kara whirled around, but Barb had already disappeared again. "Can you please rematerialize so we can talk? I want to know why you bought all this stuff."

The feather tickler rose from the box. It tapped the table once, then pointed toward the hall, and began moving in that direction. Kara followed it to the bathroom. The tiny window was foggy from the mixture of cold sleet outside and the hot steam from the radiator below it. The tickler set itself down nicely on the sink. Kara waited.

On the window, in the fog, letters began to appear. C-H-E-A-T. Then a dollar sign. Then L-O-V-E.

Why did Barb insist on using such crude methods of communication when she could talk things out like a living person?

"Someone cheated on someone they loved with a sex worker? Is that what happened to you and your girlfriend?"

The tickler rose and tapped the sink angrily. Wrong guess.

"Someone cheated someone out of money, but they loved them?"

The window pane rattled in the wooden frame. She'd gotten it wrong again.

"I don't know what you're trying to tell me. Is there some rule that says you can't say things directly?"

A downward diagonal on the window now, followed by a straight line. The start of the letter Y. Yes.

Kara picked up the tickler. "All right, can we cut it out with the big show? I take back what I said about wanting you gone, okay? I'm sorry. I'm just mad you bought all this stuff."

She returned the tickler to the box in the kitchen and moved the whole box to the back of her bedroom closet. She glanced again at the return label. SRS Services, Inc. Between the nondescript sender and the plain, discreet packaging, she should have guessed what was inside.

Barb appeared at the end of the hall, coming into being with a shimmer, at first so transparent Kara could see the wall behind her, but as she came closer, Barb solidified. Under her eyes were dark circles, and her skin looked sallow.

"Is it hard to do that?"

Barb nodded. "I'm sorry I used your credit card again. Don't be mad. I swear I have a reason."

"Are you going to use that vibrator with someone from a dating app in my bed while I'm at work?"

"What? Whoa, no!"

"Okay," Kara said, feeling tired, "then I don't care."

"It doesn't bother you if someone charges a lot on a credit card?"

"Does it matter if I say yes? You'll do it again the next time you want something anyway."

"If you'd let me start that German shepherd puppy breeding business, I'd have plenty of money on my own. I could have had a whole litter to sell by now."

Breeding and selling puppies had been one of Barb's earlier suggestions for making an income of her own. If Kara hadn't been opposed on moral grounds, her lease would have prohibited it anyway. After that, Barb had decided to become a famous livestream gamer, but when the camera couldn't pick her up, that dream had died, too.

"I told you before," Kara said wearily. "People these days get their dogs from rescue organizations."

"Okay, fine, but the charges. I didn't mean me specifically. I meant, someone in general. If someone you know charges up a big bill, does that bother you?"

Hilary had tended to use credit cards way too frequently. Her philosophy had been that it was easier to charge everything and make one payment at the end of the month, but she often forgot to keep track of how much she was charging and usually overspent. When they went through their bills at the end of the month, Kara would lecture her, and Hilary would patiently listen and nod, until Kara realized Hilary already felt terrible about it. Kara's lecturing only made her feel worse. The solution had been a shared spreadsheet where they kept track of every purchase. It had been tedious—and for Kara unnecessary—but it had helped Hilary keep her spending in check. It had been an easy way to fix the tension between them caused by money.

"Hilary used to charge a lot. It was annoying, but as long as it never got us in deep debt, it wasn't the end of the world. What's this all about? What does this have to do with cheating?"

"You have to trust me."

"I can accept that there are reasons you're doing the things you're doing," Kara said neutrally, "but at some point, I'm going to need concrete answers."

"You'll get them when you need them."

"Why cock rings and handcuffs? Isn't that a little…I don't know, cliche? And what was the whole point of writing on the window if you're just going to talk to me now?"

"If you weren't such a chucklehead, I wouldn't have to do this magic show. What's your IQ, anyway? I thought lawyers were supposed to be smart."

"Barb, what on earth are you talking about?"

"I thought the dirty toys would be the tipping point. Obviously, I was wrong."

"Does this have something to do with Valentine's Day?" Kara asked. "It's about to be the anniversary of your death."

"Jesus, Kara, you're real sensitive sometimes, you know that?" Barb stomped toward Kara's bedroom and slammed the door.

Apparently, they couldn't talk about how the ghost was dead.

Kara gave Barb a few minutes, and when she hadn't come out, Kara crept down the hall to the bedroom and knocked softly on the door. It still didn't latch properly, and it fell open enough for her to see Barb curled in a ball on the bed.

"Hey," Kara said as she sat beside her. "I didn't realize it was such a sore subject. I didn't mean to upset you." Barb didn't answer or move. "I should be more sensitive, you're right. I'm sorry."

"It's fine," Barb sniffed.

"It sucks. It really sucks. And you're allowed to feel like shit about it."

"Yeah?" Barb uncurled enough to look at her. "Hey, yeah, I am, you know? Being dead sucks." She punched Kara lightly on the arm. "And I gotta stick around here, cooking up magic shows to try to get you to understand stuff that's right in front of your face. You think I don't work, but let me tell you, Susie Q, this is a hard job. It takes a lot of creativity."

"Using the feather tickler as a pointer was a really clever touch."

"I thought you'd like that."

CHEAT, LOVE, $. No, that wasn't the order. It had been *CHEAT, $, LOVE.* And a bunch of sex toys. And all Barb could tell her was that the explanation for how these pieces fit together was right in front of Kara's face.

Barb must have known that Hilary was prone to racking up credit card debt when she asked if Kara minded that. But Hilary had never cheated on her, and she'd never cheated on Hilary. The cheating came right before the dollar sign, though, so those two concepts had to be connected somehow. Cheating through money, maybe, instead of cheating through sex. Could it refer to identity theft?

But what did love have to do with that? Maybe Barb's girlfriend was the one who cheated with money, and then she fell in love with someone else. Or maybe Barb herself was the cheater.

"You lied to your girlfriend about money. That's your unfinished business, isn't it?"

"Oh, Kara, you still think this is about me?"

No, she thought it was about Barb's girlfriend, who was Nan, Rosalind, or Sonia. "You had the package sent to you as a gift from me, so I thought…"

A package full of sex toys. Kara went over them again in her mind, trying to put the pieces together, but the cock rings remained the outliers. Everything else had been skewed toward women's bodies and sexuality. Did someone in the equation have a penis?

Maybe that was the unfinished business? Sonia had said it was common for queer women back then to have some relationships with men. Maybe there was a man in this story that they hadn't yet talked about. Or maybe someone was trans?

"Okay, I give up," Kara said. "Why cock rings?"

"You're so dense sometimes." Barb knocked her knuckles on Kara's head to see if anyone was home. "Because they didn't sell diamond rings."

"And you needed diamond rings because…"

Barb made an impatient rolling gesture with her hands as if to say, *Come on, come on, you're almost there.*

Because the cheating and the money and the love were connected to Nisha and her missing ring, not to Barb.

Angie had broken up with Nisha and thrown the ring, and Nisha had never really explained why. But now Kara could see: one of them had committed a financial betrayal that had ruined their relationship.

Angie was the one who'd taken her ring off first. No one threw away an engagement ring because they were upset about something they regretted doing. That wasn't the behavior of someone guilty. That was the behavior of the one who'd been betrayed.

Nisha had been the one carrying guilt from their relationship. Nisha was the one who'd betrayed Angie. She'd done something with money—credit cards, since Barb kept using Kara's without permission, probably to make a point—and it had ruined their love.

Kara expected that solving a huge part of the mystery of Barb's haunting would bring her satisfaction or at least relief. Instead, she felt burdened with this knowledge of Nisha's private affairs. She hadn't spoken to Nisha in weeks, but Barb wouldn't remain trapped as a spirit just for Kara to exercise her deductive powers.

"You want me to confront Nisha about how her relationship with Angie fell apart."

❖

Nisha was on the living room sofa with her laptop, a calendar, and a host of differently colored Post-Its spread out around her. She'd spent the past week working on plans, doing research, sending texts, and she felt more organized and in control of her life than she had in over a year.

Starting yoga teacher training and talking to Carter about her ideas for expanding her makeup business had been the first steps to a new path. Toward the end of her relationship with Angie, Nisha hadn't had enough money to keep up with their lifestyle. More importantly, she hadn't been able to communicate that to Angie. They were interrelated problems that had caused the dissolution of the relationship, but Nisha understood now that only one was solely in her control: how much money she earned and how much she spent. While she could have—and should have—tried to express what was going on to Angie, communication was a two-way process. As much as she'd idealized their relationship, the reality was that they'd never been good at telling each other what they were really thinking and feeling.

If they had, Nisha would have known that Angie didn't really want to put down roots in Chicago, and her move to Seattle might not have been such a shock.

She'd try to remember what she learned from their relationship because it would be a useful lesson if she ever got into another one. For now, what she could fix on her own was the financial situation.

"Guys, can you come in here, please?"

Suni and Maddie were in the kitchen, making one of Maddie's flavorless curries that Suni seemed willing to eat for the rest of her life out of duty and love.

"Have a seat." Nisha gestured to the armchairs in which they'd sat the day she told them she'd slept with Kara.

That was when she thought she'd ruined her life. It turned out, she had only ruined her friendship with Kara. She missed it, deeply, and if Kara called tomorrow, she'd happily hop in a cab and rush over to talk through everything. But she knew now that she didn't need Kara to be able to survive. She was pretty tough and resourceful on her own.

"As you know," Nisha told her friends, "I've been concentrating my energies on things other than dating right now. Because—well, because dating turned out to be a disaster. I've been doing a lot of thinking about how everything with Angie fell apart and how I've been crashing at your house ever since, and what you said, Suni, about how I was too financially dependent on Angie."

"I told you that you should never have said that," Maddie said. "That was none of your business."

"Sorry," Suni mumbled.

"But in a way, you were right," Nisha said. "Whether I stay single or get into a relationship again, I want to be able to stand on my own, so I've been taking some steps in that direction. You know how I always talk about my yoga teacher Carter?" They nodded. Of course they knew about Carter. Nisha was always spouting off some philosophical insight they'd said in class. "They helped me sign up for yoga teacher training, and I already completed half of the anatomy requirements. Carter got me a discount on the training, and the rest..."

Nisha blew out a breath now because this was a big decision for her.

"The rest I'm paying for by selling my engagement ring."

She anticipated Suni telling her it was an ill-conceived plan because there were a thousand yoga teachers in Chicago, but she didn't say anything.

Maddie, on the other hand, said, "That's wonderful, Nish! That's a huge step!"

"There's more."

She turned her laptop to face them, and on screen was the homepage for a new website advertising her services as a makeup artist for weddings, special events, and film shoots. "I reached out to some people I know, and I have three bookings already." She held up the calendar to show them the dates with appointments marked in green pen with pink circles around them. "I know freelance makeup and yoga aren't exactly the most stable career paths, but if I keep my job at the Wolfman, it should be a nice extra boost."

She spun her laptop around and typed a new address in the web browser. She turned it back to them.

"And to advertise and make sure I'm setting myself up for success, I launched this."

It was her new YouTube channel, where she'd posted videos about beauty makeup techniques. She planned to do beauty tips for wedding season in early June and a series on monster makeup and horror around Halloween. She'd also done a confessional talking about her journey and her philosophy on how makeup wasn't in opposition to the principles of yoga but a complementary way to bring out the best qualities in a person. The video already had ten thousand views and counting.

"What do you think?"

Suni came over to her and gave her a giant hug.

"I am so proud of you, choti behan."

"Really?"

Maddie nodded and joined them, and Nisha felt good being sandwiched between them. "It's great to see you planning for the future like this."

"There's one other thing," Nisha said. "I'm moving out."

Maddie gaped. Suni shot a fist in the air and said, "Yes!" After Maddie swatted her, she said, "I'm kidding. We've loved having you with us."

"I hope it won't be a problem that I won't be paying rent anymore, but I think it's time."

"Where will you go?" Maddie asked.

"I thought about selling the second ring to use as a security deposit on an apartment of my own, but I think there's probably a place where I can be more useful right now."

CHAPTER NINETEEN

"I t'll be a few more minutes while they finish the paperwork," a nurse told them as she checked Nan's blood pressure. "You're looking good, Ms. Galt. You excited to go home?"

Nisha had gotten used to seeing the droop on the left side of Nan's face. The speech therapy made her more intelligible, and she was supposed to help Nan continue her exercises at home. The paralysis in her left arm, though, was going to take longer to improve. Nisha had learned it was a matter of timing and practice. The sooner Nan started using her arm again and the more frequently she did her physical therapy exercises, the more likely it was that she'd recover some mobility. The longer she waited to use the arm, the more likely it was that the paralysis would remain. And Nisha wanted to see Nan back to full strength as soon as possible.

The doctor came into the room, flipping through Nan's chart. "Ms. Galt, we're just about ready to let you out of here. I bet you're looking forward to that."

"Damn right," Nan said.

The doctor looked among the visitors. Oleg had driven Nisha to the hospital with a fresh set of clothes for Nan. Sonia and Carlos had met them there. "Which of you is going to be providing primary care?"

"She lives alone," Sonia told him.

"Not anymore," Nisha said. "I'll be staying with her from now on."

"We never talked about that. You don't want to make a hasty decision. She might need round the clock care, right, Doc?"

"It's not a hasty decision," Nisha said. "I've been thinking about it since she was admitted."

"What's your relationship?" the doctor asked.

"Look, I know she's not really my grandmother, but she feels like it. What I've learned the past few months, listening to her and Barb and Sonia tell their stories, is that we can make our own families. The way I see it, Nan needs someone to look after her, and I love her, so why shouldn't I take care of her?"

"Do you work full-time?" Carlos asked. Then to the doctor, he said, "Will we need a daytime nurse? I've been calling around to find someone."

"I work mostly weekend nights." Nisha hadn't expected so much resistance to her plan. In fact, she'd expected Sonia would be grateful to have a problem taken off her lap.

"I will take care of her at night." Oleg looked at Nisha in solidarity and nodded. "In America, we make our own families. She is my family now."

Nisha beamed and leaned her head against his shoulder. He put an arm around her. There they were: Nan's adoptive grandchildren.

But, of course, they were making plans without asking the person whose opinion mattered the most.

"What do you say, Nan? Do you want to be roomies with me?"

"You're going to give up your life for a sick old lady?" Nan asked.

"I'm not giving up my life. I'm finding a new path for it. And it's not forever, right?" She looked at Carlos, who had offered to pay for home nursing after he'd learned how important Nan was to his mom. "Just until you get back on your feet."

"No parties after ten."

That was as close as Nan would get to officially accepting Nisha's offer. The doctor went over the discharge plans with her, explaining Nan's various prescriptions, symptoms to watch for, and handing her printed sheets of physical therapy exercises.

Nisha invited Sonia and Carlos back to the apartment because their little group had grown so close during Nan's hospitalization, and it seemed anticlimactic for them to part company now. Carlos declined, saying he had to pick one of his kids up from a basketball game, and he kissed Sonia good-bye before he left.

"He's a good boy," Nan said.

"Because of you and all this. It's brought us a lot closer." Sonia patted Nan's shoulder. "I better get home before *Jeopardy!* is on."

"Fuck *Jeopardy!*" Nan said. "Not the same without Trebek."

"You just don't like smart women."

"Are you calling yourself dumb?"

Nan and Sonia's bickering continued as the group made their way out to the parking lot. Oleg helped Nan out of the wheelchair and into the passenger seat of his car. Sonia finally relented and agreed to come over.

They walked slowly down the hall to apartment 505. Oleg was guiding Nan, who was still unsteady on her feet, and the slow pace was killing Nisha, who sensed that at any moment the door to 503 might fling open and Kara might come out.

Oleg suggested they play a game of cards, to which Nan responded, "How the hell am I supposed to play cards with only one hand?" Her cantankerous attitude was a good sign. She'd been too docile the past few weeks, and Nisha had missed her fire.

While Oleg was dealing cards, Nisha's mind was focused squarely on the apartment next door. It was after six. Kara was probably home by now. Barb was probably calling for pizza delivery.

It seemed silly that they were a wall apart.

"Hey, Sonia, would you like to see Barb?"

Sonia looked uncertain. "Have you?" she asked Nan.

"Yeah." She tipped her head side to side while pumping her good arm, simulating walking, then she knocked on an imaginary door. "I saw her, and then—" She tapped her head and gestured fireworks exploding. She clutched her chest and collapsed backward in her wheelchair. "Not a good idea."

"Come on, guys, you were so close," Nisha said. "Can't you get over Prince Charles and Camilla by now?"

"You told her that?" Nan asked Sonia. "Rosie was such a drama queen. Di had been dead almost ten years!"

"What is going on?" Oleg was utterly confused.

"Such a long story," Nisha said with a roll of her eyes. Then to Nan and Sonia, she said, "Rosalind's not here, so you don't have to worry about that. But since Barb can't leave the apartment, would it be so awful if you went over there to talk to her?"

"She gave me a stroke!"

"I gave her a heart attack!"

"The apartment is cursed, apparently," Oleg said. "Maybe no one should live in there."

"Oh, come on, that was all coincidental timing," Nisha argued. "She's lonely and misses her friends."

"What about Kara?" Nan said to Nisha. "Would it be so awful if you talked to her?"

She wasn't sure what she'd do or say if she saw Kara, and it was a much greater possibility now that she was going to be living in the building again. Kara didn't seem like the type to hold a grudge, so surely they could be polite without it being uncomfortable if they ran into each other in the mail room.

But whether they could be friends again, the way they had been, was a different story. In some ways, it was a blessing that things had fallen apart because Nisha had pulled herself together. She was proud of the opportunities she was pursuing.

"No," she said to Nan. "It'd be fine."

"Pack 'em up!" Nan yelled to Oleg. "The party's going next door."

Kara wasn't home yet, and Barb seemed surprised but happy to see them. She and Sonia hugged for a solid minute while Oleg asked, "How do they know each other? You said she was Kara's cousin from Wisconsin." Then Barb looked at Nisha and mouthed a thank you.

Nan and Barb were less physically affectionate, but there were no adverse effects on Nan's health from being in the same space again.

They set up their card game, and Barb ordered a pizza, just as Nisha had anticipated. It was fun and light, no heavy discussions about anything, until Oleg got a call from the emergency service line that a dishwasher was flooding the kitchen of another apartment and excused himself.

"Well, now that we can talk freely," Nisha said, "I just want to know why Sonia thinks she killed Barb and which of you was living here with Barb at the time."

"Rosie," they all said.

"Although I lived here for a little bit," Nan remembered, "until I moved next door. Remember, we had that party for Jimmy Carter's inauguration here?"

"You think you killed me?" Barb asked Sonia. "Why did you say that?"

"I did, remember? When we did that murder mystery play for the community park theater. My character was the one who shot you."

"Wait a second," Nisha said. "You said you couldn't help with Barb's unfinished business because you were responsible for her death. You said, 'I killed her,' and you meant...in a play?"

"Oh, you're good!" Barb slapped the table and hooted with laughter. "That's real bueno!"

"So dramatic," Nan scolded. "You scared this poor girl into thinking you were a murderer."

"You told her I was a gang leader," Sonia said.

"You didn't run a Puerto Rican gang?" Nisha asked.

Barb hooted again.

Nisha was starting to feel like the odd duck. "Why'd you say all that stuff?"

"I embellished," Nan said with a theatrical wave of her hand.

Sonia shrugged. "I wanted you to be interested enough to keep investigating, so you could figure out Barb's business."

The front door opened then, but Oleg wasn't back yet. It was Kara, coming home from work, and she stopped in her tracks when she saw their makeshift party at her kitchen table.

"Hellooooo," she said with surprise. She caught herself. "Nan, it is really wonderful to see you out of the hospital." She gave Nan a small kiss on the cheek. "Sonia, it's nice to see you again. I hope you brought flan."

Nisha was sitting next to Sonia and expected to be greeted next. Her stomach muscles clenched tight. This was the moment she'd been dreading and waiting for at the same time.

Her mind flashed to an image of Kara, nude, writhing in ecstasy underneath her.

"Speaking of unfinished business," Barb said. "You guys gonna go talk in the bedroom or what?"

❖

Nisha perched on Kara's bed like she was scared to touch anything. She was staring at the floor, clearly uncomfortable, and it made Kara wonder why she'd come over in the first place if she didn't want to talk.

Kara leaned against the dresser and crossed her arms over her chest. "You look good, Nish."

"Thanks."

"If you'd have told me Nan was getting released, I'd have gone to help you."

"We managed. Oleg was there. And Sonia's son Carlos."

Kara was out of things to say, and to be honest, it stung a little that Nisha didn't need or want her help.

"We don't have to have a big conversation," Nisha said. "We can just let it be."

"Don't you think we have a lot to talk about?"

"Like what?"

It was like a bomb fell out of the sky and exploded around them, but somehow the only thing it destroyed was Kara's heart. Surely Nisha didn't think so little of their night together?

No, of course she didn't. Kara could trust that she knew Nisha. She was protecting herself, and she had no reason to.

Kara crossed the room to sit beside her. "Nish, we connected. What we shared was special."

"It was?"

"It wasn't for you?"

"Yes, of course it was for me. It was everything for me. But you had made it clear you didn't want to get in a relationship, so I thought it was just sex for you." Nisha shifted slightly, trying to get comfortable without getting too close. "I wasn't going to be that desperate person begging someone to love them. Besides, I didn't think I deserved to be in a relationship again."

So that's what had happened. Nisha had assumed Kara wasn't interested and hadn't bothered asking because she didn't feel worthy of love in the first place.

Not that Kara had been much better. She'd made a lot of assumptions, too.

"I know the truth. About you and Angie."

"I wondered when Barb would tell you."

"She didn't. She wouldn't. It was more like she thought me knowing was connected to her unfinished business, and I figured it out on my own."

"So," Nisha said, squaring her shoulders, "what's your impression of me now? Do you hate me?"

"Does it matter?"

"A lot."

Kara knew what it was like, waiting for judgment to rain down. Hating yourself more than anyone else hated you. It was how she'd felt after Hilary died and they couldn't even list Kara as the deceased's wife in the obituary. She'd hated herself for hurting Hilary with her refusal to marry, and she'd seen herself as a villain who had wasted Hilary's remaining years and crushed her dreams. It had taken a lot of therapy to work through those feelings of self-loathing.

Nisha didn't deserve to feel that way, especially not over something as trivial as money.

All Kara's thoughts and feelings came bubbling to the surface. Her love for Hilary, her admiration for Nisha's resilience, her begrudging affection for Barb, and her growing love for Nisha. Nisha had made a mistake, and it had cost her everything. She must have felt a jumble of emotions—regret and anger at Angie and fear at being found out and self-recrimination. And Kara had been pushing her away, pushing her family away, because she thought she had lost everything, and the only way forward she could see was to do everything differently this time. And it hadn't worked.

Despite all her attempts to avoid intimacy, she had fallen in love with Nisha.

"I could never hate you."

"You couldn't?"

"Did you want me to say that, yes, I hate you?"

"You have no idea how much I regret fucking everything up and how much I wanted to tell you about it. If I had just been honest with

Angie or maybe if I had just worked more hours, maybe none of it would have happened."

"I guess I don't really know the details. I've only worked out that you made some kind of betrayal with money."

"I took out two credit cards she didn't know about and racked up fifteen grand in debt. I'm still paying it off."

"Okay, that's a lot of money, but I don't see why Angie called off the wedding and walked out on you over it. I know I wasn't around when you were together, but it seems to me that you couldn't have been right for each other if it ended in such a mess." Kara shrugged.

"I've been thinking about that, too," Nisha said. "I've been thinking about how I've blamed myself entirely for our problems when maybe the real problem wasn't the money itself. Maybe it was our communication, and that's something both of us were responsible for."

It was nice to hear Nisha had some perspective and self-forgiveness on the matter.

"I thought I deserved everything that's happened in the last year," Nisha said. "I thought it was my punishment."

"I think your sentence has been served, Nish. Time to forgive yourself. Anyway, Hilary used to charge up our credit cards, and we'd fight about it. We just made a spreadsheet to track our expenses, and it solved the problem."

"Ugh, you're so normal and easygoing." Nisha leaned into Kara's side, and it felt good. Like home. "God, I missed you."

"I missed you, too," Kara said, squeezing her. "I missed you so much."

"I need to tell you something else," Nisha said. "I'm moving in with Nan to take care of her. It's time I got out of Suni and Maddie's and got my own life."

"Aren't you just trading one couch-surfing situation for another?"

"I thought about that, but honestly, I love Nan, and I want to do this for her. I've been thinking about all the stories she tells. I was going to ask her and Sonia, and maybe Barb, if they'd tell their stories, and we could make video interviews or something. Kind of a documentation of queer history."

"I know someone at the LGBTQ library who might be interested in a project like that," Kara said. "I'll have to get you in touch with him."

"You'd do that?"

"Yeah, I think it sounds like a cool idea."

Do not say something cheesy. Do not say something cheesy.

"I'd do anything for you," she couldn't resist adding.

"Why?" If Nisha heard how much like a lovestruck twelve-year-old Kara had sounded, she didn't show it. She asked the question with a light, joking voice.

But this wasn't a light moment for Kara. It was time to lay her cards on the table.

"Because I'm in love with you."

CHAPTER TWENTY

Kissing Kara was like coming home. Their bodies melted together, and every caress, every shared breath was a reminder to Nisha of how hard she'd fallen and how right they were together. She'd have gladly stripped naked and enjoyed every inch of Kara's body for the rest of the night if it weren't for the ghost and two old ladies playing blackjack in the other room.

"I want you," Kara murmured as she kissed Nisha's neck. "I have wanted you since the first time I saw you."

It wasn't true. Kara had been on the prowl that night. But Nisha liked the idea of being special enough to make Kara abandon her plans.

"I love you, too," Nisha said. "I didn't know how to tell you."

"I can't believe we wasted all that time when we could have been doing this all along."

"Wait, it wasn't a waste of time." She was trying to be serious, which was hard to do when Kara was cupping her breast. "The past month, I really got some things together."

"Like what?" Kara kissed her way down Nisha's throat, like her mouth and the hand under the sweater were trying to meet.

"I started a beauty lifestyle brand and a freelance makeup business, and I'm in training to be a yoga teacher."

Kara stopped and looked up. "You serious?"

Nisha nodded. "It was like suddenly I could just see so clearly what I needed to do to find my way, and now I feel like I'm on track to actually accomplish goals and pursue happiness, not just…exist."

"You're incredible," Kara said. "Really, you're just so amazing. I want to know all about what a 'beauty lifestyle brand' is and I definitely want to see your yoga moves, but—"

"But we should really get back out there before they start talking about us," Nisha finished. "Or Barb makes herself invisible, so she can watch."

Kara gave Nisha one last kiss, slow and deep, and they got to their feet to return to the kitchen. "To be continued," Kara pledged.

Back in the kitchen, the blackjack game was still going. They were betting with real cash, and Barb was putting things she'd bought with Kara's credit card in the kitty as collateral. Nisha waited to see if Kara got mad, but she just shook her head over the whole thing.

They were dealt into the next hand, but before they could start playing, the intercom buzzed and Barb rushed to push the button to unlock the lobby door.

"Pizza time?" Kara guessed. "Just promise me it's not that deep dish stuff."

"Do not mock the Chicago deep dish," Nisha said with pretend seriousness. "It is sacred."

"It is a sloppy mess."

Instead of a delivery person at the door, it was Miss Pythia. She threw her hands wide and yelled, "Surprise!"

Kara gasped. "We were so worried about you. You—you vanished, and nobody knew where you were, and—"

"Rosie, get your ass over here!" Sonia called. "The bet's a dollar."

"She was gone," Nisha said, in case they'd all forgotten or she was losing her mind. "We talked about calling the police and filing a missing person's report."

"Jesus Christ, Rosie," Barb said, "why'd you scare the kids like that?"

Miss Pythia sat in the chair Oleg had vacated. "I relocated to Pilsen because the rent's cheaper."

Nisha and Kara looked at each other, stunned.

"Did the rest of you know this?" Kara asked.

"Well, yeah," Barb admitted. "It's not such a big whoop."

"Why on earth didn't you tell us?"

Miss Pythia shrugged. "If you knew where to find me, you'd come ask me how to get rid of Barb, and we had to make sure you'd have enough time for everything that needed to happen."

"So this was all some mind game with us?" Kara looked pissed, where Nisha was feeling confused more than anything.

"Sort of, mija," Sonia said, "except Barb really is a ghost."

"My last night as a ghost," Barb said, and the mood in the room soured a little. "But, hey, don't be sad, okay? Look what we got. These two kids, they got us all back together."

The four friends put their hands in the middle of the table, one on top of the other.

"Promise me when I'm gone," Barb said, getting a little choked up, "that you're not gonna let dumb stuff keep you apart anymore."

Miss Pythia winked at Nan. "I promise."

"I promise," Nan agreed.

Sonia promised in Spanish.

They resumed playing again, nagging when someone didn't bet correctly and yelling at each other to hurry up. They bickered the way people who had known each other a very long time and loved each other very much could do.

Nisha told them about her idea to record their stories, and they all agreed. She hoped she'd be able to get a few videos of them together, too, because their chemistry really was something special.

"They found out I didn't really kill Barb," Sonia told Miss Pythia.

"You tell them what happened between her and me yet?"

"I thought I'd let you do that," Barb said. "I had to drag it out so they'd have time to figure out their own shit."

"Are they in love yet?" Nan asked.

Barb looked between Nisha and Kara, standing side by side in the kitchen. "Oh, yeah, I'd say so."

Nisha could feel her cheeks getting warm.

"Then I guess we can tell them," Miss Pythia said.

"You know we can hear everything you're saying, right?" Kara asked.

"Do you want the mysterious, spooky story, or the real one?" Miss Pythia asked her.

"Let's go with the real one."

"It's not very exciting. Sonia and Barb were a thing. Then Sonia moved into her house, and Nan moved in here for a while, but Barb and I were a thing. So Nan moved next door. Then one day when I was at work, Barb had a heart attack and died. That's it."

"That's it?" Kara asked. "Four months of research and running all over the city trying to find information, and—I hired a private investigator! You made it sound like there was some huge, special story waiting to be uncovered."

Nisha put a hand on her arm. "It *is* special. It's their history."

Kara threw up her hands.

"Better sit down, Susie Q," Barb said to Kara. "After the pizza, it's gonna be time for me to check out. Last chance to play a hand with me."

❖

When they'd eaten dinner and cleaned up the poker mess, the atmosphere grew somber.

"Rosie, you bring the stuff?" Sonia asked.

Miss Pythia nodded and opened a purple velvet bag. She pulled out the same baggies of herbs and flowers she'd given Nisha and Kara on their first visit to her. She asked Kara to fetch a bowl and a lighter.

It was time to perform the ritual that would send Barb back. Sonia and Barb went into the living room, and Nisha helped Nan follow.

"Kiddos," Barb said, "because you're not that bright, I figure you might not have figured it out yet." Barb had a lot of bravado, but she was clearly shaken up over what was about to happen. "This has been fun. Really. It was kind of cool to get a second chance at life. But it's time I moved on."

"You finished your mission," Kara rephrased.

"I will have soon enough."

"So—wait—your mission wasn't to tell me about Nisha and the credit cards?"

"I thought it was to reunite your friends," Nisha said.

Barb looked at her friends. "What'd I tell you? Dense." To Kara and Nisha, she said, "My mission was to find the next pair of women who lived here who belonged together and make sure they didn't screw it up the way we did. Now that you're together, my work is done." She clapped her hands together and rubbed them back and forth, the way Kara and Levi used to when they sang, *I'm smashing up my baby bumblebee.*

"Your mission was to come back, give Nisha the ring, and tell me what Nisha had done," Kara summarized. "So I'd show her that it didn't matter to me."

"Oh, mija, you are so smart sometimes but sometimes so clueless," Sonia said. "She wasn't here to give Nisha the ring. She was here to keep the ring hidden."

"So I'd have to ask for it," Nisha surmised. "And when I asked for it, I'd meet Kara."

"You have me to thank," Barb said.

"And your friends? All the traipsing around I did? All the subterfuge about your past?" Kara asked.

"You brought us back together," Nan said. "We will never be able to thank you enough for that."

"And you gave us one last chance to see our beloved Barb." Rosalind put an arm around Barb's shoulder. "This has been a real gift."

"Now, kiddos, this is the hard part. It's time for me to go." Barb smiled sadly at Kara. "You're gonna get what you've wanted this whole time." She began to flicker in and out of view.

"I don't want you to go." Kara choked on the words and blinked back tears. "I'm going to miss you too much. I don't want you to leave."

Nisha put her arm around Kara's waist. She was the one who had said they needed to give Barb time. She'd befriended Barb, and she wanted to preserve all her stories from the past. But now she said, "Kara, it's time to let her go."

Rosalind started dropping herbs into the bowl, one by one.

"I have one more thing to say," Barb said to Kara. "You guessed right about the 'cheat' part of the message on the mirror, but not about the love part. I didn't mean that Nisha loved Angie. I meant that you and Nisha loved each other, and I hope you told each other. I want you to promise you'll be good to each other. Because this thing that we have"—she gestured to them all—"it's special. It has to be protected. Don't take it for granted."

"I won't," Kara promised.

"You neither," Barb added, pointing at Nisha.

"I promise."

The pace of Barb's flickering had slowed. She vanished for a full second before she reappeared, clutching her stomach like she was in pain.. "It's getting hard for me to stay here."

"We love you, Barb," Rosalind said.

"Love you, honey." Nan wiped her eyes with her good arm.

"Te amo." Sonia's voice was barely audible.

Barb vanished completely.

"Is she gone?" Nisha asked quietly.

"She's lost her ability to manifest," Rosalind said. "We'll finish this ritual and help her cross to the other side."

With shaky hands, Kara lit the herbs and stepped back as the smoke began to spiral upward. Rosalind asked them all to stand in a circle holding hands while she and Sonia recited the verse in Latin.

A brilliant ball of light appeared in the middle of the room. In the center of it was Barb's silhouette. It came and went so quickly Kara wasn't sure she'd really seen it, and then the light flashed out, the smoke dissipated, and the room was silent.

Nisha stared at the space in the living room where the light had been, transfixed. Rosalind collapsed onto the sofa. Kara felt the loss physically. Barb, the slob she'd never wanted in her house, had become a dear friend. She wasn't sure what life was going to be like now that she was gone.

As she looked around the room, though, she saw what Barb had given her in exchange. Three amazing, strong women had been reunited in friendship, women Kara hoped she could call her friends. Nisha had forged a new path for herself. And they'd found each other when they least expected it. What a magnificent person Barb had been to have left behind such a legacy.

Finally, Sonia said, "I definitely missed *Jeopardy!*"

CHAPTER TWENTY-ONE

One Year Later

Kara had already dressed in the suit and oxfords Nisha had picked out for her. She'd called Levi to wish him luck at the junior high dance. She'd tidied up the living room and started a load of laundry. She'd done all that, and Nisha still wasn't ready.

"At this rate, we're going to miss the opening speeches!" Kara called in the direction of their bedroom.

"Okay, okay, I'm coming." She came limping into the living room, one foot in a white high heel and the other still bare. "How do I look?"

She was wearing a pale blue dress with a fluffy skirt, something that looked out of the 1950s. Her hair was done in an elaborate curly style, pinned above her neck. She looked like she'd stepped out the pages of a vintage fashion magazine.

"You look amazing," Kara said, leaning in for a kiss. "Put your other shoe on, and let's go."

There was a knock at the door. Kara opened it to find Oleg with a man on his arm.

"George, my boyfriend," he said with pride. "He's hot, no?"

Kara allowed a moment for greetings before herding them into the hall. As she turned the lights out, she paused for a moment to smile at the picture of Hilary that was sitting on a shelf in the living room. She knew Hilary would approve of tonight.

Once the door was locked, Kara contemplated physically shoving everyone into the elevator. If the traffic patterns worked in their favor, they might still make it.

They pulled up to the library with just enough time to take pictures in front of the fancy photo backdrop, and Kara was glad because she selfishly wanted a picture with Nisha looking as gorgeous as she did. More importantly, she knew Nisha would want a record of tonight.

In the lobby, they found Suni and Maddie and introduced them to Oleg and George. Kara was doing most of the diplomatic work. Nisha was a bundle of anxiety who kept staring at the door.

When Harold came over, she calmed somewhat, but when he asked, "Are they here yet?" Nisha started to pace again.

Finally, the door opened, and Sonia, Nan, and Carlos came in. Nisha rushed over to them, kissing cheeks, and bringing them back to meet the rest of the group.

"I guess it's time," Harold said. "Let's get started."

Kara and her friends found their seats in the front row while Nisha, Sonia, and Nan went with Harold up on the stage. Each chair in the audience was lined with a program, which Kara picked up with pride.

The LGBTQ Library Presents
Titillations: Video Documentaries of Our Lesbian Past
By Nisha Rajchandra

"This is so cool!" Maddie squeaked, giving Kara's leg a squeeze of excitement.

"Little sis does it again." Suni's voice was more level, but Kara had come to recognize when she was expressing happiness.

To her left Carlos said, "I hope Nisha knows how grateful I am that she did this with my mom. It means so much to me to learn about her this way."

Kara smiled up at Nisha on stage. She was nervous about how the public would react to the screening, but she'd said to Kara many times how happy it made her to have a gift of stories to share with Sonia's family. In the year since she'd approached the library with the idea for this project, she'd really taken a leap, turning it from a home video recording on her phone to a series of professionally produced documentary shorts, of which tonight's interviews were just the beginning. After the screening, Harold was going to announce a continuation of the project where anyone in the community could come and have their story recorded and added to the series.

"We're going back to your place to celebrate afterward, right?" Maddie asked.

"Yes, and we will have a lot to celebrate." Kara's eyes were still trained on Nisha, who caught her looking and smiled.

Harold made his way to the podium and greeted the audience. He gave a short speech about the library and the project, citing the appropriate grants they'd won to make it happen. Then the lights dimmed, and the video began. First was Nan's interview, in which she talked about the bars they'd used to go to as a way of finding each other in a world before being out was publicly acceptable. Sonia talked about the conflict she'd felt between her family's Catholicism and being queer, and she mentioned several times that she questioned whether she was fit to be a mother. Kara couldn't help looking at Carlos, who looked like he might cry over that.

Sonia's video was about halfway through when the door opened and someone said, "Am I too late?" in a voice better reserved for yelling for a taxi.

The whole room turned to look. It was Rosalind, who called out, "Nisha? Where are you?" as if there weren't an event going on.

On stage, Sonia shook her head and said, "Damn Rosie."

Rosalind's was the last featured interview, so Kara supposed she was allowed to make sure she got herself settled. Kara waved her over to an empty seat in their row as people in the crowd shushed them.

To Kara's surprise, Rosalind's interview wasn't the last part of the program. Afterward came a photo slideshow with old pictures of the women, mostly featuring Barb, and the last image said the project was dedicated to her memory.

After the videos, Nisha spoke for a few minutes about how she'd come up with the idea. She mentioned how hard it had been to get the participants to stop making stuff up, which got a laugh from the audience, and said that once they began telling the truth, their real stories were even better than their fictional ones. She, Sonia, and Nan took some questions from the audience. Kara could have watched Nisha in the spotlight all night. She was eager for what was going to come next, but she loved seeing Nisha get her chance to shine.

When the last question had been asked, Harold took the podium again and asked everyone to stay in their seats for another minute. He nodded at Kara.

She tapped the pocket of her jacket once for certainty and then hurried over to the stairs.

She heard Maddie ask, "What's going on?" On stage, Nisha looked at her with confusion.

After she climbed the stairs, Kara took a deep breath. This was not a moment she wanted to rush through. She gave herself a second to check in with her feelings, something Nisha had taught her to do.

Are you sure about this?

Never been more sure in my life.

She trotted over to Nisha, took her hands, and helped her stand up. Then she dropped to one knee. The audience started screaming in anticipation. She reached into the pocket of her jacket and pulled out the velvet ring box.

Nisha's hands came up to her cheeks, and her eyes filled with tears. "Oh my gosh, you're not? Are you really?"

"Nisha Rajchandra, will you marry me?"

About the Author

Jane Kolven is the author of three contemporary romance novels. She believes in the power of popular literature like romance to bring about social change. Jane's stories feature a variety of LGBTIQA people finding happiness—because everyone deserves love. Having lived in six states and two countries, Jane currently resides in Pontiac, Michigan. She can be reached at jane.kolven@gmail.com or on Instagram and Twitter as @JaneKolven.

Books Available from Bold Strokes Books

A Good Chance by Ali Vali. Harry, Desi, and Desi's sister Rachel are so close to getting everything they've ever wanted, but Desi's ex-husband is coming back to get his revenge and rip apart their chance at happiness. (978-1-63679-023-7)

A Perfect Fifth by Jaycie Morrison. Streetwise pianist Zara Keller and Lady Jillian Stansfield couldn't be more different; yet their connection brings a new awareness of who they are and what they truly want in their lives—including each other. (978-1-63679-132-6)

Catching Feelings by Ana Hartnett Reichardt. Andrea Foster expected to catch a lot of pitches from the Alder Lion's star pitcher, Maya, but she didn't expect to catch feelings. (978-1-63679-227-9)

Defiant Hearts by Lee Lynch. In these stories, you'll find your lovers, friends, and lesbians you wish you knew—maybe even yourself. (978-1-63679-237-8)

Love and Duty by Catherine Young. All Princess Roseli wants is to marry her three lovers, but with war looming, she must instead marry Princess Lucia to establish a military alliance between their planets. (978-1-63679-256-9)

Murder at Union Station by David S. Pederson. Private Detective Mason Adler struggles to determine who killed a woman found in a trunk without getting himself killed in the process. (978-1-63679-269-9)

Serendipity by Kris Bryant. Serendipity brings jingle writer Annie Foster and celebrity pop star Bristol Baines together, and their undeniable attraction keeps them close, but will their different paths drive them apart? (978-1-63679-224-8)

The Haunted Heart by Jane Kolven. A ghost, a ring, and a quest to find a missing psychic—it's a spell for love. (978-1-63679-245-3)

The Rules of Forever by Nan Campbell. After reconnecting at their high school reunion, Cara and Lauren agree to embark on a textbook definition friends-with-benefits relationship, but trying to keep it uncomplicated is harder than it seems. (978-1-63679-248-4)

Vision of Virtue by Brey Willows. When virtue and desire come together, be prepared for sparks in this next installment of the Memory's Muses series. (978-1-63679-118-0)

Cherry on Top by Georgia Beers. A chance meeting leaves Cherry and Ellis longing for a different life, but when Ellis's search for truth crashes into Cherry's insta-filter world, do they have any hope at all of a happily ever after? (978-1-63679-158-6)

Love and Other Rare Birds by Angie Williams. Ornithologist Dr. Jamie Martin and park ranger Rowan Fleming are searching the Alaskan wilderness for a bird thought to be extinct and they're about to discover opposites really do attract. (978-1-63679-108-1)

Parallel Paradise by Mayapee Chowdhury. When their love affair is put to the test by the homophobia of their family, community, and culture, Bindi and Rimli will need to fight for a chance at love. (978-1-63679-204-0)

Perfectly Matched by Toni Logan. A beautiful Cupid named Hannah, a runaway arrow, and just seventy-two hours to fix a mishap that could be the best mistake she has ever made. (978-1-63679-120-3)

Royal Exposé by Jenny Frame. When they're grouped together for a class assignment, Poppy's enthusiasm for life and love may just save Casey's soul, but will she ever forgive Casey for using her to expose royal secrets? (978-1-63679-165-4)

Slow Burn by Missouri Vaun. A wounded wildland firefighter from California and a struggling artist find solace and love in a small southern town. (978-1-63679-098-5)

The Artist by Sheri Lewis Wohl. Detective Casey Wilson and reclusive artist Tula Crane are drawn together in a web of passion, intrigue, and art that might just hold the key to stopping a killer. (978-1-63679-150-0)

The Inconvenient Heiress by Jane Walsh. An unlikely heiress and a spinster evade the Marriage Mart only to discover true love together. (978-1-63679-173-9)

A Champion for Tinker Creek by D.C. Robeline. Lyle James has rescued his dad's auto repair business, but when city hall condemns his neighborhood, Lyle learns only trusting will save his life and help him find love. (978-1-63679-213-2)

Closed-Door Policy by Erin Zak. Going back to college is never easy, but Caroline Stevens is prepared to work hard and change her life for the better. What she's not prepared for is Dr. Atlanta Morris, her gorgeous new professor. (978-1-63679-181-4)

Homeworld by Gun Brooke. Headed by Captain Holly Crowe, the spaceship Velocity's crew journeys toward their alien ancestors' homeworld, and what they find is completely unexpected—and they're not safe. (978-1-63679-177-7)

Outland by Kristin Keppler & Allisa Bahney. Danielle Clark and Katelyn Turner can't seem to stay away from one another even as the war for the wastelands tests their loyalty to each other and to their people. (978-1-63679-154-8)

Secret Sanctuary by Nance Sparks. US Deputy Marshal Alex Trenton specializes in protecting those awaiting trial, but when danger threatens the woman she's falling for, Alex is in for the fight of her life. (978-1-63679-148-7)

Stranded Hearts by Kris Bryant, Amanda Radley, Emily Smith. In these novellas from award winning authors, fate intervenes on behalf of love when characters are unexpectedly stuck together. With too much time and an irresistible attraction, anything could happen. (978-1-63679-182-1)

The Last Lavender Sister by Melissa Brayden. Aster Lavender sells her gourmet doughnuts and keeps a low profile; she never plans on the town's temporary veterinarian swooping in and making her feel like anything but a wallflower. (978-1-63679-130-2)

The Probability of Love by Dena Blake. As Blair and Rachel keep ending up in the same place despite the odds, can a one-night stand turn into forever? Or will the bet Blair never intended to make ruin their happily ever after? (978-1-63679-188-3)

Worth a Fortune by Sam Ledel. After placing a want ad for a personal secretary, a New York heiress is surprised when the woman who got away is the one interested in the position. (978-1-63679-175-3)

A Fox in Shadow by Jane Fletcher. Cassie's mission is to add new territory to the Kavillian empire—murder, betrayal, war, and the clash of cultures ensue. (978-1-63679-142-5)

Embracing the Moon by Jeannie Levig. Just as Gwen and Taylor are exploring the new love they've found, the present and past collide, threatening the future they long to share. (978-1-63555-462-5)

Forever Comes in Threes by D. Jackson Leigh. Efficiency expert Perry Chandler's ordered life is upended when she inherits three busy terriers, and the woman she's referred to for help turns out to be her bitter podcast rival, the very sexy Dr. Ming Lee. (978-1-63679-169-2)

Heckin' Lewd: Trans and Nonbinary Erotica by Mx. Nillin Lore. If you want smutty, fearless, gender diverse erotica written by affirming own-voices folks who get it, then this is the book you've been looking for! (978-1-63679-240-8)

Missed Conception by Joy Argento. Maggie Walsh wants a relationship with Cassidy, the daughter she's only just discovered she has due to an in vitro mix-up. Heat kindles between Maggie and Cassidy's mother in a way neither expects. (978-1-63679-146-3)

Private Equity by Elle Spencer. Cassidy Bennett spends an unexpected evening at a lesbian nightclub with her notoriously reserved and demanding boss, Julia. After seeing a different side of Julia, Cassidy can't seem to shake her desire to know more. (978-1-63679-180-7)

Racing the Dawn by Sandra Barrett. After narrowly escaping a house fire, vampire Jade Murphy is unexpectedly intrigued by gorgeous firefighter Beth Jenssen, and her undead existence might just be perking up a bit. (978-1-63679-271-2)

Reclaiming Love by Amanda Radley. Sarah's tiny white lie means somehow convincing Pippa to pretend to be her girlfriend. Only the more time they spend faking it, the more real it feels. (978-1-63679-144-9)

Sol Cycle by Kimberly Cooper Griffin. An encounter in a park brings Ang and Krista together, but when Ang's attempts to help Krista go spectacularly wrong, their passion for each other might not be enough. (978-1-63679-137-1)

Trial and Error by Carsen Taite. Attorney Franco Rossi and Judge Nina Aguilar's reunion is fraught with courtroom conflict, undeniable chemistry, and danger. (978-1-63555-863-0)

A Long Way to Fall by Elle Spencer. A ski lodge, two strong-willed women, and a family feud that brings them together, but will it also tear them apart? (978-1-63679-005-3)

Barnabas Bopwright Saves the City by J. Marshall Freeman. When he uncovers a terror plot to destroy the city he loves, 15-year-old Barnabas Bopwright realizes it's up to him to save his home and bring deadly secrets into the light before it's too late. (978-1-63679-152-4)

Forever by Kris Bryant. When Savannah Edwards is invited to be the next bachelorette on the dating show When Sparks Fly, she'll show the world that finding true love on television can happen. (978-1-63679-029-9)

Ice on Wheels by Aurora Rey. All's fair in love and roller derby. That's Riley Fauchet's motto, until a new job lands her at the same company—and on the same team—as her rival Brooke Landry, the frosty jammer for the Big Easy Bruisers. (978-1-63679-179-1)

Inherit the Lightning by Bud Gundy. Darcy O'Brien and his sisters learn they are about to inherit an immense fortune, but a family mystery about to unravel after seventy years threatens to destroy everything. (978-1-63679-199-9)

Perfect Rivalry by Radclyffe. Two women set out to win the same career-making goal, but it's love that may turn out to be the final prize. (978-1-63679-216-3)

Something to Talk About by Ronica Black. Can quiet ranch owner Corey Durand give up her peaceful life and allow her feisty new neighbor into her heart? Or will past loss, present suitors, and town gossip ruin a long-awaited chance at love? (978-1-63679-114-2)

With a Minor in Murder by Karis Walsh. In the world of academia, police officer Clare Sawyer and professor Libby Hart team up to solve a murder. (978-1-63679-186-9)

Writer's Block by Ali Vali. Wyatt and Hayley might be made for each other if only they can get through nosy neighbors, the historic society, at-odds future plans, and all the secrets hidden in Wyatt's walls. (978-1-63679-021-3)